WITH THIS KISS

Suddenly, Karina found his arm around her shoulder. With just a little tug, he bought her up against him.

"Come here, Karina. I'm tired of waiting for what I really want." He tilted her head back and his lips met hers. This was no tentative kiss, seeking a path, charting untried waters. This was the kiss of a man who'd covered that ground before and knew what to expect, knew what he wanted.

The surpressed passion in Karina sought release. She responded as she'd never thought to respond to him again. Her body knew, if not her consciousness, the delights to behold in his arms.

BOOK YOUR PLACE ON OUR WEBSITE AND MAKE THE ARABESQUE ROMANCE CONNECTION!

We've created a customized website just for our very special Arabesque readers, where you can get the inside scoop on everything that's going on with Arabesque romance novels.

When you come online, you'll have the exciting opportunity to:

- View covers of upcoming books

- Learn about our future publishing schedule (listed by publication month and author)

- Find out when your favorite authors will be visiting a city near you.

- Search for and order backlist books from our line catalog

- Check out author bios and background information

- Send e-mail to your favorite authors

- Join us in weekly chats with authors, readers and other guests

- Get writing guidelines

- AND MUCH MORE!

Visit our website at
http://www.arabesquebooks.com

WITH THIS KISS

Candice Poarch

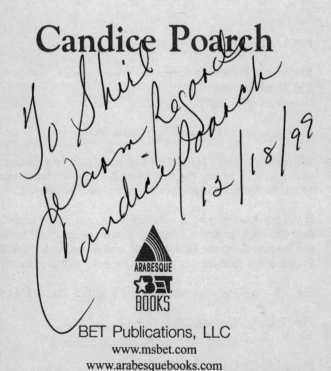

To Shiil
Warm Regards
Candice Poarch
12/18/99

ARABESQUE
BET BOOKS

BET Publications, LLC
www.msbet.com
www.arabesquebooks.com

PINNACLE BOOKS are published by

Kensington Publishing Corp.
850 Third Avenue
New York, NY 10022

Pinnacle, the P logo, and Arabesque are Reg. U.S. Pat. & TM Off.

First Printing: January, 1998
10 9 8 7 6 5 4 3 2

Printed in the United States of America

Prologue

August 15

Peaceful moments didn't come often to Phoenix Dye. As an FBI special undercover agent, he lived life on the edge. He had to weigh every word he uttered, every move he made. An error could mean his death. Little time was left for relaxation.

It seemed like only yesterday when he'd argued vehemently against the forced vacation his supervisor, Joe Greenly, had insisted he take before his next assignment. Joe had said, "Your job is stressful, Dye. Everybody needs downtime." Reluctantly, Phoenix gave in. He realized now that he'd become so jaded by his job he needed to pull back to reevaluate his life.

He would need to thank Joe when he returned.

Now, six weeks later, he wondered how a world-weary man of twenty-seven could fall in love with an innocent twenty-one-year-old in such a sort time span? Then, too, who could tell about affairs of the heart? He'd seen relationships that went nowhere—people who loved each other one moment and hated each other the next. Yet, as he leaned against the old oak tree watching Karina Blake busily pack leftovers from their late afternoon meal, he could no more give her up than he could his right hand. As he listened to the shrill of the mocking bird and contemplated the cloudless, blue August sky, the ambiance seemed almost as foreign as it was welcomed. He was a far cry from the restless, wild eighteen-year-old teenager who couldn't shake the dust of Nottoway, Virginia, from his shoes fast enough. After being ostracized by many of the townspeople, he'd thought never to return. But after being out in the world, witnessing the worst a person could see and sometimes wondering why anyone would want to bring a child into this world, home didn't seem so bad anymore, and being with Karina made him see past the vile to the beauty.

She had been thirteen, with only a bare hint of womanhood peeking through, when he'd left. Now, she was the most unexpected thrill of his visit and the reason for his newfound tranquility.

Her carefree life and this small town, which still clung tenaciously to old values and a strong sense of right and wrong, was the antitheses of what he saw every day. Even though many times some of the people had not been kind to him, there were many who had been more accepting.

Sitting in a field of wild clover that grew several feet from the lake, they'd enjoyed a picnic spread on an old patchwork quilt. This was a spot he would always think of as Karina's and his since they'd spent so many undisturbed, lazy afternoons there picknicking. It was only fitting that they enjoyed the same peaceful surroundings during their last day together. He'd return to northern Virginia tomorrow and soon Karina would go off to college to complete her last year.

He was deeply touched by her feelings for him. No one had ever loved or cared that much for him before.

The dangerous case he would return to would be the

last of its kind he'd work on. Since he was delaying their wedding, even if his real identity was discovered, they wouldn't be able to tie him to Karina.

As she popped the last strawberry into her mouth, Phoenix hunched down beside her and licked a speck of juice from her sweet lips. She'd barely eaten any of the ambrosial and succulent food prepared for their picnic. Phoenix had hardly touched his either, and the little that he did eat felt like a huge lump in his throat. His appetite was usually ravenous in more ways than one, but unfortunately, right now food was the farthest thing from either of their minds.

Karina leaned over to reach a container. The move forced Phoenix to savor her tight, skimpy shorts, which made him as randy as a sixteen-year-old. Phoenix didn't want her to think sex was all he wanted from her so he tried to control his passion and keep his hands to himself. But the outfit she wore and their impending separation made it almost impossible, although it wasn't just a tight behind that made him dizzy; it was Karina and all that she encompassed. He loved it all. From her gentle touch on his brow when he was tired to her understanding nature, the flutter of her hands when she was excited or nervous, and her cute quirks.

He plucked a clover sprig and trailed it down her neck and shoulder as she smiled back at him.

He opened his arms to gather her in, for he didn't want her out of his reach even for a few moments.

"You've pulled a lucky clover!" she exclaimed.

"What?"

"It's got four leaves . . . for luck."

"Then good things and good luck will be our motto."

Karina pushed him down until he was flat on his back, then she leaned on him and gently and leisurely pressed her lips to his. "I'm going to miss you so much. I don't think I can wait until Christmas to see you again," she whispered, a sadness edging her voice.

"Christmas will be here before you know it." He tightened his arms around her, kissed her with a desperate edge, and tried to make himself believe his own ineffective words.

"We should elope." She looked at the diamond he'd given her to seal their engagement.

"Your brother and my mother would feel cheated." Although his gut instinct kept telling him to marry Karina *now*—before he left—he wanted her to be free for her last year of college, not married to someone she wouldn't see for months on end. Phoenix relied on his intuition. He had to in his line of work. But for once he wasn't going to heed it, and hoped he wouldn't live to regret it.

She was so young, so innocent—their courtship so hurried, and the love so intense. He edged his long fingers up the skimpy pink knit top she'd tied below her breasts. ". . . and then it will be May . . ." He kissed her again. ". . . graduation . . ." He slipped the pink and blue shorts down her shapely hips, caught her buttocks in his large hands, and ground them against his manhood. ". . . then we'll marry. We'll be together forever and have three beautiful children, all the spitting image of their beautiful mother." His case would be over and she'd be safe.

"We'll have at least one son to take after his handsome dad." Her eyes were soft with love, her voice thick with longing.

He turned her over, pulled his shorts off, and fumbled with the prophylactic. He eased into her feeling, as if he'd touched a piece of heaven. "I still feel like I'm robbing the cradle," he murmured.

She wrapped her slim legs around his waist and moved her hips to accept more of him. "Do I feel like a baby?"

He groaned. "No, you're a twenty-one-year-old hussy."

She wiggled as if to push him off.

Phoenix laughed and slid deeper. "But you're mine"—his voice held a desperate edge, all humor gone—"and I love you. I love you more than I've ever loved anyone." He sealed it with a kiss.

"Just promise me you'll come back. Promise me tomorrow," she said tightly.

On the very brink of ecstasy, he sucked in a breath. "With this kiss, I promise you all our tomorrows together," he pledged and surged into the most explosive climax of his life.

What was this elusive feeling called love? he thought. He couldn't begin to explain why he needed Karina so or why it felt so—right. He only knew that loving her was as necessary as breathing.

December 20

The four-month assignment in the Midwest was finished, the case closed. Phoenix pounded on Johanna Jones's door. She had moved to Alexandria, Virginia, after graduating from college a year earlier, for a position in a large hotel chain. She wanted to own her own hotel one day, which explained her bare apartment. Every spare penny was put aside to that end. Instead of putting his furnishings in storage, Phoenix loaned them to Johanna until she had the opportunity to buy her own. He accepted her offer to keep all his things until he returned.

Eager to collect some clothing and drive to Nottoway to see Karina, not even the unseasonably cold temperature or the packed airport he'd just left dampened his mood.

Johanna answered the door in a comfortably well-worn knit sweater and faded jeans. "Well, look who the wind blew in. Merry Christmas." She pulled him in and gave him a kiss on the cheek.

Phoenix picked her up and whirled her around. "Merry Christmas to you," he said as he put her back on her feet.

"You're certainly full of Christmas cheer." She laughed.

"On my way home. But first I need some clothes. Thanks for keeping my things for me."

"Anytime. I'm glad you're spending more time there."

She stepped back. "You know where I keep your things, go on."

Phoenix started to the spare bedroom. "Mind if I take a shower?"

She waved a hand. "Help yourself."

Phoenix picked out some clothing, took a speedy shower, and hastily packed. He came back into the living room with his suitcase.

"Are you going to tell me what has you so happy or are you going to leave me in suspense?" She poured a cup of tea for him.

Phoenix stopped, grinned what he knew was a lovesick silly grin. "Okay, I'll tell. I'm on my way to see Karina Blake."

She shook her head, her smile fading. "Why?"

"You see before you a man in love." Comically, he put his hand on his chest. "We're getting married this summer. I can't wait to see her."

"You're kidding?"

"No, it's true."

"Phoenix?"

A queasy knot settled in his stomach at her unsmiling and serious tone. "What is it?"

"Maybe you should sit down," she said.

"What is it?" He couldn't move.

"Well, I don't know how to . . ."

"Come on, out with it," he snapped.

"Karina's married."

"You're lying." He looked into the eyes of Karina's best high-school friend—the woman who had been his own friend for the last three years.

"I'm sorry. I didn't know . . ." She held out a hand toward him. Phoenix stepped back.

"She's marrying me this summer." His world spun on its axis. He believed in Karina—loved her. She loved him. She couldn't possibly be married.

"She married Victor Wallace in September."

"You're wrong. I'm going to Nottoway to find out what the hell is going on."

"You can't, Phoenix." Johanna grabbed his arm. "She's married and she's pregnant. You can't go."

For a fleeting moment, he wondered if the baby was his. "I have to go."

"You can't go. She's three months pregnant and there's a good chance she could loose the babies. She can't be upset. The doctor put her on complete bed rest. She's having triplets."

Three months, Phoenix thought. He'd left four months ago.

Chapter 1

March, 10 Years Later

"We've got to find a husband for mom." Kara Wallace's voice drifted toward Phoenix Dye on the sunny and breezy spring day. Usually when he heard one sibling, he knew the other two were close by.

He sat in the comfortable wing chair by the open window of his bedroom reading the paper he hadn't had the time to read earlier in the day. Along with the scent of sweet honeysuckle, the window invited in the sounds of buzzing bees, chirping birds, and the children's urgent conversations.

The triplets still amazed Phoenix. They were the first set he'd ever met. He didn't know if it was a blessing or a curse that they lived next door to him. A possible blessing was that "next door" was at least a half mile away. His mom had complained long and hard that they were the terrors of Nottoway.

They often roamed throughout the area, claiming it as their personal territory since they were the only children there. And today as they passed his house, he placed the paper on the table and looked out at them.

"I don't see why." Karlton, the one with the more serious nature, hooked a thumb in his jean pocket. "Dad'll come back."

"I don't think so. He left a long time ago." That statement was from Karl, the more personable one. "Anyway, Mrs. Jones said Mom needed a man around the house to help her run the restaurant and to take some of the pressure off her."

Gladys Jones, Phoenix thought disgustedly. Darn, if the woman didn't nose into everybody's business. What she needed was plenty of grandkids living close by to keep her too busy to venture into everybody else's affairs. Phoenix didn't know how she'd reared the two wonderful daughters who'd moved away or the great police officer, her son, Emmanuel.

Phoenix's mom should have warned him that Mrs. Jones was the terror of Nottoway.

Now he smiled at seeing the pet squirrel perched on Karlton's shoulder. "What about Sheriff Dye?" he said.

At the mention of his name, Phoenix's humor evaporated as quickly as water on a hot sunny day.

"You only like him because he's a sheriff and you want to be one when you grow up." Kara's pigtails bobbed as she clambered along with her brothers. The pigtails and the dainty flowers on her T-shirt were her only concessions to femininity. "But we wouldn't be able to have any fun with him. We need somebody to take care of Mom and to stay out of our way."

No doubt so they could continue their mischievous behavior, Phoenix thought.

"I think we should choose Mr. Wilkins," Karl said, the tallest of the three.

Phoenix choked on his laughter. Their mom, Karina Wallace, would really thank them for that match. Mr. Wilkins was at least eighty.

"Isn't he a little old?" Kara puckered her forehead.

"He's nice and *he* wouldn't give us any trouble. He could do the paper work or something." Karl jumped over a dead tree limb.

"I think Mr. Jordan would be better," Karlton added.

"He's Miss Drucilla's boyfriend. She might shoot Mr. Jordan if he got out of line. We wouldn't want her mad at us. Besides she'd never bake us anything good again. And we couldn't do any more fun stuff over there," Kara, always the leader, added.

Phoenix had heard of Miss Drucilla's adventure at teaching Tylan Chance's wife, Clarice, how to shoot when she was having some problems with an intruder. Actually, Phoenix was renting the house that Clarice had bought when she moved to Nottoway.

"Aren't there any younger men around here?" Karl asked.

"They're all married," Kara answered, taking the squirrel from Karlton. "It's my turn, now." She perched the squirrel on her shoulder. It stayed there all of thirty seconds. "Anyway, didn't you hear Towanna say all the good men were taken?"

"I still think Mom should marry the sheriff." Karlton looked toward Phoenix's house at the announcement, but obviously didn't see him.

"We don't want her to marry anyone but Dad, but we have to think of what's best for her. And Mrs. Jones knows everything. Have you ever known anyone who knew more than she did?" The squirrel ran down Kara's arm.

"The sheriff," Kalton insisted.

"I saw Mrs. Jones telling him about his job Sunday at church." Kara raised her head toward the heavens, disgusted. "She even teaches him."

"If she can't marry the sheriff, then Dad needs to come home. I don't want anybody else," Karlton persisted stubbornly.

"I want Dad back, too. But we barely see him at all since

he left. And you have to admit it's better at home since he and Mom quit fighting."

"Besides, we have Uncle Jonathan."

"He's Mom's brother. She can't marry him," Karl added.

"Let's give Mr. Wilkins a try. I'll tell you what we'll do. We'll call him and tell him Mom wants him to come to dinner at the restaurant tomorrow night," Kara coaxed.

"And she'll pay for it," Karl piped up.

"I thought the man was supposed to pay," Kalton said.

"Mom owns the restaurant. Besides doesn't Ms. Thompson pay for her dates? At least that's what she says sometimes at Uncle Tylan's store when she's asking them out."

The children gradually walked out of hearing distance. Phoenix knew how difficult it was to be without a father, but he was sure their mother wouldn't appreciate their matchmaking attempts. And there was no excuse for a father neglecting his children, regardless of the difficulties of a failed marriage. Children still needed both parents.

His own father had died when Phoenix was very young, but he was lucky that Luke Jordan included him in his family as if he were his own. Still it wasn't the same as having your own dad.

All in all, Phoenix had to admire the crafty children. Karina's children.

They could have been his, Phoenix thought with sudden longing as he straightened and went back to his paper. If only Karina had waited for him. Turned out that she thought he wasn't going to amount to much. He'd probably been her last fling before settling down with the man she really loved.

He'd avoided her since returning to town. Actually, he'd vowed never to return to town at all after the fiasco with her. But he'd burned out at the agency. When Johanna, Gladys Jones's oldest daughter, had told him the sheriff's position had opened, although he hadn't jumped at the chance, it seemed worth a try. It was only a temporary slate.

He'd have to run in an election in November. Although he was taking a risk in leaving the agency, it was worth it.

He liked the small town atmosphere where everyone knew each other. Something he hadn't appreciated when he was younger. And he was tired of watching his back and dealing with a group of people who just didn't care. He wanted to work at a job that gave him the opportunity to reach children so he could make a difference in their lives before it was too late.

The only problem was, some of the good citizens of Nottoway didn't quite trust him. As a teenager he'd been known to cause trouble a time or two, but he'd never indulged in an actual crime. They remembered his late-night drag races and the arrogant swagger that gave the impression he was the baddest teenager around. The worst he'd actually done was run with the wrong crowd. When he realized their pranks were more than he was willing to indulge, he left the bunch; however, some of the people in the community never let him disassociate himself from the group. He remembered they had set a field on fire one fall and destroyed two acres of peanuts. Since he had an alibi, Sheriff Gaines had dismissed him. Darlene Thompson admitted they were on their way home from a movie. Truthfully, they had been in the back seat of a car making out. Was she a hot number! He'd been a virgin that night and was so nervous, he'd put his condom on before the date to keep from having to fumble with it when the time came.

He'd always dated the hot ones in high school. Even though the daddies and mothers hovered around the "good" girls, he caught more than one looking his way wishing he'd ask them out. He hadn't given them the opportunity to say no to him—until Karina.

She didn't say no. She married another man. He'd never left his heart so opened to a woman since. And he didn't plan to ever do it again. That's what he got for dating above himself. He'd just been her playmate.

Since his return, they'd only met infrequently and in passing, both of them seemed eager to avoid lengthy conversations.

What could he say, anyway? "Why didn't you wait for me? Why did you marry another man and have his triplets when you could have waited and had my children?"

It was times like right now that he regretted not having children. Kara was the spitting image of her mother's nutmeg complexion. While Karina's hair was cut short, her daughter wore pigtails. Phoenix remembered Karina wearing them as a child. Even her facial features and expressions could have been Karina's at that age. He could also tell that Kara would be taller than her mom.

Phoenix knew it would be foolish to ask questions eleven years after the fact. He needed to let bygones be bygones.

But how many nights had he lain, heart nearly splitting for missing her, remembering how it had been? How many nights had he awakened in a cold sweat from dreaming about her? Eleven years was a long time to miss a woman. So why couldn't he let the memory die? She couldn't have been as perfect as that memory. He needed to quash his obsession for her once and for all.

Phoenix slammed the paper on the table. Distance and time had elevated the feelings that were once there instead of blunting them. It was time he exorcised those feelings. And he'd do it by ceasing to avoid her. Once he was around her, he'd see her flaws. A good place to start was her restaurant. Everyone for miles raved about it. People came to sample the delights from as far north as Richmond and as far south as North Carolina. He could use a good meal, although Miss Drucilla kept him amply supplied now that Tylan had married and had a wife to cook for him.

Boy did Tylan Chance luck out. A beautiful teacher who thought the world of him. And Tylan loved her equally in return. How rare a love like that was in this day. And she was pregnant with their first child. Every time Phoenix stopped by the One Stop Gas, Garage and Convenience

Center, the proud papa-to-be had something to say about his wife and preparations for the coming child.

Something turned sour in Phoenix's stomach. Once, he'd loved like that.

It was time for him to put a end to this obsession.

Phoenix had picked up Towanna Jordan, his date, as a cover. His stomach churned as he drove up the stately drive that was lined with towering oaks and reached the restaurant. It was readily recognizable that the yard and gardens with blooming azaleas, tulips, and paper whites were well kept—the antitheses of its previous existence.

Mrs. Castle, the former owner, had always served the best in country cuisine: fried steak, chicken, grease-laden greens good enough for a heart attack, but she never cared about the upkeep of the grounds or the building. She maintained it with the minimum attention necessary to keep the building inspector at bay. Phoenix often remembered her saying, "People don't come here for the building, they come for my cooking!"

But he had to admit that the fresh coats of paint, the repaired columns, along with all the other restorations, added charm. If the food was at least as good, then Karina wouldn't have any problems with customers, which obviously she didn't if the packed parking lot was any indication. He hoped he'd be able to get a table without having to wait half the night.

"This place is packed every time I come here," Towanna said. "I'm so happy she's doing well."

"They say the food's the best around," Phoenix added with a bored tone.

"Oh, it is. I come here a lot, now that I've moved back. Are you going to be okay?" she asked, not fooled for a moment.

Phoenix spared her a brief glance. "I'm fine. I hope we

won't need reservations. I didn't think to call ahead." He'd never had to make reservations before.

"You're with a friend of the owner. You won't have any problems," Towanna said saucily as she unbuckled her seat belt.

"Nice to know people in high places." A half-smile pulled his lips as he exited the car and walked around to open her door.

Inside the restaurant, the cream-colored walls, rich draperies, a profusion of plants, and cut flowers all combined to bring the outside in. Different kinds of pictures set the mood in each room, from simple landscapes to florals. Each one seemed to have a soothing scene. People knew they were there to relax and enjoy the food and the atmosphere.

Immediately, Karina greeted them with menus in hand. She looked gorgeous in a teal blue silk dress that flared out from the waist to just above her knees. She still had a liking for high heels, which only seemed to emphasize her shapely legs. Around the delicately rounded neckline she wore the pearls her brother, Jonathan, had given her as her high school graduation gift. And at thirty-two, she was every bit as striking as she'd been at twenty-one. He could say even more striking now that she'd matured gracefully, and her eyes and lips were every bit as delectable as he remembered—and more.

"Good evening," she said automatically and stopped dead in her tracks once she noticed the arrivals. But she recovered quickly. "It's good to see you Towanna ... Phoenix."

"You know how much I love coming here. We don't see enough of each other since you opened. That has got to change, girlfriend."

Karina smiled and hugged Towanna. "It will as soon as my assistant arrives. I'm so happy you've transferred to the local bank branch. We can see each other more often."

"I'm looking forward to it."

"Don't I get a hug, too?" Phoenix asked. "After all, it's been a while for me, too. Let's see, eleven years?" As he talked he gathered her in his arms. She stood stiffly within the circle.

Always the devil, Karina thought. She gave him a quick peck on the cheek and stepped back, perching the menus in front of her for protection. "Do you have reservations?" Karina's smile felt so brittle, she expected her face to crack any moment. She knew very well that they didn't have reservations.

"No, we don't," Phoenix answered. "Do you have room for us?"

"We should be able to squeeze you in. Let me take a look." Karina walked over to the hostess stand and hoped the tremble in her hands wasn't noticeable. She flipped through the reservation book and couldn't find a space for them. She didn't want them spending any more time than necessary over their food. Although she was pleased to see her friend, she didn't like seeing her with Phoenix. Why couldn't he have stayed away?

She looked through the book again and noticed a faint line drawn through one reservation in the non-smoking section.

"I have a table available in the non-smoking area."

"That will be fine," Phoenix spoke up.

"Follow me, please."

Gallantly, Phoenix held the padded oak chair for Towanna.

After Karina had seated them, she stopped at some of the other tables to exchange small talk and pleasantries with her guests. Whenever she glanced toward Phoenix, Towanna was making intimate gestures with him in her usual playful manner. An envious pang tore through Karina. She didn't know how she made it without collapsing. As soon as she could make an escape, she asked Tracy Beard, the cashier, to seat the new guests while she attended to business in her office.

Tracy looked at Karina askance and slowly nodded, "Sure. Are you okay?" she asked with a puzzled frown.

"With a packed restaurant, I couldn't be better." Which was the reason for the cashier's confusion. Karina had never left the seating to her when the restaurant was so busy. Her policy was to greet each guest, thereby helping to preserve the nostalgic, comfortable feeling that urged them to return. It wasn't the food alone. She needed to escape to give herself time to gather her wits.

She thought she was over Phoenix. After his departure all those years ago, the promised phone calls and letters never arrived. She'd put him out of her heart after she tried to find him to inform him that she was pregnant with his child. It was only three weeks after he'd left, and she'd been informed that his number was unlisted. When she'd written him, the letter had been returned with a "no forwarding address." She'd been devastated and berated herself for being foolish enough to trust him. Finally, Victor Wallace, who had been mooning after her for some time, had asked her what was wrong. They were at the Ice Cream Parlor where she'd eaten with Phoenix numerous times. She'd burst into tears and run out of the shop. When he caught up with her, the sordid tale escaped.

She didn't want to bring shame on Jonathan, her brother, who'd forgone his master's degree to take care of her when their parents died. He'd done everything right. How could she screw up so? How could she have believed Phoenix when he said he loved her and wanted to marry her?

Victor had said he loved her and would marry her now. Soon after, they discovered she was pregnant, not with one child, but with three. Victor hadn't batted an eye at the news, but had been a supportive partner. The marriage had lasted almost ten years. Their divorce was finalized a year ago.

And now entered the man who never took any responsibility for what he'd done with her that lazy summer so long ago, which still seemed like yesterday. And with his honed maturity, he was even more attractive now than he was eleven years ago. The specs of gray in his hair didn't detract at all from the handsomeness of his sienna features.

"Karina?" A knock sounded at the door, snapping her out of her preoccupation.

"Yes?"

A harried Tracy opened the door. "We have a slight problem out front."

"What is it?" Karina rose from her chair.

"Well, your date is here," she said slowly.

"My what? I don't have a date." Perplexed and annoyed, Karina rounded the desk.

"Look, you go and handle it." Tracy turned and quickly went back to the foyer.

Presenting a hostess facade, Karina briskly trod to the entrance. Mr. Wilkins had taken a seat. But she didn't see anyone who could possibly fit the title of "her date."

"Who are you talking about?"

Tracy pointed to Mr. Wilkins. "Mr. Wilkins claims you invited him to dinner."

"What! Has the man lost his mind?" Karina whispered, looking at the man in horror. He was the most lecherous eighty-year-old bachelor in Nottoway.

Tracy shrugged her shoulders, laughed, and deserted.

Karina walked over. "Good evening, Mr. Wilkins. May I help you?"

It took a minute for him to stand, even with the assistance of his cane. "I'm here for our date. You've invited me to dinner."

"You must be mistaken," Karina said bluntly.

"No, you promised. Are you going back on your word? The triplets called me yesterday and said you wanted me for your date this evening. And I'm here." He tapped the cane on the floor in irritation. With added benefit of his raised voice, the sound was loud enough for the entire restaurant to hear it and a sudden quietness hovered in the air as ears strained to listen, eyes bulged to see.

Karina was going to be minus three children tonight. "Could you please accompany me to my office so that we can straighten this out?" The thing to do was to get him away from the crowd.

"The only thing I want is a table with you at it with me." He would have to have a strong voice, even if the rest of him was frail, Karina thought.

Provoked by his obstinacy, Karina snapped. "We're much too busy for me to sit to a meal this evening."

"Your kids promised a meal and said that you'd take me home." He'd gotten loud again.

"You're a grown man," Karina whispered. "You know better than to believe children about something like this."

"I got my grandson to drop me off . . ." he began again, even louder. By now, the guests were straining their necks to see what was going on. If she didn't quiet him, it would be all over town by tomorrow.

"All right," Karina cut in. "I'll give you a complimentary meal, but I won't be able to join you. I'll call you a cab when you're finished."

"But . . ." he started.

"This is as good as it gets. Either you take what I've offered, or I can call that cab right now!"

Reluctantly, he acquiesced.

Karina looked at the reservation list again. The only table available was the one next to Phoenix and Towanna. She escorted Mr. Wilkins there. "Someone will be with you momentarily." Good business dictated that she stop at Phoenix's table. He was caressing Towanna's hand.

"Is everything to your liking?" she asked. Her professional smile was back in place.

"Everything's wonderful as always," Towanna answered.

Phoenix didn't say anything. He kept his eyes trained on Towanna. But Towanna had enough to say for the both of them. "I tried lamb chops the last time but this time

I'm experimenting with something different, the salmon with Riesling sauce."

"You'll love it."

When Phoenix reached up and wiped a speck of food off of Towanna's upper lip, it was more like a caress. Karina tried to ignore the intimate contact and the knife in her stomach.

Phoenix smiled to himself. He could always tell when she was irritated about something. Her hands would flutter more than usual as she talked. She was gesturing big time.

Their main course arrived and Karina moved on to the next table. He'd ordered stuffed flounder.

"Um, this is delicious," Towanna said after swallowing a bite of the salmon. She held a forkful out to him. "Want to try?"

Karina caught his eye as his mouth closed around the morsel. He chewed as her eyes remained transfixed on him, knowing that both their minds were going back to shared memories of the many times they'd fed each other that long-ago summer, how it had often ended in a kiss, and quite often in something more intimate.

Phoenix's stomach muscles tightened as hot desire coursed through him. Once Karina had taken a mouthful of ice cream and licked a path down his chest with it. That episode had ended in the most passionate lovemaking session he'd ever experienced. And, thank goodness, the thought was broken by a waitress who approached Karina. He heard her tell the waitress Mr. Wilkins's dinner was complimentary as she left.

Phoenix took a deep calming breath. Mauve swags graced the huge window near his table, allowing him to look out into the twilight. He hoped the rushing water and the swaying trees would calm him. She was smooth, he had to admit. But didn't she always handle any situation with aplomb?

"You're my date tonight and you're brooding," Towanna pouted and touched his arm. "What's wrong?"

The perfect diversion. Phoenix pasted a smile on his face and focused his attention on her. "You have my full attention," he said. As her usual playful self, she tore off a piece of garlic bread and put it to his lips. He captured it and her finger with his mouth. A giggle escaped from her.

"You naughty man," she said. "Too bad it couldn't be more." She smiled in resignation.

"You're in an impish mood today."

"I'm pretending I'm on a real date enjoying a candle-light dinner with the love of my life."

The lone candle and the flower in the center of the table drew Phoenix's eye. Though simple, with the low lights, it lent the perfect romantic atmosphere. "One day it will be real," he said softly, wishing it for both of them.

"How you do'in," Mr. Wilkins voice cut in on his intro-spection. "A bit dark in here don't you think, Phoenix?" He turned the roller chair around in his direction. "How can I see what I'm putting in my mouth?"

"I like the lights low," Phoenix answered in a whispered voice so as not to disturb the patrons near them.

"To each his own. Who's the nice young lady you got with you?" He squinted, his eyes trying to get a better view.

"Mr. Wilkins, Towanna Jordan."

"How you doing?" He scooted toward her and shook her hand.

"You know me, I'm Luke Jordan's daughter."

With the recognition, he slapped his leg. "Well, I'll be. You've been living in Richmond, haven't you?"

"Yes, but I'm back now."

He had to scoot back toward his own table so the waitress could pass with a laden tray. "How do you like being home?"

"Just wonderful," Towanna gathered potatoes on her fork.

"Good, good. Wish my date would come over here. But, I need her to get the lights up so I can see. Don't see as good as I used to." He looked around, squinted and raised his hand. "Waitress, waitress?"

"Yes, Mr. Wilkins?" The polite waitress, whose hair was arranged in a beautiful array of braids, arrived promptly.

"Could you get my date?" With a smug gleam in his eye, he puffed out his chest.

"Your who?"

"My date, Karina." The gleam turned into a licentious grin.

"Oh!" The waitress gave a shocked exclamation and an uncertain, "Of course." Quiet footsteps muffled by the soft soles of her shoes padded across the wood floors, leaving the charming room.

Soon Karina returned in her wake, her lips pinched. "What can I do for you, Mr. Wilkins?"

"You can just set yourself down at the table after you turn up the lights some. It's too dark." He snaked out a gnarled hand to grab Karina. The wayward hand traveled too close to Karina's behind. She slapped it away and bent to whisper to him.

"If you don't want to lose this hand, keep it to yourself." She straightened. Her voice curt, she continued, "Mr. Wilkins, I'll have an extra candle placed on your table. I won't be able to dine with you this evening. We're too busy, but enjoy your meal." She walked briskly away, her stiletto heels clicking on the wooden floor.

Phoenix heard her telling the waitress, "Get Mr. Wilkins an extra candle and please have the cook put his order ahead of all the others." Her tone was acerbic. He had felt like punching the old man when he had dared too close to Karina's behind.

Gosh but was she beautiful and spirited. She drew him like a magnet. Having lost his appetite, Phoenix forced a forkful of the food that now could have been paste for all his discrimination into his mouth. Coming here had the opposite effect to what he'd intended.

Chapter 2

Phoenix looked at his watch as he walked to his mailbox. He had an hour to shower and dress for the reception Luke Jordan was holding in his honor. He pulled the mail out of the box and looked up when a piercing scream split the air.

"Help! Lord, have mercy, help me!" It was Mrs. Jones, shouting as she sprinted down the lane, moving faster than Phoenix had ever seen her move. He dropped his mail and ran toward her.

"Help!" she shouted again.

"It's okay, Mrs. Jones, Speckles won't hurt you." The triplets shot down the lane behind her in hot pursuit.

"Help! Help!" Arms flailing, the woman continued to run.

Phoenix could see something crawling on her head, shoot down her back then under her arm. The woman's arms were steadily swinging, trying to dislodge it to no avail. As quickly as she swished one spot, it darted to another.

Phoenix sprinted toward her, almost tripped over a branch, righted himself, and ran on at full speed.

"Stop, Mrs. Jones. Speckles won't hurt you." The triplets were still behind her.

Phoenix finally caught up with the woman and stopped her. A squirrel raced down her front with her still steadily fighting it, shrieking all the while as she bounced from foot to foot. Phoenix grabbed the furry animal, and before he could catch it solidly in his hand, it raced all over him. "Calm down, Mrs. Jones."

"Lord, Jesus. Thank you! Thank you!" Breathing heavily, she looked through slit eyes and saw the animal on Phoenix, swatted at it, and backed up a few paces, ready to take off again. "Get it away!"

Before the triplets caught up, the squirrel had traveled up one of Phoenix's legs and down the other, up his back, and over his head and chest. Winded, Kara detached the animal from Phoenix's shirt where it had finally landed. It hadn't unnerved him too much since he'd seen the animal with them many times as they walked across his property.

"Get it away from me!" Mrs. Jones looked as though she was about to faint.

"He's friendly. He won't hurt you," Karl said, stroking the furry animal as its beady eyes looked about.

"Why don't you take the squirrel away?" Phoenix took the woman's arm and led her over to a stump. "Rest here and calm down, Mrs. Jones."

"Lord, have mercy, I didn't know what landed on me. I went to the basement to clean a little and the critter must have gotten into my bucket, because as soon as I set it on the kitchen table, it leaped out and ran up my hand." With her hand over her heart, she paused for breath. "I'll tell you, I have a mind to make squirrel stew out of it."

"You can't cook Speckles!" Kara pleaded.

"After the fright that animal gave me, I most certainly will." Slumped on the stomp, she fanned herself with a hand.

"But, he's our pet. You just can't." Three sets of wary eyes landed on Mrs. Jones. She winked at Phoenix.

"It nearly gave me a heart attack." She let out a shuddering breath.

"Only because you were scared of it. It wouldn't harm you."

"Well, I'll think about it," she said with a teasing glint of humor in her eyes.

"You're okay now, aren't you, Mrs. Jones?" Concerned, Karlton huddled around her, not sure of what to do.

"I don't know if I'll ever be right again. What was that thing doing in the house anyway?"

"Speckle's mom died and we had to take care of him."

"Are you keeping him in the basement?" Phoenix asked.

"Yes, sir," Karlton answered reluctantly.

"Does your mother know about it?" Karina was never too enthused about animals, but maybe she indulged the children.

"We haven't told her yet. We wanted to train it first," Kara said.

"It's time you told her," Phoenix said firmly.

She put her arms around the woman. "Do we have to? You're all right, Mrs. Jones, aren't you?"

Just like her mom, Phoenix thought. Could wrap anyone around her little finger with a sweet warm touch and a pretty smile.

"I'm not going into that house with that animal in it. Don't try to sweeten me up," the older woman huffed, but everyone knew it was all bluster.

"We'll keep it locked in the basement. You don't have to go down there."

"I'll go get the car and drive you back to the house, Mrs. Jones. You kids keep the squirrel locked in the basement until your mom gets home." Phoenix now had forty-five minutes left before his reception. It wouldn't do to be late.

If it wasn't one thing, it was three with the triplets. They kept something going all the time.

The fancy, slinky silk cocktail dress that ended two inches above Karina's knees and showed off shapely legs drove Phoenix crazy all night at the reception. This time, however, he knew better than to get entangled in those shapely legs.

Phoenix decided to get some punch, went to one of the two wishing wells, picked up a fluted glass, and filled it from the fountain. As he sipped, he looked at the strings of festive garlands and helium-filled balloons floating all over the place. He had yet to partake of the buffet table, which sat laden with gastronomic delights.

Phoenix watched Mrs. Jackson, one of his favorite teachers. She was one of the few people here he could call an ally. Curiosity bought most of the others here. They'd whispered more than once that he'd end up on the other side of the law. He was pleased to prove them wrong.

"A fine party, isn't it?" Luke Jordan smacked Phoenix on the shoulder.

"It was indeed." Phoenix dragged his eyes from Karina and focused on Luke. Thank goodness the party was winding down. "You didn't have to do this, you know. It's not as though I've won an election. This may only be temporary."

"We've got to celebrate every step. Let people see you as sheriff. Then we won't have any problems with getting you elected, come November. You don't know how happy we are to have you back."

With the wooden floors polished to a high sheen, one could barely tell the reception was being held in a gym. The entire building had been changed. Phoenix was pleased to see that the town had its first library sectioned off in one part of what used to be a junior high school. Now the school was a recreation center. It had tennis courts and rooms for community classes. Nottoway had made many positive changes since he'd left.

"It's good to be back." It was hardly worth celebrating at this point, Phoenix thought.

But Luke obviously thought otherwise. He plucked up a spicy meatball that a passing waitress tempted him with. "That Karina sure knows how to cater a party, doesn't she? I wish I could get her to run the country club when it's finished, but she's got her own place."

"Um," Phoenix said, uncommitted. He dipped a boiled shrimp in cocktail sauce and popped it into his mouth.

"She's done well with that restaurant," Luke added.

"What happened with Mrs. Castle?" Mrs. Castle had run the restaurant for over thirty years before selling it to Karina.

"Went to Georgia to be near her daughter." Luke kept a watchful eye on Miss Drucilla, who was conversing with a gentleman across the room.

"How does she like it there?"

"Said it was nice to sleep in for a change. Wished all her life she could sleep in. Now that she can, she still gets up at the crack of dawn." The men shared a laugh.

When Miss Drucilla Chance ambled over, Luke took her heavily veined hand in his. She wore a peach silk dress that made her look twenty years younger than her eighty-one years. She never dressed so elegantly and appealingly before. Her infatuation with Luke must be the cause, Phoenix guessed.

Towanna and her boss, Thornton Sterns, engaged Luke in a conversation and Phoenix leaned over to kiss Miss Drucilla on the cheek and give her a hug. "How are you, ma'am?"

"Fair to middling. I'm so proud of you. Knew you'd do good." She patted his back while holding onto one hand.

"Thank you. You were always my champion."

"I don't care what anyone says. You did it all on your own." She lowered her voice, her eyes twinkling. "Now, the only thing missing is a wife. Thought you'd be hitched by now." She patted his hand with her callused ones that knew many years of hard work.

"All in good time, Miss Drucilla. I hear you have a budding romance of your own. Do I hear wedding bells?" he teased.

"Oh, go on with your foolishness." The older woman actually blushed. For years she'd believed Luke might have killed her brother, and regardless of how much Luke loved or pursued her, she'd never allow him to date her. But more than a year ago, it was proven that the previous sheriff, Hadley Gaines, had killed him. Luke wasted little time in making up for lost years.

Luke Jordan's deceased wife had been a quiet woman, not as vivacious as Miss Drucilla. Phoenix thought that, after missing his wife for several years, Luke was due some excitement, and from what he'd heard, Miss Drucilla was more than capable of providing plenty. Her husband had died in the fifties and she'd never remarried. She was due some happiness of her own. Luke was just the man to give her the special treatment she deserved. Phoenix wished them both the best.

"It's taken a long time, but I don't believe in rushing things," Miss Drucilla said.

"I wouldn't call it rushing. Luke's been in love with you more than sixty years."

"That's what he said. Man's about to worry me to death. A body can't barely move without him underfoot." Even though her tone was stern, her face held a secret smile, belying her words.

"Now, don't you look beautiful, Miss Drucilla." Karina walked up looking good enough to eat.

"You should know, after all, you picked out this dress." She turned to Phoenix. "You remember Karina, don't you? She was just a little thing when you moved away from here."

She'd grown quite a bit when he'd returned eleven years

ago, Phoenix thought. "Yes, I remember her. Good to see you again, Karina."

"How are you?" Her eyes darted away after making quick contact with him.

"He's going to make a fine sheriff," Luke cut in. "Phoenix, have you met the new bank president, Thornton Sterns?"

"No, I haven't." The men shook hands.

"Phoenix Dye, our new sheriff."

Thornton Sterns was the image of a bank president. Standing eye to eye with Phoenix placed him at six feet two. He looked to be around forty. Not a strand of his blond hair was out of place. And his tailored Italian suit fit him perfectly. All bank presidents wore the same uniform, which explained why he looked vaguely familiar.

"Welcome home," Thornton said, his demeanor a little stiff.

"Thank you."

"You're going to be bored to death around here after the excitement of the FBI."

"Trouble has a way of following you anyplace," Phoenix said.

"Why would a young man want to leave the FBI," Thornton asked.

"I wouldn't call me young, but I thought it was time for a change. You never know how appealing a quiet small town can be until you're away for a while."

"I can empathize with that, and I know you can, too, Towanna."

"I certainly can," Towanna said. "It's wonderful to be back. The pace is less hurried. That in itself means a lot to me."

Another waitress stopped by with smoked salmon on melba toast. Miss Drucilla daintily chose one, slipped it into her mouth, and chewed with a dreamy look on her face. Pursing her lips in a playful way, she said, "You make this even better than I do."

"That's impossible," Karina said. "But it's a hit at every catering function."

"I was just telling Phoenix I wished we could get you to manage our restaurant at the country club. You've done a fine job with yours," Luke said as he joined them.

"Functions like this help," Karina assured him.

"Speaking of functions, we're planning a picnic for the local bank branches this summer. The area around the river would be an ideal location," Thornton said to Karina.

"It would be. Call me next week and we can work something up with details."

"Perfect. Excuse us." He shook everyone's hand. "It was nice meeting you, sheriff. Towanna and I have to work tomorrow."

After their departure, Luke said, "Phoenix, we're going to need someone to watch the country club at night until construction is finished. Do you have anyone in mind?"

"I'll look into it." His eyes were riveted on Karina as her pink tongue peeked out to get a crumb on her lip.

Just then the band announced it was playing its last song. It was going to be a slow one.

"Come on, Miss Drucilla. Let's show these young folks how to cut the mustard." Luke grabbed her hand.

"You won't catch me on a dance floor. I haven't danced in years and I'm not about to start now."

"All you have to do is move and follow me. Excuse us." Luke pulled her away.

"I'll follow you all right. Luke, now, Luke . . . ," they heard as the couple continued on. Luke Jordan gathered the petite woman into a respectable embrace and they swayed to the music. Then looked back at Phoenix. "What're you waiting for? You've got a pretty girl standing there."

Reluctantly Phoenix held out a hand to Karina. "May I?"

With equal restraint, she stepped toward him and he

gathered her into his arms. As they danced to the slow, romantic music, the silence between them was stiffening.

"I'm surprised you came back," Karina said finally, still stiff in his arms.

"It was time." Phoenix wondered why she agreed to cater his party. She was the last person he expected or wanted to see. Except his body knew, if he didn't, exactly what they'd meant to each other at one time.

Karina felt so warm and comfortable, she smelled feminine and hot. The music flowed around them. No words were needed as Phoenix basked in the closeness with her. If he closed his eyes, he could picture them in the Ice Cream Parlor and in love. Holding her close as they waited for their burgers and fry order. What naivete, what trusting natures they had then, to be lost forever with the reality of life and the passage of time.

As soon as the music stopped, Karina hastily stepped back. "Well, I'm the hired help here," she said with a touch of nervousness. "I have to get back to work."

Phoenix scanned her from head to toe. "Where's your uniform?"

"I'm wearing it." Karina turned on four-inch heels and, with hips swaying—just enough to tease—sauntered off to greet another guest, acting as if she were queen of the palace, another sign of nervousness Phoenix knew.

"Um, um. You always knew how to pick them."

Phoenix turned toward the familiar voice of his high school friend. "Glad you could make it, Patrick." The men shook hands.

"You don't think I'd miss the welcoming festivities of my best friend, do you?"

Phoenix smiled, pleased. "How have you been?" His eyes strayed to Karina as she talked animatedly to the mayor and his mother. In no time she had the taciturn woman wreathed in smiles. Karina had that effect on people.

"Better snatch her up before someone else does," Patrick informed him with a chuckle. "She's a free woman."

"Good luck to him." Bitterness edged his voice.

"A businesswoman and a looker all wrapped up in one package. They don't come like that too often."

"Since she's such a catch, maybe you should try." Phoenix wished he'd kept his mouth shut. Though he didn't want Karina, he didn't like the idea of her with Patrick either. He was still dizzy from the dance.

"Looks like they're ready to close the buffet. I'm going to grab some before they do."

"Sure." Phoenix marched to the wishing well needing a fortifying drink.

One by one, people started to leave until Phoenix, Luke, Miss Drucilla, and Karina with her staff were the only ones left. He talked with Luke, and before he knew it, the place had been cleaned, the props taken out, and Karina had her coat on and was about to leave. He excused himself from Luke and met her at the door. "I'll walk you to your car." She looked startled.

"That isn't necessary."

"You can never be too cautious. Looks like your crew has left." He glided along with her.

"Suit yourself." Her steps were quick and perky.

"You've done well. I mean it, congratulations on your success."

"So have you." When they reached her car, she turned to him and looked up and for a brief moment her beautiful brown eyes settled on his. An insatiable urge propelled Phoenix to give in to his desire—to see if the desire pounding through him touched her even a little. As if a magnet drew him, he bent and kissed her.

Eleven years melted away. Before he knew it, he'd gathered her into his arms and she quickly wrapped her's around him, returning his ardor. The feel of her silky skin was as potent as the desire he still dreamed about—and it was every bit as real. The delicate tremble that shook her urged him to catch her bottom and grind it against himself before he remembered her traitorous nature. Suddenly, their mouths parted and he looked into the brown pools of her eyes. A soft light from the building put them in shadow.

"Ah, Karina, did he give you this?" The words were half whispered, half anger. He pressed a hand to her staccato heartbeat. "Did you desire him as much? Did you melt for him—in less than a month?"

She stiffened and pushed him away. "As if I had a choice." With shaking fingers she pushed the key into the lock and opened the door. "We aren't going to pick up from where we left off. Our relationship ended eleven years ago."

"I couldn't agree with you more." Pheonix turned and walked away. She'd had a choice. She could have waited for him.

Damn her. Why did he kiss her? He couldn't be in the same room with her two hours without wanting to devour her. He'd wanted closure, the same kind of closure and relief he felt when he'd finished a case. Loose ends always bothered him, needled at him until everything was settled. The embrace with Karina made him feel the same unease. And he no longer wanted there to be closure. Except that he'd always thought their relationship hovered in the air, incomplete. They needed to clear the air at least and make some kind of peace. And what did he do the first time he had her alone? Act like a love-struck teenager who couldn't keep his libido in check.

Chapter 3

Einstein's fingers tightened around the glass as he stared out the huge window in the old Victorian house, rage pouring through him. The death of his only brother still left him hollow inside. Even though Jimmy was older than he, Einstein was the one with the brains. He'd always looked out for his older brother. It had been the two of them against the world.

Feeling a deep, hollow pit in his gut from his loss, he grieved in silence. It was a grief that would linger until Jimmy's death was avenged. Jimmy had died in a robbery, a bullet from Phoenix Dye's crossfire.

How many times had he told Jimmy that bank jobs were too risky? Especially when white-collar crimes paid astronomically more and the cases were seldom prosecuted even if they were caught. Company CEO's didn't want their stockholders to think they were incompetent.

Now, having failed Jimmy miserably, Einstein was alone. He tossed back the bourbon he was holding and, as it burned a path down his throat, he continued to brood. Since he couldn't bring his beloved brother back, the least he could do was see that Jimmy's death was avenged. His throat tightened. But it had to be done properly.

Consciously and slowly, Einstein brought his rage and pain in check. He couldn't afford to continue to lose control. He mentally ran over his goals to keep things in perspective. Emotional people always made mistakes. He wasn't emotional and he never made mistakes.

Casey stood behind him in silence. He liked that about Casey. The older man knew how to gauge Einstein's moods. He knew when to talk and when to keep his mouth shut.

Casey had been Jimmy's cellmate a few years ago when he'd been sent to prison for theft—activities he'd engaged in since the ripe age of six.

It had taken two years to plan Phoenix Dye's downfall.

"When will Chance be hit?" Einstein asked, still brooding.

"Within the week. Stump was fairly chomping at the bit. He's been out of commission since they put him in that witness protection program a year and half ago. He's ready to pull another one. And this place is far enough out of the way to make him feel comfortable."

"Good. We'll start out with little incidents that will start the town gossiping. Dye won't be able to keep Stump in jail. He'll have to let him go back into the program. If word of Stump's whereabouts were discovered . . . well, our sheriff won't let that happen."

Why anyone would let himself identify with a name like Stump was beyond him. A man should pick an appropriate name. A name with dignity. Whereas he realized Stump garnered his name from his stature, if it were he, he'd at least pick a name that reflected some intelligence. But nothing as undignified as Stump. Jimmy had given him his own nickname. As a child, Jimmy would say, "Boy you're as smart as Einstein," and the name stuck. It had the added advantage of concealing his real identity.

"Why don't you just kill Dye and get it over with?" Casey had the gall to ask.

Einstein turned around to face him. "I don't want him to die before he's totally disgraced!" He slammed a fist against the desk and gritted his teeth. Once again he let out deep breaths and brought his emotions under control. "His good name means everything to him. Did you know that Casey?"

"No, I didn't." Nervously Casey got up from his seat, wandered the room, picking up odd pieces from the book-case, the table, and a shelf, then setting them back down, bored and ready to leave. The nervousness was not born of fear of Einstein but of sitting too long in close confinement. Casey loved his freedom.

"Always know your opponent's strengths and weakness. Then you have control. Every minute detail is significant."

"If you say so." Casey sighed and sat in the chair by the desk. "What do you want me to do about Wallace?"

"String him along. A few glasses of cheap whiskey should loosen his tongue. Make sure you find out everything you can about the triplets and Mrs. Wallace. They could prove useful."

"I ain't into hurting kids," Casey shook his head. "No way."

"The children won't be involved. We'll only use them if necessary." Einstein narrowed his eyes, concealing his anger. His orders weren't to be questioned.

"As long as they aren't hurt. If that's all, I've got a little business of my own to deal with." Casey walked to the door.

"I can't afford to have you arrested. Keep yourself clean." He signaled the end of the conversation by a flick of his hand.

"Sure. Sure," Casey said as he left.

Einstein knew that something could always go wrong. That was the chance you took with having to work with outsiders. But he owed Casey. Casey had taken good care of Jimmy while he was in prison. Still, Einstein kept a light plane at a small nearby airport. If it became necessary, he could always leave the country for a few months until things died down. Then pop up as his old identity later.

Phoenix had promised Patrick a visit too many times to evade it any longer. His move to Nottoway and familiarizing himself with his new job had taken up an enormous amount of time.

Patrick had been his closest friend in high school. He'd entered the army after graduation while Phoenix had gone off to college. Phoenix had worked full time as a hotel night auditor and had taken a heavy class load at the same time. In his senior year, the FBI had recruited at his college and he'd handed in an application, not believing that he'd actually get a shot at a job with them. He'd been shocked when they'd asked to interview him in D.C. and even more so when they'd offered him a position. It was the best offer he'd gotten. A chance to travel the way he'd always wanted to, and a job the people in Nottoway would have thought he'd be on the opposite side of. In prison instead of looking in.

Phoenix pulled up into a yard where a sculpture of a man and woman embracing warred with low grass patches and white sandy spots. Patrick sat on the front porch whittling a chunk of wood. His hands were always busy, either shaping hot metal or sculpting wood.

Phoenix surveyed the surroundings. The house, though old, held a fresh coat of white paint. On the porch huge sculptures graced opposite sides of the door.

"Long time no see." Patrick stood as Phoenix exited the car.

"It's been busy. Good to see you. It's been a long time." The men shook hands.

"Yeah, I bet they keep you hopping."

Phoenix tested an old swing to see if it could support his weight, then eased himself on it. He remembered the two of them swinging there many times, telling their tales of woe. Patrick's father was more often drunk than not when he wasn't working and had a tendency to become maudlin and sentimental. Patrick was always embarrassed when his dad would burst into tears telling him how much he loved his son. He remembered Patrick's mom always had a ready smile and smelled of lemon and spices. Mr. Stone had succumbed to cirrhosis of the liver years ago, but Mrs. Stone was enjoying her retirement.

"How's your mom?"

"Better than ever. She moved down to South Carolina with her sister—near the beach. She always loved the water."

"She always talked about moving there."

"Finally did a couple of years ago." Patrick had resumed his whittling. "Wanna beer or something?"

"A soda if you have it."

"You know where the fridge is."

Phoenix went into the house. It looked the same as it always did, except for new linoleum on the floors. He went over to an old fridge that must date back to at least the early sixties, pulled out a pop, snapped the cap, and ambled back to the porch swing.

He took a long swallow from the can. "What're you making?"

"A horse."

"For whom?"

Patrick shrugged. "Nobody in particular. You can have it if you want."

"I'll take it. You always did great work." The piece would look great in his living room. "Name your price."

"It's nothing. By the way, I've got some things for the triplets. Why don't you take them to them when you leave here?"

"Are you kidding? I don't get within shouting distance of them." There was only one set of triplets in Nottoway. And they were enough.

"Hey, they aren't so bad. No worse than we were."

"That's not saying much." Why would Patrick be making sculptures for them? He was never that close to Karina.

"Yeah, well, kids'll be kids. It wouldn't hurt for you to get to know them."

"For what?" Phoenix had no aspirations to get closer to them. Getting close to them would mean more contact with Karina. That wouldn't do.

Patrick stopped his whittling and gave Phoenix a long look. "Heard you had a thing for Karina years back."

Phoenix looked at a lone cloud floating across the horizon. Patrick had been working in New York that summer. "That was ages ago. It's got nothing to do with now."

"Heard you two were inseparable."

"A summer fling." He took another swallow and started a slow rock, pushing the swing back and forth with his feet. "So what's happening with you?" Karina was not a subject he wanted to talk about. Besides, who didn't have a lost love from some point in their lives?

"Nothing much. Lost my job three weeks ago. Stephens closed their cigarette plant."

"I heard about that." Hundreds of people from the area had lost their jobs. He knew Jonathan Blake's business had plans for expanding within the year, but the displaced workers needed jobs now.

"They offered jobs for anyone who moved with them. But I wanted to stay here. I'll find something sooner or later."

"Ever tried to sell your sculpture or woodwork?"

"Naw. Who'll buy this stuff?"

Phoenix looked at the sculptures displayed on the porch and in the yard. It rivaled the museum pieces he'd seen. "Don't put yourself down, man. This is great work."

"I give it away to friends. Ain't nobody going to buy it."

"You'll never know. Why don't you get Karina to display a few small pieces in her restaurant? When people see how great it looks there, they'll buy. I'm sure Karina will go for it. What does she have to loose?"

"Think she'll go for it?" Patrick's expression carried hope.

"Worth a try."

Patrick shrugged his shoulders and kept whittling. He held the look of a defeatist.

"Luke Jordan needs a guard for the country club at night. Keep people from running off with the supplies. It's short term, but maybe it'll tide you over until you can find something else."

"Sure, why not? That's what I did at Stephens. So how do you like the house?"

"The roomiest place I've had in years."

"Seen any ghosts lurking around?" He laughed.

"Only in the form of the triplets passing by."

"They pulled a fast one on Mrs. Chance when she first came here. Cast shadows on her window. Had her thinking a man was lurking around the place."

"They don't like her?" He'd heard they had a tendency for mischief.

"They love her. Heard Mrs. Jones talking about the place being haunted and thought they'd play a Halloween trick. Then the real stuff started when Sheriff Gaines tried to get her to leave. Got Luke Jordan in trouble."

"Yeah, I heard. Gaines killed Elonza Fortune almost forty years ago and tried to frighten Mrs. Chance from the house fearing that some evidence was left there. He tried to make it look like Luke was responsible."

"You sure did luck out. Walked right into Gaines's cushy job. Not much happens here."

"I was ready for something different." Phoenix didn't want to belabor the point, but it was more than luck. He'd paid his dues and then some with fifteen hard years as an agent. And the way still wasn't paved with gold. Plenty of people in Nottoway still didn't trust him. They were just waiting for him to screw up so they could say their famous, "I told you so's," that he'd never amount to anything.

"Ms. Chance was behind the recreation center project,

too. Heard tell she put on quite a show at the town meeting."

He and Patrick talked a while longer before he left. Reluctantly he stopped by Karina's house to deliver the packages. Her eyes widened when she saw him.

The last person Karina expected or wanted to see at her door was Phoenix Dye. He held a box that contained several objects wrapped in newspaper. Karina finally managed a "Hello." What did he want? Would he see a resemblance in the children's features? Karlton was the spitting image of him.

"Come in." Karina opened the screen door to allow him entrance.

"I was visiting Patrick. He sent gifts for your children." He stepped over the threshold.

"That was so kind of him. He's always doing thoughtful things." Karina stepped back to make room for him. As he entered, she took a quick look around the kitchen to make sure the triplets hadn't left anything out of place. She'd been rushing around dressing and didn't take the time to do anything with the house.

"Where are they?" he asked.

"They're playing outside." The house was unusually quiet without them. She felt more peace when they were around, even when they were bickering.

He set the box on the table and glanced around the room she'd shared with her husband. It was a modern, cheerful room, decorated with yellow and green wallpaper and yellow curtains. She had pots of herbs in the huge window over the sink. Had Victor come up behind her and kissed her on the neck while she was preparing breakfast? Did they spend quiet evenings on the porch watching the children play, or did they snuggle together on the porch after the triplets had gone to bed? Through the pain, Phoenix was envious of the shared intimacy they'd had together and wondered why it all ended.

"I know you think it's safe here but it wouldn't hurt to

keep a watchful eye on them. Danger lurks everywhere these days."

"This is a pretty safe neighborhood. Nothing ever happens here. Besides everyone's always keeping an eye out for them."

"You can't always count on that." Phoenix didn't know why he'd said anything. Her children were her responsibility. But he was back in Nottoway because he cared and he could make a difference. He wanted her children safe, and it just wasn't safe leaving children unattended nowadays. Maybe he was more cautious from his experiences even though his mom never had to worry while he ran around with his friends. Everything had changed from yesterday.

"Are you implying I'm negligent with *my* children?" Hackles raised, she leaned slightly forward.

"I'm not criticizing you, I merely saying you should be more careful about their safety. They shouldn't be allowed to run around without adult supervision." However, what he really wanted to ask her was why she married another man so soon after he left town. Her energy and spirit had always intrigued him. It was only one of the things that had precipitated his falling in love with her. With the anger, Phoenix felt sadness for what could have been for both of them.

"Just how many children have you raised, Sheriff?"

"None, but I've seen plenty of them in body bags."

Karina's temper snapped. "Don't you dare try to frighten me about my kids. They've been safe playing in this neighborhood for years. And they aren't alone out there. When they're away from me, the three of them play together. I don't need you coming here from the big bad city telling me what to do with my kids! We live in a nice, safe community with caring neighbors. Furthermore—"

"Leave our mom alone!"

"You can't arrest our mom!"

Karina threw her attention toward the door. The triplets stood there with varying degrees of fear and anger. She walked over to them, her heart pounding. "He's not here to arrest me. We were just having difference of opinion. Just like you do sometimes. I'm fine. Really."

"I didn't mean to cause a ruckus. Take it or leave it. I was just giving . . . forget it." Phoenix walked toward the door. "Didn't mean to upset you. I've got to get going." At the door, he faced Karina again. "Before I go, I wondered if you'd mind displaying some of Patrick's smaller sculptures in your restaurant. He's lost his job and any sale would be a help."

Karina massaged her forehead. "I'd love to. I'll call him tomorrow." Protectively, the kids moved over to their mom as Phoenix left.

He hadn't had a decent thing to say to her since he'd returned from Washington, and now the first thing out of his mouth was a criticism. Well, the very first was a kiss. She straightened, tingling from awareness and anger. Karina didn't have the time for his nonsense. He hadn't mentioned a word about not contacting her when he'd left, and she wasn't about to let him know how upset she'd been at his desertion by mentioning it now. But he wasn't about to get away with criticizing her concerning her children.

"He's not going to try to arrest you later is he, Mom?" Karlton asked.

"Of course not. He was just concerned about you playing alone. You are careful to stay together when you go out in the woods aren't you?"

"Sure."

"Good." Karina hugged them and remembered the gifts. "Look at what Patrick sent you. Sheriff Dye dropped them off for him." Karina reached into the box to distribute the packages. Each was labeled with a child's name. "Open them quickly, I'm dying to see what he sent."

Kara ripped the paper to uncovered a ballerina. "It's beautiful!"

After seeing that, the boys tore into theirs. Karl uncovered a carving of a man on a motorcycle and Karlton, a sheriff wearing a tin badge on a horse.

"You have to call him and thank him for the gifts and then write your thank you letters." It was another ten minutes before Karina could start back to her bedroom to finish dressing. "Maybe you should stay close to home where Mrs. Jones can keep an eye on you. I wouldn't want anything to happen to you."

"Oh, Mom, we aren't babies. We'll be careful."

"Stay close to the house just the same."

As Karina walked toward the bedroom, she heard Karlton say, "I told you he wouldn't arrest Mom . . ."

While she pulled on her clothes she wondered if maybe she'd overreacted to Phoenix's suggestion. She thought back to what he'd said about children in body bags. Karina shuddered. If anything happened to the triplets . . . They were her life. She'd gone through such a difficult time during her pregnancy, worrying about having to marry a man who wasn't their father and then later about losing them. The doctor had demanded bed rest for her after the third month. It was a long arduous ordeal. But she and they had pulled through, without their father.

Victor Wallace had been a godsend. Their natural father couldn't have done a better job with her during her pregnancy. He'd waited on her hand and foot. And once they were born, he'd spent many nights rocking them to give her a much needed break. The children were never on the same schedule for a time. While one was sleeping another one was up.

When Mrs. Jones arrived, Karina put on her makeup and left with a last warning for the triplets not to wander off.

*   *   *

It must be the day for reminiscing, Karina thought when her ex walked into her office a little before noon. Karina was going over the Monday order the chef had started for the secretary.

"You're looking good as ever, Karina."

"Thank you, Victor." Though she didn't love Victor as much as she should have, their separation had been a painful ordeal.

"Your place is real nice, too. You always did have class."

"Have a seat." Karina pointed to an empty chair across from her. "How have you been?" She hadn't seen him in months. Now she waited for the pain to come. When it didn't, she almost felt guilty. She should feel something more for the man she'd been married to for nine years.

"Great. I'm starting a business of my own."

"That's wonderful. What kind?" She was happy for him.

"We're not sure yet, but Casey is getting some people together to go in for something big. We may buy that shopping mall that closed down and open it again. Put in a few stores. There's still a market in that area."

"Sounds good. It brought a hardship to the community when they closed that center. You have a ready market. I hope things go well."

"How are the children?" he finally asked.

"They miss you." Lately they hadn't said much to Karina about his absence, but she heard them talking among themselves about it.

"I miss them, too. Been meaning to drop by, but you know how it is."

Since the separation, there had always been something to interfere with his visits. Although he wasn't their natural father, he was the only father they knew . He'd been so supportive when they were tiny, Karina couldn't demand any more from him than he'd already given. She realized that her inability to love Victor was the catalyst for their divorce. Giving up on waiting for Karina's love, Victor finally started having affairs with younger women to compensate for the void. It seemed he wanted to sever all ties with her.

"I know I owe you a lot for everything you've done, but it would be great for you to see them. They love you and don't understand your absence."

"You don't owe me anything. If you let me, I'll even take them out maybe next weekend."

"They'll love it." It wasn't Victor's fault that she'd never loved him the way she loved Phoenix. She felt guilty that she couldn't make him happy enough to stay. She'd owed him happiness in his home.

"Heard Phoenix is back. Have you told him?" His eyes were half closed. His face expressionless, keeping Karina from reading his thoughts.

She didn't pretend to misunderstand his statement. "No. There's no point in that, is it?"

"I guess not. Tell you what, I'll call you."

"I won't say anything to them until you call." He had promised to visit them in the past but failed to show up, disappointing them so many times. She didn't want to see any more disappointment in their faces. They shouldn't have to pay for her mistakes.

Karina felt pulled in opposite directions with the triplets on one side and Victor on the other. She owed so much to both.

Phoenix ran out of the house. He was late for his date with Darlene. As usual. He saw Karina pull up in her driveway and the triplets walking down the lane to their house. He should have known better than try to give Karina advice. She had never lived in the city as he had. She didn't understand the trouble that could lurk at any corner. Out here even he didn't lock his own car most of the time when he was home. He wouldn't have dared do that in Washington.

Phoenix opened the car door and got in. Before he could stick the key in the ignition he felt a crunch and something wet seep through his trousers. He yelped and jumped out the car. A yellow gooey mess of cracked eggs greeted his eyes. "Those conniving, scheming!" This was too much. They needed a firm hand. He looked up the lane. They were too far for him to run after. Phoenix ran in the house to grab paper towels to clean the seat then took another shower and dressed again. He called Darlene.

"Darlene . . ."

"Just forget about coming over. I'm on my way out."

"Wait a minute, I ran into some trouble. I'm just going to be a little late . . . hello, hello?"

Dog-it. Phoenix slammed the phone back on the hook. He headed for his car and Karina's . . . again. He didn't plan to take any sass from her this time. She needed to keep a tighter rein on those children. It'd cost him his date with Darlene. Not that he was in love or anything, but she was someone to spend some time with. You didn't keep women like her waiting. Added to that misfortune, he now had a dry cleaning bill and only hoped the mess wouldn't leave a stain.

Irritated at his dilemma, Phoenix pressed Karina's doorbell while leaning one hand against the doorjamb.

Karina opened the door wearing a shirt and jeans, looking as if she'd hastily pulled them on.

"Yes?" She stepped aside to allow him into the house.

Once over the threshold, Phoenix confronted her. "Those children of yours put eggs in my car seat, which I sat in. They've cost me a pair of good slacks and a date," he said between clenched teeth.

"Eggs?" Her eyes widened as she covered her mouth with a hand.

"Yes, eggs." He glared back at her.

"I'm sor . . . sorry." Her lips twitched, her eyes lit up. "Of course, I'll pay your cleaning bill."

"I don't want you to pay for my cleaning. I want you to keep them away from my place!" He lashed out, her humor adding fuel to his temper.

"They were frightened that you'd arrest me. They were trying to protect me in the only way they knew. But, I don't condone this behavior and I'll deal with them."

Phoenix relented a little. He tried to remember that he was just as protective of his mom as a child, too. He could understand their dilemma, but that didn't solve his ruined pants or his frustrating night ahead without a date.

"Why don't you talk with your husband and have him help you handle them," he suggested in a more agreeable tone.

The humor left her eyes. "He's my ex-husband and that's none of your concern."

Phoenix sighed. "Look, I know it has to be tough raising them alone, but these children are his responsibility, too. You should see that he lives up to it." Phoenix didn't know why he even cared. Karina had a choice that wasn't available to his mom. His father died, while Karina's husband was alive.

He'd come over spitting mad. As he looked at her small, proud stature and thought of the huge responsibility of three children heaped entirely on her shoulders, he wanted to protect her. Her shoulders had straightened more and the weary look on her face had turned to determination by the time he'd finished talking.

"Is he at least paying child support? There are laws now to see that he does."

"You don't need to concern yourself about my children's welfare. Please bring me your cleaning bill and I'll reimburse you."

Phoenix had the urge to kiss the annoyance and hurt right out of her, but kept it in check. "Look, I'm not the enemy here. I just want to . . ."

"We'll be fine. The children won't bother you again. If

you'll excuse me, I'll see to their discipline." She held the door for him.

Left with no other option, Phoenix sighed and left. The door shut behind him. Talk about touchy. He hoped all divorcées weren't as prickly.

Chapter 4

Resentment boiled over in Karina at receiving a lecture from someone whose character should allow him to be the last person to deliver lectures. Oh, he could sugarcoat himself as well as the next one. He'd certainly done so before. But in the end, it spelled disaster for anyone gullible enough to be taken in by him. Karina took deep breaths in an effort to control her anger as she heard Phoenix's car pull away. He was certainly generous with giving her advice on duties and support payments when it was really his responsibility to help take care of them!

Face heated with anger, Karina wielded the vacuum with excessive force as she swept the carpet. Where was all that responsibility and caring eleven years ago when she really needed it? Her chest tightened with the bottled up emotions. She couldn't even tell him. Couldn't vent her anger on him. Karina couldn't even confide in her friends about it. Her brother, Jonathan, didn't know Phoenix was the triplets' father, even though she thought he may have suspected. The only person who actually knew about the children's parentage was her ex and her doctor, neither of whom she could talk to.

By the time she cooled down even a little, she'd vacuumed the kids' bedrooms and hers. However, Karina's own reservations surfaced as the anger began to abate. Had she made the wrong decision in not telling him later? When Patrick returned from New York, he'd kept in contact with Phoenix and he always made a point of letting her know that. She could have corresponded through him. Yet, why should she have? He'd made promises he had no intention of keeping. So why would he be concerned that he'd left her pregnant and frightened. Or that he had three children who desperately needed him? Besides, she'd been married to Victor by then.

Karina heard sounds in the kitchen and she marched in to confront the children. They were fixing bowls of cereal, something they were content to eat regardless of the time of day.

"Sheriff Dye was here." Hands on her hips, she walked into the room.

All motion stopped.

"It seems someone put eggs on his car seat." Karina moved forward and sat at the table. "Would you know anything about that?"

The triplets looked guiltily at each other.

"Well, somebody has to protect you," Kara said, chin tilted.

"That was a stupid stunt I don't approve of."

"Uncle Jonathan said to take care of you while he was on vacation. We have to look out for you. Dad's not here, anymore," Karlton added.

"You're children," Karina snapped, then felt a heavy weight on her chest replacing the anger. "Sit down, please. All of you." Chairs scraped back as they all sat at the round oak table. "I don't want you to worry about me. Any problem I may have with the sheriff, I can take care

of. If not, then I'll get your Uncle Jonathan's help. You
don't have to worry about it. I'm the adult here. Not you."

"But, Mom, you always say that families should look out
for each other," Kara reminded her.

"And you think you can help me by pulling stupid
stunts—and on the sheriff? Putting eggs in the sheriff's
car is wrong. You're lucky he only came to me to talk about
it. If you have a problem with something, come to me.
Don't do anything I won't approve of."

"I bet if we talked to the sheriff, he'd leave you alone,"
Karlton said.

"I'm not in any trouble. You are. I want the three of
you to go to his house and apologize for what you did."

"Ah, Mom. Do we have to?" Kara asked.

"Yes, you do. And you also have to raid your piggy banks
to pay for his cleaning bill."

"Mom," Karl said, "we're saving for skates."

"Maybe you'll remember that the next time."

"That's not fair," Kara pouted.

"It's not fair that he has to pay for cleaning his clothes
either. Now go apologize."

"Do we really have to?"

"If you don't, you can do dishes and go without your
Nintendo for a month."

"Oh, all right."

Chairs scrapped as they pushed back from the table.
They marched off as if going to the gallows. Karina shook
her head with a small smile and a touch of sadness. They
shouldn't have to worry about her. With a dependable
male around, they wouldn't have those worries.

Yet, she could see Phoenix now, the outraged male
who'd probably demand blood tests before he even
believed her. That would panic the children. As if they
didn't have enough instability in their lives already. Then
he'd demand visitation rights and get the children depen-
dent on him before he'd pick up and leave again. No,
thank you. They didn't need any more disillusionment.

The stress of single parenting and running a new business was taking a toll on Karina. Sometimes she wished she could afford to relax, not worry about making a profit, or whether they had enough supplies to last the weekend if they got an unexpectedly large crowd, or who would cover a station if a waitress called in sick. Or God forbid, if the chef became ill. Karina could prepare any dish the chef did and could pinch hit anywhere, but handling both the customers and the kitchen would be tedious. Still, this was her dream and she'd rather be where she was than any other place.

Karina sighed. Wishing wasn't going to change a thing. She got up to put the milk back into the fridge.

Phoenix was in the bathroom rinsing the eggs out of his pants when he heard movement in his room. He crept to the door and eased it open. It opened noiselessly because he'd greased the hinges a week ago. Darn, he'd left his gun on the dresser. He crouched low and moved stealthily into his bedroom and stopped.

Karlton was examining his gun.

He should have locked it up, but they'd never come in his house before.

"Put the gun down on the bed, Karlton," Phoenix said quietly.

After hearing his name, Karlton jerked and turned, causing the gun to point toward Phoenix.

"Son, put the gun on the bed," Phoenix repeated calmly, his heart in his throat. Pent-up fear was crushing him, but he remained outwardly calm.

"I . . . I just wanted to look at it." Karlton stammered as he placed the weapon on the bed.

Phoenix walked over, picked it up, and unloaded it. After he checked to make sure the chamber was empty, he handed the gun back to the boy.

Karlton's eyes lit up at the unique opportunity. He

turned it over and over in his hand, studying the instrument, pointing it toward the dresser as if he were going to shoot. "It's heavier than I thought," he finally said.

"It's a dangerous weapon, not a toy. It kills people." Phoenix gathered up the clip, locked it up, and went to his closet to pull a homicide crime scene book from the shelf. Most of the book wasn't suitable for a child.

Karl walked up behind him. "What are you doing with a gun?"

"You're in big trouble, Karlton, and you are, too, Sheriff Dye. Mom doesn't want us handling guns," Kara said from the doorway.

"I was going to show your brother some pictures. Would you like to see them?"

The stubborn stance evaporated at the chance to see something unique she could tell kids at school about.

"Okay. Can I hold the gun, too?"

"I want to hold it," Karl said.

Phoenix handed the gun to him for a minute and then to Kara.

When they finished examining it, he put it in the locked safe he kept for the gun and turned the lock. "I want you to understand that guns are serious weapons. They kill." After opening the book, Phoenix flipped past some of the gory scenes and found the page displaying an exploding water bottle. He sat beside the children on the bed. "Take a look at this picture. This container is full of water. When a bullet hits the plastic bottle, it explodes. Imagine what it does to a person's body."

"Did you ever shoot anybody?" Karlton asked eagerly.

"I have. To save someone else's life or to save mine. A police officer or a sheriff is given authority to save and preserve life."

"Did you kill them?"

"It's not something I've ever wanted to do. But I have. It's my job to protect the public. It's not fun or exciting."

Phoenix waited for that to digest before he asked, "Why are you here?"

"Mom made us come apologize," Karl answered.

"Next time knock before you enter."

"We did knock. You didn't answer. And we knew you were here. We thought you couldn't hear us," Karl answered.

"Don't ever go in someone's house without permission." A shudder passed through Phoenix at the thought of shooting one of the children. He didn't let the panic intrude in his voice. "What if I'd hurt one of you, thinking you were intruders? You can always come back later."

"Karlton wants to be a sheriff like you. We won't tell Mom you let us hold the gun this time," Kara said.

"You can tell her. Don't keep secrets from your parents."

"You're going to be in big trouble if we do," Karlton said.

"I can handle it. Let's go downstairs." Phoenix trooped after the kids. Just because he didn't get along with their mother was no reason to take it out on the children, he decided. They even tried to protect him. Phoenix didn't know the last time anyone tried to protect him from anything.

They sat on the edge of the couch. He never spent much time with children. He knew soda was his favorite beverage at that age, but adults were supposed to think healthy. "Would you like some milk?"

"Do you have any cookies? We didn't get to eat our cereal," Karl stated hopefully.

Didn't Karina fix real food for the children? Why would they need to eat cereal for supper when she ran a restaurant?

Phoenix didn't have cereal in his cupboard. He wasn't a parent, but he knew they didn't need cookies if they were hungry. He scrounged around in his kitchen to see if he had anything quick to fix. He did have eggs, cheese, and ham. That should be filling enough. "How does ham and cheese omelet sound?"

"You can make omelets?" Karlton asked.

"Sure."

The boy looked at him in wonder. "Great, you do know everything."

"Not as much as Mrs. Jones. Or Dad, either," Kara added.

"No one knows everything. Why don't you go wash your hands so you can help me. Set the table or something." Phoenix quickly squashed what could turn into a sibling squall. Loyalty was an admirable trait.

When the three of them ran off, the phone rang. It was Darlene with a change of heart.

"I've decided to forgive you. Why don't you come on over?"

"I'd love to, but something's come up. Maybe another time." After her unreasonable tone earlier, Phoenix didn't want to go out any longer. Besides the kids were entertaining.

"I might not be available."

"My loss." Phoenix put a great deal of false reluctance into the statement before they disconnected. Since Karina, every woman had come up lacking—including Darlene. With the three children, Karina was working her way under his skin again. He couldn't afford to let that happen. He'd be sure to keep the children and Karina separated in his mind.

"We're ready." Kara was getting into the spirit of things.

"Good. Karlton, why don't you get the cheese, eggs, and ham out the fridge. Kara, you can get the oil out the cabinet and the pan from the stove drawer. Karl, the dishes are in that cabinet. You get to set the table."

They worked companionably at fixing the meal. He even let them mix the ingredients. The triplets talked nonstop. Karina must not have a dull moment when they were around. He needed to call her so she wouldn't worry about her children.

When he did call her, he had to reassure her several times that they weren't an imposition. She seemed reluctant but finally agreed. Surprisingly, she didn't blast him about the gun either.

After they'd cleaned their plates, Karlton apologized. "We're sorry we messed up your pants and car. We were scared you'd arrest Mom and we wouldn't have any place to go."

Phoenix was taken aback. He'd never looked at it from their point of view. Just that they'd caused a problem, but not at why, even though it was part of his job. He'd always taken up for his mom when he was growing up. Karina was their security blanket. They wanted to know she'd be protected from harm's way. "I wasn't going to arrest your mom. You know, if you're scared, you can always talk to me. I'm just a field away."

"You're neat," Karlton said.

Phoenix never realized how special a kid could make you feel. "You're pretty neat yourself." He rubbed the boy's hair.

Surprisingly, Phoenix had an enjoyable evening with the children. He'd never realized youngsters could be so entertaining. Since returning home, he was learning an entirely new and fascinating world.

After the triplets left, he went over some of his cases. One in particular, an accident that had occurred just before he'd arrived, caught his attention. It had been a one-car accident. The car struck a tree at high speed. Still recuperating in the hospital from several broken bones and a cracked skull, the teenager, Howie Martin, was lucky to have come out alive.

As a teenager, Phoenix had raced on the very same stretch of road. It had a two-mile area before hitting two curves, then another mile straight. Even now he could feel the vibrancy of the car and the pumped adrenaline of the race. Thinking of the disaster that could have resulted, Phoenix shuttered. Now, he also realized how very lucky he and his friends were to have survived unscathed.

He also didn't want another teenager hospitalized from a drag-racing accident in his town. It could affect innocent people. At any time there was the chance that anyone returning home after work or an evening out traveling late at night on that road could meet with an accident.

Phoenix drove the official sheriff's car but did not use his siren or cartop lights. As he neared the favorite drag-racing area on Trundle Road, he saw several car lights ahead. Phoenix slowed the vehicle as he heard Emmanuel's voice crackle over the radio.

"I'm chasing the robbery suspect toward Trundle Road. Is anyone in that area?"

"I am. What kind of car is he driving?"

"A green nineteen-ninety Camaro."

"I'll set up a roadblock along that two-mile straight stretch. It'll give him plenty of time to stop," Phoenix informed him.

"Good. We should be there in about five minutes."

"Barbara?"

"Yes, Phoenix," the night dispatcher answered.

"Is another car in this area?"

"I am," Stan replied.

"Set up another road block in the other direction to keep anyone from coming through."

"Will do."

Phoenix turned on his siren. He'd deal with the drag racers another night. He couldn't take the chance of anyone being in this area tonight. And the cars ahead of him sped off.

"What's going on, Barbara?"

"There's been a robbery at Tylan Chance's store, Sheriff."

"Was anyone hurt?" Phoenix asked.

"No."

"Notify Dinwiddie County that they're approaching the county line, just in case he breaks the block." There was no telling what could be around the curve on dark country roads.

He heard Emmanuel's voice on the radio.

"I just passed Russel's farm. He'll be there in a minute," Emmanuel said.

Phoenix put the car in the middle of the road, lights flashing, and got out of the vehicle.

"He's slowing," cracked over the line.

When the car came to a standstill, a short man exited the vehicle.

Phoenix breathed a sigh that there wasn't an accident.

"Stand beside your car with your hands up," Emmanuel's authoritative voice shouted. The man turned toward the car and placed his hands on the top. Emmanuel and Phoenix approached with their weapons drawn. Emmanuel made quick work of cuffing and searching the man.

Stan's car drove up behind Emmanuel's.

Then the man faced Phoenix.

"Stump!"

"Phoenix! It's so good to see you again," Stump said as if they were meeting at the supermarket instead of a chase.

"What the hell is going on?" Phoenix roared. It was Hal Waters, but he'd always gone by the nickname of Stump. It had taken a lot of fast talking to get his management to put the man in protective custody. "How the hell could you risk your cover by pulling a stupid stunt like this? Don't you know there are people out there who want you dead? Or have you forgotten that?"

Hal twitched, sheepishly. "I know, but Casey said it'd be a safe enough job. Said the town didn't have a sheriff and I was sure to get away in the middle of the night. I didn't know you were here, else I wouldn't have come."

"You better thank your lucky stars I was here else you

probably wouldn't have lived through another day. Who the hell is Casey?''

"Someone who pulls small jobs here and there. I ain't ratting again.''

"You've got more trouble than Casey right now. As soon as your prints go through, you're going to have a virtual army here to see that you don't live to do another job or snitch on anybody.'' Phoenix pulled a pad out of his pocket and dated it before writing "Casey" and "Hal Waters" on it.

"It was supposed to be an easy job. I could pull it and be back in West Virginia in no time.''

It was a warning, Phoenix thought. Someone was telling him they knew where he was and could get to him anytime.

"It's the feel of it. I had to feel the tumblers crack in my hands again. To see if I still had the touch.'' The man's eyes were glazed as if he were in the midst of an orgasm. "Oh, Phoenix. I had to do it,'' he said beseechingly as if Phoenix could understand such nonsense.

Phoenix raked his fingers through his hair. This damn day held one problem after the other.

"The loot's all here,'' Stan hollered out.

"I didn't take much. Well, maybe just a little bit.''

"Didn't the program get you a job?'' Phoenix asked.

"They did. A horrible job, Phoenix. Boring, boring, boring. I'm fixing radios, televisions, and VCRs. That's an insult to my skills.''

"At least it keeps you alive.''

"You call fixing TVs a living? There's no creativity. No challenge for my brain. It's not like picking the best locks ever made.'' A dreamy look crossed his features. "Oh, the sweet feel of the tumblers in my fingers. Now, that's living. But, I've got it out of my system, now.''

"You know, if you weren't a key witness in the Farentino case, I'd leave you to your own devices,'' Phoenix said exasperated.

"Oh, but you're a knight at heart. You could never leave

the weak to the vultures. That's always been your strong point."

"Emmanuel, isolate him at the precinct. I want you—and only you—to see to him until I can take care of some things."

"Huh?"

"Just do it," he barked.

"Sure thing, Sheriff."

"I'll drive behind you." Phoenix turned to Stan. "Stan, you wait for the tow truck. Give the goods to Emmanuel. He'll record them."

As he followed Emmanuel, Phoenix wondered who Casey was. He had to make some phone calls.

"I don't want any interruptions for a while," he said once he'd arrived at the precinct. He closed his office door before he seated himself behind his desk and dialed a number he knew from memory. His old boss at the agency.

"This had damn well better be good," Joe's familiar gravelly voice answered.

"Why the hell haven't you retired yet, Joe?"

"Dye? Tell me you're tired of hicksville and ready to come back. Your slot's waiting for you."

"Nothing doing. But I do have a problem." Phoenix heard a rustle of covering and springs creak in the mattress as Joe sat up in bed.

"Shoot."

"Hal Waters pulled a job in my town tonight. We caught him with the goods in no time, but I think his cover's blown. He had to have been sent here as a warning. From whom, I don't know."

"Why do you think that?"

"Some guy named Casey convinced him that this town didn't have a sheriff and a robbery would be easy to get away with. Could you check to see if you have anything on a Casey connected to his case?"

"The name doesn't ring a bell."

"I need you to get him back ASAP."

"You'd think the fool would have more sense. Farentino's lawyer is trying to get the case reopened. If they knock him off, we wouldn't have a case. I'm going to send Grady and Howell to pick him up. Give me your number and you can arrange a rendezvous."

Phoenix rattled off his number.

"Sit tight. We'll have him out of your hair before daybreak. You going to have any problems on your end?"

"I'll take care of things here. Do you remember Mina Walsh? A budding romance was going on there before the trial. She's in the program, too. Maybe you can talk to her and see if she wants him around. He seemed to calm down in her presence."

"That is a thought. We'll look into it."

The last thing Phoenix needed was for his cases from the agency to follow him here. He'd thought to put an end to the budding crime already here, not create more problems. But first things first. He had to call the district attorney to clear Hal's transport back into the program.

Groggily, Percy answered on the fourth ring.

"Percy, I've got a problem. There was a robbery tonight at Chance's store. The man who pulled it is in the witness protection program."

A pause, then a sleepy voice came over the line. "He risked his protection to pull a small town robbery?"

"There's no accounting for common sense here. Anyway, everything was recovered. I need you to do a null pross on this one. There are a lot of people who want him dead. He won't make it in this area over a couple of days. If his fingerprints and picture go through, we'll have a war on our hands. Especially since their attorney is trying to get the verdict overturned on some technicality. With him dead, if a retrial's ordered, there won't be a case."

"I don't see why we can't null pross. I don't want a war here. A lot of innocent people could be hurt."

"You don't know the half of it. This saves me some

paperwork. If you didn't go along, then the FBI would step in."

"Sure. I'll be there soon to take care of the paperwork."

The quicker they got Stump off his hands, the better, Phoenix thought. It crossed his mind that maybe he needed to get more officers in, but then Casey had access to him at any time if he'd wanted to kill him.

It felt like Grand Central Station, because soon the phone rang again. "Sheriff Dye here."

"Hey," Grady's familiar voice rang on the line. "I knew you couldn't lay low for long."

"I tried," Phoenix sighed.

"The agency's in your blood."

He hoped not. "How are things on your end?"

"Keeping us busy. Not like the pampered sheriff."

"Maybe you need to find yourself a small town." Phoenix thought of the triplets, Mrs. Jones, and Mrs. Bright. None of them allowed him a moment's peace.

"And miss the city? No way. We should get there around daybreak."

"We'll be waiting for you." They hung up and Phoenix settled in to wait.

"He robbed the store and you let him go?" Gladys Jones parroted.

"We had no choice, Mom," Emmanuel answered.

"Stay out of this, Emmanuel. You'd never do something so stupid. I'm talking to the sheriff." She put her hands on her ample hips. "Now, that man could come back here and rob any of us blind in the middle of the night and even kill somebody next time. If we wanted that, we wouldn't need to pay you the steep salary you get out of us."

"He's never hurt anyone. Actually, the gun he carries around never has bullets. But the store employees don't know that. He's not coming back. The FBI is dealing with him. They have jurisdiction over us." Phoenix didn't know why he was going into details. After the sleepless night, he only wanted to go home to bed. He never should have stopped by Tylan's store.

"We pay you to deal with it." Mrs. Jones still wasn't finished. "If you think we're going to vote for you as sheriff in November, think again."

"Mom," Emmanuel tried again.

"You also pay them," Phoenix added, knowing she wouldn't listen to any of his responses. She wanted her son, Emmanuel, in the sheriff's seat.

"I said stay out of it, Emmanuel."

"No, I'm not, Mom. Come on, let's go. Let him do the job you're paying him to do. You're causing a scene." He grabbed her arm gently and tugged her out of the store, under a stream of protests about her giving him birth and she was still the boss and Emmanuel agreeing to it all as he nudged her on.

"I'll do more than cause a scene if he keeps letting criminals go. I'll get him out of—" The door slammed on her last word. But Phoenix knew exactly what she was about to say. He also knew plenty of people in town felt likewise. He could never outgrow his past. Regardless of the positive things he could do for the community, they would always remember the bad boy from high school. Hell, if he considered what high school students were getting into now, he'd be considered a saint. Well, not quite, but close.

He had his work cut out for him if he planned to win the election.

Chapter 5

"Mrs. Jones is a champion in our corner. She's never short of vindictive words for our fair sheriff. Everything is going just splendidly." Einstein picked up a brandy snifter and swirled the brandy around. "You see, it isn't grand developments that can bring a man down, it's the little things that pile up bit by bit." He took a soothing swallow of the fiery liquid.

Casey never understood all the nonsense Einstein spouted, but he'd been good to him, and Einstein's brother had been his best friend. Casey felt he owed the man something. Besides, Einstein was always generous with money. Gave him some start-up loot and paid for a nice place for him to live when he got out of the joint. Nicest place he'd ever lived in. And Casey had to admit, the man was a genius. Casey would have killed the sheriff and gotten it over with. But not Einstein. He always took his time with stuff. Planned things.

Casey liked this little town. He rented a place in Petersburg, close enough to answer Einstein's calls and still be able to start his own business on the side. Lots of potential here—especially for criminal activity. Not like the city where he had all sorts of competition to contend with. With his skills, he'd never be caught by these country bumpkins. Yep, he had lots of ideas for business here.

"Now, I think we're ready for the next leg of our journey. Do you have the people lined up to help you appropriate the supplies at the country club?"

"Yeah, it's all set to go."

"Good, good. And are these people trustworthy?"

"They don't want to go back to the joint any more than I do."

"Excellent. Then let's schedule it in a week. That will give the good sheriff ample time to relax and think his troubles are over." He looked up at a large portrait of his brother. "It's only a matter of time before your death will be avenged, Jimmy. I'll enjoy every minute of watching the good sheriff suffer."

Karina stifled a yawn as she watched the children eagerly search for Easter eggs. They all had attended sunrise service at church this morning and she'd been up since four thirty.

Now, she and some of the ladies were in the kitchen getting things ready for the party while some of the parents entertained the children outside.

Luke Jordan's granddaughter's birthday fell on Easter Sunday this year and he had pulled out all the stops for the party. Upon her arrival, Karina was surprised to see Phoenix, but she should have known he'd be there. All the children hovered around him.

It was the perfect day for outside activities. The temperature was in the mid-seventies. Flowers were in full bloom and the green leaves on the trees were a welcome sight, if not a pollen nightmare for hay fever sufferers.

"Phoenix is a natural with children, isn't he?" Clarice Chance commented. Earlier, he'd helped the younger children search for eggs. Now, between innings as umpire for the softball game the older children were playing, he threw a happily screaming three-year-old in the air and caught her. While one little boy waited for his turn, he jumped from foot to foot singing the commercial jingle "Nacho, Nacho man, I want to be . . . a Nacho man."

"Is he singing what I think he's singing?" Towanna asked.

"Well, 'nacho' and 'macho' do rhyme. At three he really doesn't know what macho is. But he knows he loves to eat nachos."

Everyone had a good laugh off that one.

"I can't believe it. Phoenix is actually singing 'Nacho Man' with him. All the children love him." Clarice smiled back. "I'm so lucky to have him as a tenant. He doesn't give me a minute's trouble. And he keeps the house more immaculate than a woman."

Karina thought about the inch of dust that often covered her furniture. Mrs. Jones constantly lamented about it. Lately, however, Karina had made an effort to do a little more. But she just didn't have time to dust every day, and finding the time to spend with her children held precedence. Actually, Mrs. Jones never had to work outside the home a day in her life. She didn't have to baby-sit for Karina now, but she felt the children would be deprived if she didn't sit for Karina while their regular sitter was out of town tending to her sick sister. Karina was grateful. But she could do without the criticism. And whenever the woman cleaned, Karina spent days trying to find things.

"I suppose he is." She also knew she had to be careful of what she said around the woman. Although Mrs. Jones had a warm heart, she was a notorious gossiper. She'd certainly had her share to say about the new sheriff. Karina went back to the table and resumed packing the gift bags. Mrs. Jones also didn't understand why Emmanuel hadn't gotten Phoenix's job. She refused to understand that

Emmanuel needed more time on the force before he'd be ready to be sheriff.

"Well, I know one thing for certain. All the women just love Phoenix Dye. He's so sexy and fine and not full of himself. You know how some men can be when they're that good-looking. He's like my Tylan—just a good solid man."

"You can say that again," Towanna added. "If we weren't such good friends, I'd go after him myself. Lord knows how hard good men are to find nowadays." She sighed. "But, the spark just isn't there." Towanna joined Karina at the table. "I thought you and he might hit it off once, Karina."

"Do tell," Clarice joined in. "You never told me about this."

"That was the summer I did my business internship in D.C.," Towanna continued. "Mom wrote telling me how a person couldn't separate the two of you. According to her, a person didn't see you unless he was nearby. Jonathan was away most of that summer, wasn't he, on some business?"

"He was preparing for an expansion and needed training before delving into it," Karina added, wanting to end the conversation about Phoenix.

"Whatever happened to Phoenix and you?"

Karina shrugged her shoulders nonchalantly. "It just didn't work out."

"That's such a shame. Both of you are wonderful people. You would have been great together," Towanna said.

"Every single woman and their mothers from miles around love him." Clarice eased out the chair to get a glass of milk. "Still, there are a few opinions not quite so enamored of Phoenix."

"They don't count. If they hold childhood skirmishes against him, it's their loss," Towanna said.

"Gosh, I'll be so glad to get over this morning sickness.

I don't know why they call it 'morning sickness' because it's an all-day occurrence for me."

"Some man must have named it. You know how they get everything backward," Towanna suggested.

"Wouldn't it be great if you and Phoenix discovered you were still in love, married, and lived happily ever after?" Clarice added, returning to the table.

"Girl, that only happens in fairy tales. But it would prove interesting. A modern-day Cinderella," Towanna said dreamily.

"Too bad life isn't a fairy tale," Karina forced herself to say, using what she hoped was her normal voice. Phoenix was the last person she wanted to talk about. "Anyway, with my luck, he'd end up turning into a frog instead of the prince."

"I wouldn't have thought that Tylan and I would marry either. When I moved here, we blended like oil and water. And look at us now."

"I don't know. He could be my frog any day." Towanna fanned herself as if she were about to swoon.

They laughed at her antics.

They heard shrieks and looked out. A group of the kids were pouring water over Phoenix's head.

"Will you look at that? I tell you, he'll let those kids get away with anything. He has to be cold." Towanna shook her head and walked back to the table.

In no time, Miss Drucilla bustled in with Phoenix close behind. He stopped at the door, refusing to enter.

"Towanna, get a towel for Phoenix before he catches his death from getting so wet. It's not summer, you know. I don't know why you indulge those children so." Miss Drucilla fluttered about clucking like a mother hen. She was prettily dressed in a blue shirt-waist dress with a white lace collar. She was never seen without her brown opaque stockings and on her feet she wore walking sneakers.

"I'm going to get a shirt and pants out of my car. I keep them there for emergencies." Phoenix slipped the sodden shirt over his head and squeezed the excess water out of it. He stood by the door almost shivering from the cool temperature. Karina's eyes followed him as he walked to his car and grabbed a T-shirt and jeans. When he returned to the house, Towanna handed him a fluffy green towel and he went to the bathroom to change.

"Can you believe he promised the winning team they could pour a bucket of water over his head?" Miss Drucilla said in a reprimanding voice. "And they did."

Karina's mind was still on Phoenix's chest as he wiped dry. It was even more powerful than she remembered, honed by years of maturity. She'd run her hands through the thick hair that tapered toward his belt buckle so many times. She'd loved the contrasting feel of it against her tender breasts. Her nipples puckered at the thought. It had been so long since she'd made love. Not since Victor left, well over a year ago. And by the time he'd moved out, their times of intimacy had been few and far between. And never as good as it had been with Phoenix.

"Did you hear me, Karina?"

Karina jumped. "Yes, Miss Drucilla?"

"I asked if the gift bags were finished?" Miss Drucilla asked impatiently. "What in the world is wrong with you?"

"Only two to go." Karina decided to ignore the last question.

"Good, good. You can help Phoenix distribute them." She put her hands on her hips for all of two seconds. "Lord have mercy, if those kids aren't a busy lot. They're going to be plum tuckered out by nightfall."

Luke walked in and grabbed Miss Drucilla around the waist.

"What in the world? Oh, stop your foolishness," she blustered. "You're too old to carry on so. And around the children, too."

Luke winked at them and kissed Miss Drucilla on the cheek. "You've been gone too long. I'm missing you, woman."

She slapped his hand with the dish towel as Phoenix walked back in. "Get on outta here." The woman actually blushed. Frazzled, she patted her hair, forgetting what she was about to do.

Just then, Kara ran up. "Sheriff Dye, you promised."

"That I did. All right. Hold on a minute. I'll be right with you."

"Is all that stuff for us?"

"You weren't supposed to see it," Miss Drucilla finally found her tongue. "Go on back outside."

"Okay, are you coming, Sheriff?" She grabbed his hand and pulled, giving him no option but to follow.

"Well, where're you off to?" Miss Drucilla wanted to know.

"On a hike. We're looking for ferns. Trisha doesn't believe they grow around here. But they do, and I'm going to show her the spot by a stream."

"Be back in half an hour," Miss Drucilla called out. But before Phoenix could get ten feet, Mrs. Bright grabbed his attention. He motioned Kara on.

"Phoenix, some strange people have been passing my house." Every bit of ninety, with chubby cheeks and a soft teddy bear look, Mrs. Bright always had a friendly smile, even though she tended to go for the unusual.

"Did you recognize any of them?" Phoenix helped her to a nearby chair.

"No. But I think you should check it out. They had no business on my road, passing by my house and they actually slowed down as if they were searching for something." Her hand clutched her heart. She shuddered. "I'm just so frightened that they'll come by and kill me in the dead of night. I didn't get a wink of sleep last night. I don't think I'll be able to sleep tonight either."

"What time did it happen?"

"Around midnight."

"I'll have a car drive by your house tonight."

"Thank you so much. And I'll be waiting for him. Tell

him to come on up and I'll have a nice cake baked for him." The woman ambled on and Phoenix joined the children.

Miss Drucilla bustled in, peeved. "Why that woman clutters up his time with nonsense, I don't know." She grabbed a kitchen towel. "I wouldn't put up with it for a minute." She traipsed out into the yard again.

Karina got up to observe what the children were doing. Kara had one of Phoenix's hands and Karlton was on the other side of him. Some of the parents went with the group, but Karina noticed that all three of her children hovered around Phoenix. Even though Karl didn't grab his hand, he didn't let anyone else get next to him, either.

"If that girl of yours hasn't taken a liking to that man. He's so patient with her, too," Miss Drucilla noticed. "She's not going to let him go. At least he'll keep them out of our hair for a spell. I guess we're going to have to take the bags out. Give us a chance to get the table set up."

A deep sense of dread washed over Karina. Oh, Lord. What in the world drew her children to Phoenix? Three weeks ago they didn't even like him. But she knew. There was a bond that distance and time could never erase. And she couldn't tell him anything at this late date. Even though she was depriving her children with her silence. She couldn't afford to let them get attached to him and have him leave in a year or so, breaking their hearts. He said something to Kara and she smiled up at him, looking happier than Karina had seen her look in a long time. Little girls needed their dads to make them feel special. Karina closed her eyes on the sight.

"What is it, Karina?" Towanna had walked up behind her. Karina didn't hear her approach. "Something's been bothering you all day. Is everything going all right with the restaurant?"

Karina cleared her throat. "It's going just fine."

"So, what has you so preoccupied?"

"I guess it's just the first day I've had off in ages." And instead of her children spending the time with her, they're spending it with their father who couldn't have been bothered with them as babies, or just didn't care.

"You work too hard. You need more help at the restaurant."

"It'll get better. Robert's a great manager and he's almost ready to go it alone. In a few weeks, I should have more time to spend with the children, thank God. As a matter of fact, Robert's handling the buffet crowd today. I'm going by later. But, he's ready for it."

"Good, because it's time we got together for lunch. Just relax and talk the way we used to. We haven't done that for a time."

Karina smiled. "I'm looking forward to it."

"Let's set the table." Towanna squeezed her shoulders lightly.

Karina rushed into the restaurant, tense and late. Her children had quibbled about having to leave the party before everyone else. They fussed about not being able to have any fun because she worked all the time. And they did it all in front of Phoenix. Finally, he'd suggested that he would keep an eye on them and bring them home when the party was over and Towanna had offered to help him since they knew her so well. Karina thanked them for their gesture, but refused. And a battle royal ensued. Finally, under the pressure of the five, and guilt because she did spend an enormous amount of time at work, Karina had reluctantly given in. Her children had hooped and hollered, jumping around Phoenix and, in no time, ran off with him when the words had barely passed her lips, enveloping her in even more guilt.

Envy had settled in Karina's stomach. She wanted her

children to have fun and enjoy themselves. On the other hand, she was envious that, after spending so many years of loving and caring for them, their affections were so easily alienated from her to their father. "Get a grip, Karina," she told herself sternly. She knew her children's affections weren't estranged. They enjoyed a man's attention. With Jonathan away, and Victor's refusal to spend time with them, they needed him. Which bought up another sticky topic. Should she tell Phoenix about them?

Absolutely not. It would only hurt them more when he left.

"This place is packed," Robert said as he passed. "But it's going well."

"Do we have enough of everything?"

"Yes, we do. You didn't need to come in. You should have taken the day off."

Robert had run several restaurants around the country. He really was ready to take over. But, Karina still wasn't ready to give up her baby completely. Not during a busy shift. She had to make it a success. Her future, and her children's future, depended on it. Robert went off to greet another guest.

Robert was six feet two, every woman's dream, lean and handsome, but for one small flaw of a nose that had been broken during a high school basketball game. It only enhanced his masculine good looks. He'd received a basketball scholarship for college, knowing he wanted to manage restaurants. Since college graduation, he'd traveled throughout the country and managed several, but now he was ready to return to Nottoway. Karina was happy when she'd received a call from him several weeks ago asking if she needed help. It couldn't have come at a better time. He needed a few weeks to close up things on that end and two weeks ago, he arrived in town and immediately came to work. She no longer had to work fourteen to sixteen-hour days.

Karina was grateful that his size and good looks didn't

intimidate the men, but his professional and friendly demeanor helped them relax and enjoy his presence. He'd even made several positive suggestions since his arrival. As a result, more items had been added to the menu, the restaurant carried a better selection of wines, and now Karina was advertising for more weddings and small banquets.

Robert passed again. "I'm having a problem with Mrs. Higabothum."

"What is it?"

"She's upset that her husband brought her here for dinner on their anniversary."

"She doesn't like the food?" Karina knew Mr. and Mrs. Higabothum, proprietors of the Ice Cream Parlor, never ate out.

"I don't think it's that. She thinks her husband likes your food better than her's."

"Let me handle them." Karina walked over to the couple.

"I'm so happy you're joining us," she began.

"I just don't see why we had to come here for dinner," the woman lamented.

Her husband put a hand on hers. "The food is good here."

"Are you saying I don't cook good food?" She snatched her hand away.

"Of course not," Karina piped up to diffuse the tension. "I can't wait for church activities when you bring your famous lemon chess pies and fried chicken. It's the best I've tasted. I understand it's your anniversary. How many years have you been married?"

"Forty years," the woman answered. "And he never said he didn't like my cooking in all those years." She rolled her eyes at her husband who looked at the ceiling, resigned to not knowing what to do at this point.

"I think he loves your cooking but he didn't want you to have to cook for your fortieth anniversary."

"That's what I tried to tell her." Mr. Higabothum nodded his head.

Mrs. Higabothum sniffed and pursed her lips.

"He just wanted you to have a special day where you didn't have to work. Let's face it, a woman's work is never done. This way you can enjoy a meal with your husband and not worry about having to do the dishes afterward."

"That's it exactly." Mr. Higabothum eased his hand back on his wife's. She didn't move hers away this time and Karina could detect a slight softening in her countenance.

"It's not many marriages that make it to forty years anymore. Most of them don't make it to ten. It's a special time for you two, indeed."

"Well, if you put it that way." She looked shyly at her husband.

"So, what will you two lovebirds do this evening?"

"We're taking in that new movie at the new movie house," Mr. Higabothum answered.

"Oh, you'll love it. I'll go and let you enjoy your meal. Just let me know if you need anything." Karina walked off noticing that Mr. Higabothem had scooted his chair a little closer to his wife's. Karina was pleased their table faced the river, which lent a pleasing, relaxing view with the flowers in full bloom.

"Robert, have the chef make a special dessert to celebrate their anniversary and maybe have the staff sing to them. I think they'll like that gesture. Make them feel special."

"That's a perfect solution. I should have thought of that."

The triplets rushed out of the car as soon as Phoenix arrived home. Mrs. Jones called while he was at the Jordan's saying that she wasn't feeling well and wouldn't be able to keep them tonight. Phoenix left a note on Karina's door and bought the children to his house.

"Have you ever been married?" Kara asked.

"No, I haven't," Phoenix answered with a sneaky suspicion of where the conversation was heading. They were checking him out for husband material.

"Have you ever been engaged?" Karl wanted to know.

"Once."

"Why didn't you get married?" Kara asked.

Phoenix thought of Karina and their engagement eleven years ago and how quickly he'd fallen for her. He wondered if she had kept the engagement ring or thrown it away. Money was tight then and he'd cleaned out his bank account to purchase it for her. "It just didn't work out."

"Why not? You'd make excellent husband material," Karlton said formally.

Phoenix smiled. "She didn't think so."

"Who was she?"

"Enough about my love life. What do you want to do?" Phoenix slid the key into his door and soon everyone was in the house.

"What's to eat?" Karl said.

"You can't be hungry. You ate plenty at Luke's."

"I bet my mom will marry you," Karlton declared.

"Don't be too sure of that." He could hear the police scanner clicking away from upstairs.

"Oh, boy. Can we go listen to that?" Karlton asked.

"Sure." He looked up from the cereal and milk he took out for Karl. After the last visit he'd stocked up.

"Do you have a computer?" Kara asked.

"No, I don't."

"How can you live without a computer?" Karl asked. "We get to mail messages to other children all over the country. It's fun."

"It helps with homework, too. If we need information on a topic, we just look it up over the Internet. You really live in the Dark Ages don't you?" Kara frowned.

"You have to get more modernized. Living without a

computer is like driving a horse and buggy," Karl said over a mouthful of cereal.

"I think you're getting carried away." Phoenix rubbed his hair. "Maybe one day."

"Happy anniversary to you," the crowd began to sing. The chef prepared a trifle for two and set a rapidly melting candle in the middle.

The couple was beaming as Karina placed the dessert in front of them.

"Oh, isn't this just wonderful," Mrs. Higabothum gushed.

"Certainly is," her husband responded.

After the song was over and the couple blew out the candle, the staff departed, but Mrs. Higabothum held onto Karina's hand. "This has been a wonderful anniversary. And the food was delicious," she whispered. "Not as good as mine," she informed Karina, "but, I think it would be a good idea for Daddy and me to eat here now and then, now that I've tried it. Nice to get away from kitchen duties now and then." Karina often wondered why she called her husband "Daddy."

"You're welcome back any time. And I hope the two of you have a wonderful anniversary." Karina kissed the woman on the cheek, hugged Mr. Higabothum, and left them to enjoy their desert.

"You have a customer for life," Robert said.

"I hope so."

Chapter 6

Phoenix stopped at the One Stop Gas, Garage and Convenience Center for his morning cup of coffee. The brew at the police station was simply awful. Patrick was there eating an egg sandwich.

"Just getting off, Patrick?" Phoenix went over to the pastry area, grabbed a fresh doughnut, and poured a cup of the steaming aromatic liquid.

"Yeah. Pretty slow night."

"How's the new club job working out?" Phoenix took his first sip and pulled out a chair to join him.

"Just fine. Thanks again for thinking of me."

"Anytime." Phoenix bit into his doughnut and watched Tylan Chance approach.

"You have to get yourself a wife so you can get decent meals." Tylan grinned from ear to ear. "I don't have to eat junk food for breakfast."

"Now that you're married you think everybody's supposed to be sharing your glory." Phoenix grumbled, not at his best first thing in the morning.

Tylan shrugged. "Spread the happiness around."

"And I suppose Clarice gets up and cooks breakfast for you every morning," he said with a grin. The idea held some merit.

"Not exactly." Tylan scratched his head. "Now that she's pregnant, I get to cook breakfast. Women's lib and all."

"Isn't life something," Patrick lamented.

"How is Clarice?" Mrs. Jones came out from behind the canned goods.

"Still complaining of morning sickness."

"Try some chamomile tea."

"Feeling better today?" Phoenix asked her. She seemed to have made a miraculous recovery in so short a time.

"Lot's better. Must have been something I ate yesterday." A smirk appeared on her face as she faced Phoenix. "How did the kids work out? Did they give you any trouble?"

"Not a bit."

"I suppose they wanted to marry you off to Karina. They talk about it all the time." A calculating gleam rose in her eyes as several heads turned in their direction. She'd said it loud enough for everyone to hear.

"Not a bad idea," Patrick said.

Phoenix gave him a pained look. "I'm sure Karina wouldn't thank them for their efforts."

"Well everybody knows she needs a husband." Mrs. Jones grabbed a chair and sat as if she had nothing better to do. "No one's coming around to see you, either. Maybe it wouldn't be a bad idea after all. That is, unless there's something between you and Towanna?" the woman asked with keen interest.

"When I find someone, you'll be the first to know." *Darn, nosey woman.* She had no business keeping an eye on what was going on in his house.

"I'm ready to go, Gladys," Mr. Jones called. "I got to get to work."

"I'll talk to you all later," she said as she carried her things to the front of the store.

"Playing daddy now?" Tylan asked after Mrs. Jones left for the cash register.

"That woman doesn't have enough to do. She called in sick last night and I ended up keeping the triplets for Karina."

"They're sweet kids. A bit active, but good."

"Yeah."

"Thinking of kids, are you ready for your first game?" Tylan asked.

"We most certainly are." Phoenix smiled

"What group do you have?" Tylan filled his cup with coffee, then pulled out a chair.

"The nine- and ten-year-olds." With time to kill, Phoenix joined him to get out of the way of people passing by.

"You know that was a novel idea you had of getting the three counties together to compete in these games. That way they won't have to play the same teams over and over. How did the boys end up playing without Kara? She's so competitive?"

"She's playing soccer. Bill Dragon, my deputy, is coaching the girls' soccer team. He has a niece on the team and Luke's granddaughter, Kara's best friend, is on the team."

"You're getting to know the triplets well, aren't you?" Tylan asked.

"How can I not? I'm next door and they feel the entire neighborhood belongs to them." A grin crossed his lips. "Towanna came by to drop off the uniforms the other day and arrived before I did. The little scamps told her they'd take it because I didn't like women stopping by my house."

"They didn't." Tylan roared with laughter.

"They most certainly did. I had another long talk with them. It seems that's all I'm doing lately is talking to them. Did you have that problem when you were dating Clarice?''

"No. Then, too, they stayed with Jonathan a lot then. Their father had just left and I think they still harbored thoughts that he'd come back.''

"They definitely don't believe that anymore." Phoenix told them about the date they fixed Karina up with. The men had stitches in their sides by the time they finished laughing.

"They could choose someone a lot worse than you. You're bringing about a lot of good changes. You know Hadley Gaines never did a thing but sit on his butt most of the time. Things are really looking up. Thornton Sterns is bringing about some good changes also. The last bank president didn't do anything for the community but take its money. This guy's diving right in. Even starting a savings incentive program for children.''

"Tell me about it. We needed something like that. Most kids don't think about saving at all. Or anything about money for that matter.'' Phoenix got up. "Well, I have to get to work. Talk to you later.''

Phoenix left a few minutes after Mrs. Jones. As he drove to the station, he thought about the computer the triplets insisted he needed. He had never stayed in one place long enough to invest in a computer before. Now that he was putting down roots . . . Get it together, Phoenix. You can't be thinking of getting a computer because Karina's children thought you needed one. Those children and that woman stayed on his mind much too much of late. They missed their father and were trying to use him as a substitute, and it just wasn't going to work.

When Phoenix reached an intersection, a blue minivan streaked by, driving at least seventy in a forty-five mile zone. He turned on his siren and pulled out behind it. He knew exactly who that car belonged to. She still drove as recklessly as she had eleven years ago. In no time, he caught up with her and she pulled over to a stop. Phoenix searched on his dash for his ticket book, wiped the dust off it before leaving his car to approach Karina.

"Good morning. May I see your license and your car registration please? Do you realize you were driving seventy in a forty-five mile zone?"

"Do we really have to go through this? You know who I am."

"Standard procedure."

"Look, I realize I was going a little over the speed limit, but couldn't you just give me a warning this time?"

"I'm sorry. I can't show favoritism."

"A warning isn't showing favoritism," Karina said, knowing the chances of her getting a break were slim to none.

"How long have you been driving? Thirteen, fifteen years? You're well past the time for a warning. Speed limits are posted for a reason. Have you thought about what would happen in a collision around these blind curves?"

Peeved, she rummaged around in her purse and retrieved the items, then shoved them in his hand. Phoenix opened his new ticket book to the first ticket. He'd never written one before. He hadn't had the time to deal with it in the past, there were so many other things that needed doing. He hoped he wouldn't have a problem filling the damn thing out. But he kept getting distracted by Karina's fingernails tapping on the steering wheel in irritation. And that spirited anger spitting from her beautiful brown eyes.

Karina had left for the restaurant right after the school bus picked up her children. Fuming, she had snatched the dreaded ticket from Phoenix when he finished and roared off . . . within the posted speed limit. She entered the quiet building, barely noticing Patrick's sculpture of an old man fishing in the river that was located in the restaurant's foyer. It was her favorite sculpture, usually had a calming effect on her. That peace failed to present itself now that she had a ticket to pay that she could ill afford. Added to that, her insurance might increase. God, she hoped not. Phoenix didn't have to give her a ticket. He did it just to be annoying. He knew she always drove a tiny bit too fast. He probably sat around waiting for the opportune minute. She'd tried to stay within the speed limit after he returned because she knew she couldn't put anything past him. If her mind hadn't been clouded with worries of profits, she would have paid more attention to her driving.

Profits were only one of many of her worries. The children were becoming much too attached to Phoenix. She lay awake nights wondering how to end the attachment and then wondering if she should. But now profits held precedence.

Who would have thought a year ago that her restaurant would be thriving? In the beginning she'd been reluctant to take on such a huge responsibility. She'd heard Jonathan say a hundred times that he wished there was a nice place nearby for lunch and dinner where he could take his clients. The restaurant business was a risky field to be in. She'd thought long and hard before she undertook the venture. With more businesses entering Nottoway, the town needed a nice restaurant and Karina knew she needed employment. She'd always loved to cook and the restaurant business intrigued her. It was better to labor at something she loved.

She knew Jonathan would have been happy to give her a position at his company, but there's that special something about having a business of her own. Karina hadn't realized how much *time* the restaurant would require.

And now, she needed to go over her budget again to see if she could finally afford to pay herself a salary. She had little choice with only enough funds in her savings account to cover about two months worth of expenses. For the first few months, she'd lived off her savings, however, now her savings were dwindling. She would have been able to pull a salary by now if she had not hired Robert. She could handle Robert's salary just fine, but squeezing in hers was a problem. Still, Robert was worth the sacrifice.

As she scanned and calculated figures, it looked as though she'd have it this month, but next month would be a problem unless she was able to pull in a few more of the banquets she had advertised for. Karina couldn't complain.

She heard a noise in the outer room and looked at her watch. It should be time for Judy, who came in early to prep for lunch. Instead of Judy though, Robert walked through her office door.

"Why are you here so early?"

Robert took his windbreaker off and hung it on a peg in her office. "Judy called in last night asking if I could prep for her. Her little girl had a high temperature. She's taking her to the doctor. She'll be in before noon, though."

"Children get everything that goes around at that age." The worries of a working parent, Karina thought.

"I wouldn't know since I never had the urge to have any." He turned up his nose at the thought.

"I know, a born bachelor."

"That's right. I can't imagine having the little pesky beings to deal with every day. You can't sleep in until they're eighteen." Robert shuddered at the inconvenience of it all.

"I get to sleep in. Besides, they're worth it. I wouldn't give mine up for anything." Karina glanced lovingly at the pictures of her children on her desk.

"To each his own. So, did you see Towanna yesterday?" He asked eagerly.

"Yes, I did." Karina glanced at her figures again.

"Well," he continued annoyed, "is she seeing anyone?" He perched a hip on the edge of her desk.

"Why don't you ask her?" She put her papers down and gave him her full attention, a teasing smile tugging at her lips.

"Just testing the field to see if any competition is out there." He drew in a deep breath. "I just might ask her out."

"Towanna loves children." Karina raised an eyebrow.

"I'll change her mind," he said with certainty.

"I don't think so. Maybe being around a few nieces and nephews will wear on you," Karina teased, though she didn't understand how anyone could dislike children.

"I want to take *her* out, not her family."

The phone rang and Robert said, "That's my cue to start working."

Karina picked it up the receiver.

"Good morning. This is Riverview Restaurant. How may I help you?"

"Ms. Wallace?"

"Yes?"

"This is Corrie Taylor. My daughter is working on the prom breakfast committee. They would like to have it at your restaurant. We know you aren't normally open that time of the morning, but the parents would feel so much better knowing they're at your establishment than at a club or God only knows where. Lord, they can get into all sorts of danger these days. The advertisement in the Sunday paper said that you do banquets."

"What time were they thinking of?" Karina sent up a prayer and whispered to herself, "Thank you, Lord."

"Probably from right after the prom to nine in the morning."

"How many people are we talking about?" She wrote furiously on a form.

"About five or six hundred juniors and seniors with their dates. All of them won't be there at the same time. We're getting to the point where we need more than one high school in this county."

"I think a buffet would work well for them. Why don't I work up some possible selections and prices and the committee and parents can come by to discuss selections."

"That sounds wonderful." The woman sighed. "They waited until the very last minute to plan this."

"I'm sure we can work something out to suit them. I'll call you tomorrow afternoon." An idea came to Karina. "If the parents wouldn't mind supervising, I have plenty of rooms upstairs if the seniors would like to stay over for the night in sleeping bags. The boys could have a separate floor and that way they'd have the entire night of fun without parental worry."

"Oh, that sounds fabulous. I'll talk to the seniors and the parents. I'm sure they'd love those arrangements. There's so much to worry about now."

"I agree."

They hung up and Karina started pulling out price sheets and working up numbers.

"Who was that?" Robert asked from the doorway, a chef's hat perched on his head. He had his shirtsleeves pushed up and had covered his clothing with a white full apron.

"My salary for May."

"Your what?"

"The students attending the senior prom want to have breakfast here afterward."

"Great. There must be a thousand of them," he rolled his eyes heavenward.

"Five hundred anyway."

"That reminds me. You got a call yesterday about a June wedding. They know it's at the last minute, but they wanted to know if you can accommodate a dinner for a party of one fifty."

"Things are looking up."

"The note's on your desk." He fingered through some of her papers. "On second thought, I probably put it in your message box. Be right back."

In less than a minute, he was back with the details.

"I'll call her today to set up arrangements." Part of June's salary, Karina hoped. "By the way, one of us is going to have to deliver hot dogs and drinks to the baseball game for the players. The restaurant volunteered for the first game."

"Is that the team the sheriff is coaching?"

"Don't mention that man's name to me." Karina seethed.

"Uh, oh. What did he do?"

"Just to be annoying, he gave me a speeding ticket this morning," she snapped.

"You weren't speeding by any chance, were you?"

"That's beside the point. Plenty of people speed and don't get tickets. He could have issued a warning."

"Maybe it's a love pat. You know how, when kids fall in love, instead of kissing, they hit each other?"

"Don't be ridiculous. That man knows perfectly well how to say whatever he pleases." He certainly wasn't at a loss for words during their summer fling, Karina thought. She'd lived to regret all his words. He talked her into trusting him quickly enough.

"Anyway, spending money on those little monsters seems a waste to me."

"Let's hope the parents remember us when they're selecting a restaurant for dinner and their functions. Remember the seniors are not adults yet. But a banquet will bring in good money. I'm going to need the extra money to pay for the ticket." She sighed. "I'm going to go by the Higabothum's when I leave here at five to pick up the ice cream. After I bring it here I'm going home to spend an evening with my children. Think you're ready to handle it alone tonight?"

"Sure."

The jukebox Karina was so familiar with was playing when she entered the Higabothums's Ice Cream Parlor. The cute white tables and pink chairs were the perfect image for the establishment. A few children stood at the bar ordering sandwiches to go with their treat. The Higabothums's parlor was very popular because they served their own home-made ice creams. The secret recipes had been in their family for generations. When Karina asked them to make a special flavor for the restaurant, they were eager to comply.

"Well hello there, Karina. Haven't seen you in a coon's age. Heard that the restaurant was doing great. I was just telling Daddy we have to return there. I enjoyed my dinner," Mrs. Higabothum said.

"Please do. How are you?"

"Just fine."

Out of her peripheral vision, Karina watched Phoenix approach the bar. Her lips tightened at the sight of that hateful, spiteful man. The unfairness of the ticket still stung.

"Well, looka here. Just like old times. How you doing, Sheriff." Mr. Higabothum shuffled in from a storage room. He wore the pink apron and hat his wife had made for the store and insisted that everyone wear. Teenage boys rebelled at having to wear bright pink, but there was no budging Mrs. Higabothum on her decision. Everything had to match.

"How are you?"

"I remember the two of you coming in here just like it was yesterday. Ordering sandwiches and playing the same song on the jukebox to dance to while you waited. I bet we still have that record in there, don't we, Daddy?"

"Shore do."

"And Karina, you're just as pretty as ever. Phoenix was always a handsome, sly devil. I knew you'd do good. They said you weren't going to amount to much, but I remember how you used to help me lift things and clean the snow off the walk for me and Daddy and never charged us a dime. I always told Daddy, now, that's a good boy. He's going to be something when he grows up. And wasn't I right, Daddy?" Mrs. Higabothum perched herself on a chair and chattered on.

"Shore was. He was a good boy. Always knowed he was gonna do good. What can we get for you?"

"I'd like one of your special burgers with the works."

"How's your mama, Phoenix. Heard from her lately?" Neither budged from their spot to give the cook the order.

"I talked to her over the weekend. She's coming here soon for a visit."

"Tell her to drop by. I'm looking forward to seeing her. I know she likes being close to the water. Always liked the water. Used to come in here when she was a teenager and say, 'Mrs. Higabothum, I'm going to live right on the water when I leave home. Just you wait and see.' And now she does. Isn't that something, Daddy?"

"I remember when your mamma and daddy used to court, too. I was telling the Mrs. all them years ago that you and Karina used to court just like they did. Come by for them sandwiches and ice cream and always eyeing each other. Certainly is a shame you didn't marry. Thought you two were made for each other. Those children of yours, Karina, are the sweetest children. When Jonathan bought them by, they helped out just like Phoenix used to do. Didn't I say so, Daddy? How's Jonathan enjoying his vacation?"

"We got a card from him the other day and he loves it. It's the first one he's taken in years."

"I know he was nervous about going away for so long. But a body needs to get away now and then. And I told him so, too.

"Daddy, why don't you go over there and play that record in the box for them. Let 'em dance like they used to do. We still got it. It sure is nice to see you two together again."

"Please don't trouble yourself." Pressed close against Phoenix was the last place Karina wanted to be. "I need to pick up the ice cream."

"No trouble at all. You have enough time for one dance." Mr. Higabothum shuffled over to Phoenix and Karina to urged them over to the dance floor.

"I need to get my sandwich . . ."

"I'll get it fixed while you dance. Gonna take a few minutes, anyway." Mrs. Higabothum finally slapped the order into the serving window.

Mr. Higabothum continued to coax them toward the dance floor and went to the jukebox in search of the song Karina remembered like yesterday.

"I really can't stay," Phoenix said.

"But, I thought you said you were on your way home."

"I am . . ."

"Good, then. You don't have a wife or anything waiting there. I haven't heard that song in a long time. Be nice to hear it again and see you two dance to it. Yes, sir-re, just like old times."

Jeffrey Osborn's soothing voice singing "We're Going All the Way," was not what Karina wanted to hear. So many problems occurred because they hadn't.

First Karina was a little stiff with the feel of the familiar body next to hers. Soon, however, her body seemed to have a mind of it's own throwing logic and reason out the window. The mellow words of the song and the enticing music prompted long-lost feelings to encase her within their cocoon. Phoenix's arms tightened around her and she snuggled closer, both of them moving slowly to the sensuous beat. Being in Phoenix's arms was like coming home from a long journey that had taken her away far too long.

Nothing existed but them. It was as if they were alone in the world together. Karina closed her eyes and could almost smell the lake where they lounged on a blanket in the hot August heat. She could almost feel his gentle touch, his kisses.

She caressed his muscled chest. Breathing in the masculine scent of him, she felt large, sure hands caress her back while intense desire spread through her.

"We have to talk," Phoenix whispered in her ear.

Karina stiffened. "About what?"

"Ssh. Later." He eased her head back to resting on his shoulder.

Karina felt a feather kiss. What did he want to talk about? What did he know? No! He couldn't possibly have found out about the children. The earlier mood had left.

The song ended and Karina was shaky. Phoenix didn't look any better.

One of the little boys Phoenix coached broke the ice by saying, "You don't even know how to dance."

Phoenix gathered enough wherewithal to say, "And I suppose you can teach me?" With his hands in his pocket, he seemed so self-assured, not the mass of emotions that was Karina.

"Sure I can. All you did was stand in place and barely move at all. You're always telling us to put more energy into our plays. Maybe you can put a little more energy on the dances. The one you were doing is old."

"When you're older . . . a lot older, I'll tell you the merits of slow dancing, kid."

No one was paying any attention to Karina and she was glad for the respite. She walked over to the counter hoping to make a hasty exit.

"Now, didn't you two look just wonderful together. And both of you being single, too. Didn't they look wonderful, Daddy?"

"Um." Mr. Higabothum didn't bother with a comment this time. He had a way of ignoring his wife when she carried on too long. But then, she had enough to say for the both of them. He gave Karina a wink. "Let 'em worry about their own love life. Don't need us doin' it for 'em."

"I wasn't trying to run their lives, but a body can comment if a body wants to." She sniffed and straightened her shoulders. "Still say you looked good together." Blessedly, a couple of teenagers came in with ice cream orders for their parents and Karina took the ice cream and made some excuse to leave.

Chapter 7

It had been heaven to hold Karina in his arms again.
Her soft brown skin felt like silk beneath his fingertips.
Her petite body fitted perfectly to his. Phoenix was awash
with contrasting emotions of how delightful the dance had
been and how abruptly their relationship had ended. The
ebb and flow kept Phoenix awake for half the night. His
love of her had never completely died.

For the first time, Phoenix considered that there might
be a logical reason for what she'd done, though, for the
life of him, he didn't know what. Maybe this time . . .
Phoenix, you're a fool if you even consider a relationship
with Karina again. Then as now, he never understood how
she could have been so loving with him one month, yet
forget him . . . Karina's smile was his last thought as he
drifted to sleep.

Phoenix woke to a ringing phone.

"Phoenix, those spaceships are back."

Who would dare pull a crank call this time of night?
Phoenix looked at the digital clock. It blinked two-twenty.

He closed his eyes, wanting to doze off again. "Who is this?"

"It's June Bright. What's wrong with you?"

"Oh, Mrs. Bright." He sat up in bed and pried his eyes open. "What spaceships?" he sniffed.

"The spaceships I've been telling you about."

What the hell was the woman talking about? He vaguely remembered her talking about something at the birthday party, "Oh, the cars."

"No, no. They're spaceships this time. I don't know how long they've been here. I just got up to go to the necessary and I saw the lights out my bathroom window. You need to drive by and check it out." Her excitement carried over the phone.

First thing tomorrow, he was getting an unlisted number. The whole town knew his. "Are you completely awake?" he asked. She'd never been one for tasting the cooking sherry.

"Yes, I am. If you don't get over here, you're going to miss them. They never stay very long."

"Did you call 911?"

"What for? You're the sheriff."

It wouldn't do any good to lecture her on why they had 911 and why she should call the sheriff's office and not the sheriff's home at 2 A.M. "I'll get someone to come by to check it out."

"I'm watching them from my kitchen window. I'll fix something for the officers to eat while I wait. Well . . . do you think maybe I should keep the lights off? I don't want them capturing me. Lord knows I don't want them experimenting with my body and touching me all over." The eagerness in her voice was followed by a shuddered gasp.

"Maybe you should keep your lights off." She'd been without a man too long, Phoenix thought.

"Thank goodness I didn't turn on the bathroom lights.

Just the bedroom one in the back of the house. Maybe I'll just leave the kitchen lights off, too."

"You do that . . . In—"

"On the other hand, maybe I should cut off *all* the lights in case they have some scouts wandering around. Wouldn't want them peeping in my windows. Folks from other planets can land on our planet just like we land on theirs. They said so on the television show the other night." Cries of mingled fear mixed with excitement.

Phoenix cleared his throat. "We'll check it out. There may be some simple explanation for the lights."

"I doubt it. Mr. Harold's folks only stop by now and then, and always during the day. Nobody's got any business being out here this time of the morning. Thank goodness they landed on his property and not mine."

"Someone will be there soon." Phoenix tried to urge her off the phone. "Keep your doors locked."

Phoenix disconnected and dialed the office. "Emmanuel, Mrs. Bright is seeing her spaceships."

"Again?" Emmanuel started to laugh.

"Send a car around there, will you?"

"Sure. Want me to call you back afterward?"

"Only if you see spaceships." Phoenix hung up.

Phoenix tried to sleep the rest of the night, but instead of the rest he desperately needed, he thought of Karina's smooth skin. He trooped downstairs and got a glass of water, then glanced out the window in the direction of Karina's house. Its silhouette stood out in stark relief against the yard light. He wondered if she was sleeping soundly or plagued with a sleepless night. He trooped back to bed, put his hands behind his head.

They needed to talk. He opened the drawer and pulled out the locket to glimpse her sweet beguiling smile. Now he recalled her saying, "So you'll have something to remember me by."

He could never forget her. It was the one keepsake he carried with him when he went undercover, though he knew it was safer leaving personal items in storage. He couldn't resist having a picture of her nearby to look at, to give the occupation he'd chosen purpose when he'd wondered why he'd put himself through the danger. When he discovered she was married, he'd closed the locket and hadn't opened it again until returning home to Nottoway.

He could never bear to throw this last reminder of her away.

Her teasing black eyes, her dimpled chin, her seductive smile, her quick energy and spirit, all the little details he loved about her were reflected in the miniature photo. When she'd been his, he'd felt he could conquer the world. When he'd been on that nightmarish assignment, the only thing that made his life sane were his memories of Karina. And suddenly, when it was over and he was on his way to see her, he'd discovered she was married. Part of him died that day.

Why did she deceive him? What went wrong? He could tell whether men were lying by looking in their eyes and recognizing the little nervous twitches that came involuntarily. Or sometimes their eyes couldn't quite meet his. And then there were the hardened ones who could look anyone in the eyes and lie. He could detect those, too, because their eyes were so cold he could almost shiver at the look of death. But Karina wasn't like that.

He couldn't detect any false pretenses from her. She seemed so open and honest and full of love for him.

Still, she'd married another man as soon as he left.

Why?

Tired from a sleepless night, Phoenix walked into the office with a cup of the awful coffee the station kept, not having had the time to stop by Tylan's before work.

"A load of supplies at the country club were stolen last night," Emmanuel said as he closed the door.

"Patrick?"

"Okay, except for a giant-sized headache, he'll be fine. Someone knocked him out from behind. He was taken to the emergency room, but they sent him home."

Phoenix released the breath he didn't realize he was holding. "What did they get?"

"Basically building supplies, lumber, plumbing fixtures, and some heavy equipment."

"What evidence did you gather at the scene?"

"Just a lot of tracks. So many different vehicles were on the site, it'll be impossible to pick one out. I called Luke Jordan to let him know." Emmanuel looked past Phoenix. "Uh oh, looks like trouble."

When Phoenix turned around, he saw three of the club backers with Luke.

"Hi, Luke."

"Phoenix. Can we talk in your office?"

"Of course." Phoenix lead the way. The four men followed him.

"We're going to have to let Patrick go," Luke started without preamble. "It's not something I wanted to do. I was outvoted." Luke shrugged as if he'd given it his best shot. "I believe in giving him the benefit of doubt, but . . ."

"We haven't charged anyone yet. We're still sorting through and gathering information."

"Sorry, Phoenix, I know you recommended Patrick, but I just don't think we can trust him. He could have easily set the whole thing up," Kron said. "Hell, they stole a large compressor, a generator, power saws, drills, wood, aluminum and that's only the beginning. We can't afford to keep him."

"You may want to let my office investigate the case before you make any rash decisions. There's nothing yet to indicate Patrick was involved," Phoenix put in. "He might sue you for improper discharge or something."

"He was a little wild in high school. Always in the fast lane," Kron said.

"He's worked since he was ten years old. He's never stolen a thing in his life," Luke added.

"I don't know." One older man scratched his balding head. "Used to drive them old cars all fast and ran after those loose girls."

"So did your son." Phoenix let that sink in. "There's no sense in speculating. Let my office do what you pay us to do. As soon as we know something, we'll inform you." Phoenix hoped he didn't sound as impatient as he felt. He wanted to go out to the site before anyone . . . anyone else trampled all over the place. He knew from the investigation done so far, that people had muddled the site, but hopefully, he could find something.

"Yeah, come to think of it, you used to drive those fast cars, too."

Phoenix leaned forward in his seat. "Are you trying to insinuate something here?"

"Phoenix, we aren't trying to insinuate anything," Luke cut in quickly, giving Kron a cold look. "Hell, my boys raced, too, just like we did as teenagers. It's just these yahoos are paranoid. And until you can find out who's behind this, it'll be better to keep Patrick out of this." Luke tried a consolatory tone. "I know how it feels to be unjustly accused of a crime." A couple of men nodded. Luke had had all kinds of trouble last year when he was accused of harassing Clarice Chance.

"We're not about to cast stones at this point. We'll give you a chance to investigate and do your job. Won't we men?"

A few "humphs" could be heard.

After the men left, Emmanuel walked in.

"He's been working in security for years with no problems. Why the hell do they suddenly not trust him?" Phoenix lamented.

"You know how people talk when something happens. They remember everything from kindergarten."

"But Patrick never stole anything. Sure, we ran with the

wrong bunch for a short time, but we soon left that group. That happened in high school and shouldn't follow him as an adult. He's had an exemplary work record, which should count toward his credibility."

"A lot of folks around here don't like you. Old man Taylor never stopped talking about the peanut field that bunch destroyed."

Phoenix sighed. "Don't I know it. Anyway, they want him off the job. Good luck for them finding someone else," Phoenix snapped, then picked up the typed notes again, brows creased.

"Luke really feels bad about it. He didn't want to get rid of Patrick, but he was outvoted."

"I suppose you're right. Isn't this just grand?" Phoenix dropped the papers on his desk and got up. "I'm going out to the site."

He arrived at the country club just barely ahead of the construction workers. The supervisor was miffed at having to wait before they could get to work, but Phoenix ignored them while he searched the grounds. Not a clue would be left after the workers tramped all over the grounds.

He examined the spot where Patrick was struck over the head. When he didn't find anything there, he started pacing the area. Stacks of plywood were on one side, heavy equipment, at least what was left, was on the grounds.

A large concrete slab was over to the side. "The generator was taken from that spot," the foreman pointed out.

Phoenix walked to that area. A piece of broken metal pipe was on the ground, along with other items. Phoenix picked up the pipe. Several strands of short black hair were attached by what appeared to be dried blood. Must have been what clubbed Patrick, he thought. Patrick would faint at the sight of blood.

When walking along the side of the foundation, Phoenix picked up a cigar. He smelled an expensive brand, probably Calista Lopez or Paul Bellicoso. He slipped it into the evidence bag. It wasn't the usual brand construction workers bought. And since it was well intact and it had rained a day ago, it was dropped recently. Patrick had asthma and wouldn't consider smoking anything; he didn't even like to be in the room with smoke.

The lunch crowd had dwindled to a trickle, and the specials were going better than expected. Although quite a few customers liked the fancy dishes Karina served, many liked the meatloaf, fried chicken, and everyday country cooking. Of course, her fried chicken was actually baked to cut down on the fat content, but people seemed to love it and it was definitely a hit. Karina stacked menus behind the cash register, and heard someone enter. Before she could turn around, someone caught her from behind and kissed her cheek.

"Oh!" She whirled into Jonathan's arms. "Jonathan, you're back." She hugged her brother. "I knew you couldn't stay away for the full two months."

"Had to get back to work. Six weeks were enough." He stepped to the side and Karina saw he wasn't alone. People she hadn't met before. "Let me introduce you to Harry and Betty Kramer."

Karina extended a hand. "Welcome to Riverview. I hope you enjoy your stay in Nottoway."

"It's a lovely town," Mrs. Kramer returned. Some people wore gray very well, Karina thought, and Mrs. Kramer was one of them. The woman looked to be in her mid-fifties and the gray steaks in her short styled hair only enhanced her beauty.

"Your brother has recommended your restaurant so much that I'm dying to taste the food," Mr. Kramer said. "What's this with the never-fried chicken?"

"It's a recipe I experimented with. Lots of nice spices but it's actually baked. It's wonderful."

"I'm going to try it then. With the doctor talking about low-fat foods, I don't know the last time I've had good fried chicken."

"Remember, we are what we eat . . . Oh, dear," Mrs. Kramer gasped. "Will you look at that lovely sculpture? Do you mind if I ask where you got it?" She walked over to view it closer.

"It was made by a local artist," Karina informed her. "He does wonderful works. I have several pieces on display here. Before you leave, I'll show them to you."

"Splendid. This piece would look simply lovely in my foyer. I love the water." She turned to Karina. "Harry and I have a summerhouse in North Carolina that's right on the Atlantic. We hope to move into it next year," she said, glancing back at the sculpture.

"Actually, it's for sale," Karina said.

"Name your price." Mrs. Kramer's eyes lit up, her hand over her heart.

Karina named a price well above what she and Patrick had originally agreed on. Given his druthers, he'd nearly give the art away. If someone didn't step in and take matters in her own hands, he'd have to keep a "day job" forever.

"Sold! I do believe I got a wonderful bargain on this." The woman smiled and slipped her hand into her husband's arm.

Thank goodness someone was interested in Patrick's sculpture. The robbery at the club and Patrick's dismissal was the talk of the lunch crowd. He could use the extra income. She'd take the money by his place on her way home.

"Looks like things are slowing down. Can you join us, Karina?" Jonathan asked.

"Sure. Let me tell the cashier and I'll be right with you." Karina seated them at the prize table that afforded a lovely view of the river and left to ask Tracy to seat any last minute guests.

* * *

When Phoenix arrived home from work all he wanted was a hot shower and bed, but before he could retire, he needed to visit Patrick. After a sleepless night, he was dead on his feet.

"Sheriff Dye."

Phoenix turned impatiently toward the voice. "Yes?"

"My kite's stuck up the tree. Can you get it out for me?" Kara looked at him beseechingly.

"Not now, maybe later," Phoenix snapped.

As the child walked dejectedly toward her house, Phoenix felt guilty. It wasn't her fault he'd had what Karina used to call a bad hair day. "Kara," he called.

"Yes?" She looked at him warily.

"Look. I didn't mean to snap at you. It's been a long day. Tell you what. I have an errand to run so come back in a couple of hours and I'll fly the kite with you. Have you done your homework yet?"

"Not all of it."

"Why don't you finish it. By then I should be back. I've got some longer string in the garage we can use."

"Oh, great! Thanks." She turned and sprinted down the drive.

Phoenix took a shower to wake himself and headed to Patrick's.

Patrick was sitting on the porch with a ice pack plastered to the back of his head.

"What happened, man? Are you all right?" Phoenix asked. He didn't wait for an invitation to take a seat in the swing.

"Except for the mother of headaches." Patrick took the ice pack off his head. "I didn't do it." It looked as if it pained him to have to say that to a friend who should have known better than believe otherwise in the first place.

Phoenix felt guilty for him having to say it. Patrick may not have had a white-collar job and a college education, but he'd worked hard all his life. Phoenix and Patrick had delivered papers on their bikes together for their first jobs at ten. They'd worked together at odd jobs throughout high school.

After the army, Patrick acquired a position in security at the tobacco company and he'd worked there until it closed and moved to another state. And he worked even harder on his art, though he never tried to sell any of it. He'd thought of art as a hobby he loved to do and gave pieces away to friends as gifts, especially when he wanted to treat someone and didn't have the extra funds to buy something.

"I know." Phoenix sighed. "Can you give me anything to work with? I went out to the site earlier."

"I was making my rounds and as I neared a corner of the building, I thought I heard a noise behind me. When I turned around to see what it was, I was hit on the head. Next thing I knew police cars and Mr. Kron were swarming around me."

Both men looked up as a car drove up in the yard.

Karina wished she had called Patrick before visiting him, but she'd hoped to surprise him. Now it was Phoenix, of all people, sitting on the porch. Nothing but to make the best of it. She couldn't exactly turn around and leave like a coward.

Patrick walked to the car to greet her.

"How are you feeling, Patrick?" She hugged him.

"I'll live."

He closed the door and they walked to the house arm in arm.

"Hello, Phoenix."

"Karina." He took a swallow of his soda and pushed back on the swing.

"I've got good news for you, Patrick. I sold three of your sculptures this afternoon."

"Three!"

"Yes. And I have a nice check to hand you. They're

business acquaintances of Jonathan's. They loved your work."

Headache forgotten, he grabbed Karina and swung her around and around.

At the unexpected exuberance, Karina squealed. Patrick tumbled and, had it not been for Phoenix steadying them, they would have both landed in a tangled heap in the dirt.

"Hey, you're not ready to run a marathon yet. Take it easy. Congratulations, buddy. I'm happy for you," Phoenix said.

Patrick pumped his hand enthusiastically and grabbed him in a hug.

"All right. Enough of this."

"Lord. It wouldn't have happened if you hadn't suggested I put some pieces at the restaurant. And thanks for letting me put my pieces there, Karina. Hey, I've got to pay you a commission."

"Don't be silly. You don't have to pay me for having beautiful art displayed in my restaurant. But, I do have a few empty spaces and I need at least three more pieces. I hope you have something that goes with a water scene. I'm going to buy that myself. It was very painful for me to let go of that sculpture."

"You didn't have to sell it. I would have given it to you."

"No more giving your art away. You're a bonafide artist who should be paid for his work."

"But without you, it wouldn't have been possible." Patrick continued to look at his check.

Karina knew it was difficult for him to believe he'd made so much off the sales.

"This is more than I ever hoped to get for twenty pieces, much less for three."

"When you value your work, others will, too. Those pieces are worth every cent she paid," Karina insisted, sharing the euphoria of the first sale from one business person to another.

Since Phoenix was there, Karina decided not to linger.

She made a hasty excuse to escape when Patrick invited her to sit with them.

As luck would have it, when Karina turned the key in the ignition not even a groan sounded from the motor. She pressed on the gas and tried again. Nothing. Patrick and Phoenix walked over to see what was the matter.

"I haven't had any problems with it. I don't know what it could be," she said as she exited the car.

"Pop the hood and we'll take a look-see," Patrick said.

Karina pulled the hood release and the men looked underneath. Since Victor left, Jonathan had seen to the regular maintenance for her car. When something needed doing, he'd loan her his car and take hers to Tylan's to get fixed. Between Jonathan and Victor, she'd never had to change oil or add brake fluid—which was another mark against her flight to independence. It was time she learned more about cars. At least the rudimentary needs like how to change the oil and regular maintenance.

"Your alternator's broken. You're going to have to get it towed to the garage. Won't take long and it shouldn't cost much. I'll give Tylan a call." Patrick went to make the call.

"I'm about ready to leave anyway. I'll take you home," Phoenix offered.

"You really don't have to. I'll ride to the garage with the tow truck."

"There's no need. Leave the key with Patrick. No telling when they'll get here."

"I suppose you're right." But Phoenix would want to talk and Karina thought of the discussion he'd mentioned the other day. She wasn't ready to talk about the past.

Patrick returned. "It'll be an hour, at least, before he can get to you. Somebody broke down clear across the county on Crosstrain Road."

Karina took the car key off the key ring. "Here's the key. Phoenix offered me a ride home." Karina reluctantly handed the key over.

A light came into Patrick's eyes. "Good. I'll drop off some pieces at your shop tomorrow morning. What time will be good for you?"

"I'll be in by eight. Anytime after that will be fine." Whoever said men weren't matchmakers hadn't met Patrick, Karina thought.

They rode in a silence so thick you could drive a knife through it and when they neared their homes, Phoenix pulled into his drive, not hers.

"It's time for that talk," he said as he turned off the ignition.

"I really need . . ."

"Mrs. Jones won't mind if you're a few minutes late."

"But . . ."

Phoenix opened his door and slipped out, and before she could form a coherent objection, he had come around and opened her door. Resigned, Karina followed him into the house. If she put up a fight, he'd wonder why.

She wouldn't give him reason to ask even more questions. She hadn't been in the house since Clarice's wedding. It was still decorated with the same beautiful detail. The polished sheen of the wooden table gleamed. A lone glass drained in the kitchen sink.

"Have a seat."

Karina didn't really want to sit. She'd feel better on her feet. Nevertheless, she sat on one of the plump sofa cushions. Phoenix sat across from her, elbows on his legs, and swiped a hand across his weary face. The creases in his forehead showed how fatigued he was.

"You've got wonderful kids, Karina."

Karina fingers tightened around her purse handle. "Thanks."

"Why didn't you wait?"

She didn't even pretend to misinterpret his meaning. What could she say? That she'd tried to reach him and couldn't? What good would it do to tell him that now? He'd want to know why she'd felt it so urgent to reach him and then got married so quickly. He'd know the triplets were his. "It was a long time ago." Her hand cramping, she placed her purse on the floor by her feet.

"I know that. I still need to know. The triplets could have been mine. Hell, your children spend more time with me here than with their own father. Why doesn't he visit them? They need him."

Karina focused on the portrait on the wall behind Phoenix, wondering how she was going to live with telling the childrens' father, "You don't need to concern yourself with them. It doesn't do any good to rehash this. It's over and done with." *The triplets were his.* He was much too close for her conscience's comfort. She got up and paced to the window. Her house was in clear view. It looked as lonely in the distance as she'd felt for the last few years.

"But not complete. We need to end this . . . this distance. I have questions I need answered. One of which is why didn't you wait?"

"I tried to contact you. But all my letters were returned with 'no forwarding address,' your phone had been disconnected, and I didn't hear from you. I thought you'd written the relationship off. Maybe with distance and time I thought you'd felt that it wasn't all you'd wanted it to be. It was an unusual experience."

"We had so much love, Karina. At least on my part. I told you before I left, I'd be traveling around. You might not be able to reach me."

"You didn't say you'd disappear off the face of the earth," Karina snapped. As the enormity of what happened sank in, Karina closed her eyes in disbelief. How she'd suffered back then. And all because they didn't really know each other. In a daze she said, "I didn't even know what you did for a living. You had me in such a sexual haze that summer . . . I didn't take the time to think, much less ask questions about your life."

"My job precluded me from saying anything about what

I did. I was working on a special assignment that I wasn't allowed to talk about.''

She shook her head. ''You should have trusted me enough to at least tell me that much.''

''You could have waited until Christmas,'' he insisted. ''You should have finished your last year of college.

''I didn't see you Christmas.'' Karina put a hand to her dizzy head.

''You were already married!'' he said in a mocking tone. ''Did my proposal mean so little to you? Was what we shared so inconsequential?''

''I thought it was meaningless to you.'' Karina grasped for a chair, mind spinning. *He didn't desert her.*

''I told you I was coming back. You should have trusted me,'' his voice thundered.

''Like you trusted me,'' Karina shouted back.

Silence reigned as they grappled with their own thoughts. At least that explained why she couldn't contact him. Karina was trembling, sick with knowing that she'd suffered for nothing, all because he thought she was too young, too inexperienced to talk to her. Hadn't she read that psychologists said the number one problem with relationships was lack of communication? She would have waited had she known. So much lost. And much to sort out in his presence.

''Did you love me at all, or was it a hallucination on my part?'' His voice was raw.

''It's too late to talk about it now.'' The realization that he'd loved her deeply, regret at what could have been. Karina wasn't prepared to deal with these newfound revelations.

''I need to know.''

''I loved you.'' Her voice caught.

''Then why didn't you wait? Even if you thought I wasn't coming back, you could have waited at least until Christmas. That wasn't asking too much, was it?''

It was the perfect opening for her to tell him about the triplets, but caution and fear kept her silent.

He came up behind her, kneaded her shoulders, turned her and stroked her cheek with the back of his hand. She'd missed such gentle touches when he left. His index finger caught her under the chin and tilted her head to get a clear view into her eyes, her eyes were moist.

His voice gentled. "Karina," he whispered. "What we had was so special. We'd ignite each other just by being in the same room. I thought nothing on earth could come between us." He pressed a demanding kiss to her lips, immediately seeking entrance, and was allowed. Tongues mated, reveled in the familiar dance that drugged their senses. As breaths quickened, hands touched and caressed, they forgot the past. Only this moment counted.

She opened his shirt, caressed his chest, loving the feel of him. And Karina's world tilted while lips were sealed, Phoenix lifted her in his arms and marched upstairs to toss her on the bed. He hurriedly undressed her and she fought with his clothing. Clothes landed everywhere in their haste to be closer.

He touched, caressed, drawing the very essence of sensuality from her that only he had the power to do. Then finally, he pulled open the bedside drawer, glided on a prophylactic and was back, slowly sliding in, with some resistance, since it had been two years for Karina. Passion built and they danced the age-old rhythm to fulfillment.

Phoenix let out a shuddering breath. "I've missed this so very much, Karina. I've missed you."

Karina lifted a hand and caressed his face, a face so familiar, so dear. "I missed you."

"We had it all." He frowned. "I should hate you. I've wanted you since I came back." He kissed her again, harder this time as if to punish.

She was losing him. She felt the withdrawal when he got up. "The kids are waiting for me. I promised I would come for them before dark." He disappeared into the bathroom.

Karina heard water run and he was back with a warm washcloth wiping her intimately. He kissed her again, before disappearing again. No more lingering touches.

Karina got up, grabbed her panties from the door knob and her bra from the bed post. What the devil did they do? Her clothes were scattered all over the room. She was going to deal with what had just happened and what would happen next, once she was behind her own closed doors. But then Karina realized that what they'd just experienced was all they could ever share. She couldn't tell him about the triplets and without a reasonable explanation for marrying Victor, he'd never trust her.

By the time she finished dressing, Phoenix came back to the room, a towel wrapped around his waist. Without saying a word, or looking her way, he snapped the dresser drawer open, pulling out underwear.

Uncomfortable in the strained silence, Karina went downstairs to wait for him, not knowing quite what to say.

The tense atmosphere lasted on the trip to her house.

As soon as they arrived in her yard and parked the car under a maple tree, they heard, "Sheriff Dye . . . Sheriff Dye. We're ready."

"We were just getting ready to call your . . . hi, Mom. Why are you with Sheriff Dye?" Kara ran to the car bubbling with excitement.

"My car broke down and he gave me a lift home." Karina opened the door and exited the space too filled with memories. Her sons scampered into the back seat. Kara took the front. Enthusiastically, they waved goodbye to her as they pulled away.

In the house, Mrs. Jones had her jacket on, ready to go.

"They are certainly excited about flying that kite with Phoenix," Mrs. Jones said as Karina entered the house.

Karina pictured the glow of anticipation etched on her children's faces when they left with him. "They get exited about doing anything with him," she mumbled.

In a rare show of warmth to Karina—she often exhibited

this affection to the children—Mrs. Jones patted her hand. "They like having a man around. You know, men are like big kids themselves."

"I suppose." Karina forced a smile.

"Well, I fixed a pot roast for dinner." She donned her scarf and sweater. The wind had picked up outside. "The children have finished their homework and they've eaten dinner, so you should have a nice restful evening while they're with Phoenix. You don't get many free evenings. Why don't you take a relaxing bath and go to bed early."

"I just might do that."

"I'll see you tomorrow." Mrs. Jones left in an unusually jovial mood.

Out of the living room window, Karina saw Phoenix on a ladder trying to get the kite out the tree, the children looking anxiously on. Karl hopped from foot to foot, while Kara called up to Phoenix and Karlton held on to the ladder. Phoenix stopped a moment, said something to them. Karlton stepped back, Karl handed a stick to him. Phoenix used the stick to maneuver the kite out the tree. The wind blew it right back in.

Karina laughed.

Phoenix said something to Kara who was holding the string, while he stretched to loose the kite again. It was higher this time. What patience he had with them, Karina thought.

She turned from the scene with mixed feelings. God, what a mess. If only he'd said something—anything to her before he'd left. If only she'd been strong enough to consider having her children alone and not have married Victor. That wasn't an option at that time. Having children out of wedlock just wasn't done in small towns, at least not in Nottoway.

Deciding to take Mrs. Jones advice on the soothing bath, Karina ran her bathwater, then brewed tea while the tub filled. Once done, with tea in hand, she got into the hot water and leaned her head against the bath pillow as the bubbles wrapped around her tense body and reached high enough to kiss her chin.

To have made love with Phoenix had to be rated as one of the most asinine things she'd ever done. He wasn't a man to take lovemaking lightly—at least with her. He'd expect much more than she was willing to give right now. And he could be tenacious, headstrong, and obstinate when he wanted something. Like a dog with a favored bone. She wasn't fooled by his silence after their lovemaking. He liked to take his time to think things through before acting.

She should have used the opportunity to tell him about the children. It would be easier now than later, if he found out from some other source. But Karina could just imagine the potential fallout that revelation would bring. A hurricane would be mild in comparison. She also needed to consider his plans for the future. He'd said he was away from home most of the time on assignments. What her children didn't need was to lose one father only to settle for a part-time version now. It would be much too confusing to them and much too unsettling in their lives. But wasn't he in their lives now? Didn't he spend enormous amounts of time with her—their—children now? What a mess.

On a more positive note, it stirred her heart to know that Phoenix hadn't deserted her. How he must have suffered when he discovered she was married. A crushing blow for a man so full of pride and honor. His suffering must have equaled hers. Oh, God. They'd been so much in love. Why did things happen—seemingly small, inconsequential things—to destroy people's lives—forever. Because in the end, Karina didn't know how their situation could be salvaged without hurting them both.

The tepid water had turned cold and the bath was turning out not to be so relaxing after all. Karina started to wash. When she moved her leg, she realized anew how tender she was from her first loving experience in two years.

His touch had been like a slice of heaven. His knowing hands had remembered every secret spot on her body. How she'd missed their closeness. One difference this time was his separation from her as soon as the act was completed. Eleven years ago, he would have held her and whispered to her in his hypnotizing voice. That came with trust, and Phoenix no longer trusted her.

She could not make love with Phoenix again.

Chapter 8

"You pulled off that stunt perfectly. I'm pleased with your work," Einstein said to Casey. He swirled the cognac around in his glass. He reveled in the sweet joy of having the luxury to buy the best, and he never took his success for granted. He often remembered his childhood, a time when he could barely afford food. When he'd been forced into living on his wits on the street.

As an adult, he could afford anything money could buy. And money bought just about anything a stuffed pocket desired. Suddenly he frowned, a steely determination etching his harsh features. Jimmy was supposed to be with him, not six feet under. It was all Phoenix Dye's fault. *Your day will come Phoenix Dye and you will suffer as I have. See how you like losing something important to you,* he vowed. He pulled himself out of the gathering depression.

"It's time for phase two," he said briskly to Casey. "Put pressure on Vic Wallace for his investment share in the shopping center. He's been borrowing from you and he'll be forced to go to his ex wife for it."

"She'll just go to that rich brother of hers," Casey said with reckless assurance.

"I don't think so. Our Ms. Wallace has an independent streak. Going to her brother would be the last option for her. She works night and day to keep that restaurant functioning. She's not about to go begging to her brother for the money. Her pride won't let her. Unlike her ex."

"You're wrong this time," Casey said as if it were a challenge. "You said she's spent everything on that restaurant. She doesn't have anywhere else to go."

Einstein let it drop. He was assured of his superior logic skill. But it didn't hurt to remind Casey of that fact. "You've got a lot to learn about people, Casey. I've made it my life's occupation. I didn't get my wealth from hard work alone. But from knowing people's character and using that to my advantage," Einstein said. "Let Victor know just how painful things could get if he doesn't come up with the money."

Casey smirked a cruel smile on his lips. "I'll do that."

Einstein turned his back to signal the meeting's end. He watched Casey approach his car. Plotting the demise of Phoenix Dye sent a savory warmth flowing through his veins. The success was getting closer. Oh, the joy of it all. Who said vengeance wasn't sweet? It certainly wasn't a man who ever got it.

No one ever said a restaurant owner had to be the sounding board for prospective customers. But that was Karina's role as she listened to Tina Landrum spill her problems.

"I shudder at the thought of barbecued ribs at a wedding reception." Tina took a sip from her second vodka and soda. "Can you imagine guests dressed in their silks and lace eating ribs?" She shuddered. "Or the bride wearing a white dress with grease and red sauce dripping down the front." She finished on a high screech.

Karina agreed with the woman. Ribs weren't the best

choice for a wedding reception, but as a businesswoman she would deliver whatever the customer requested.

"I've got three weeks, mind you, *three weeks* to plan a wedding." Tina continued. "I mailed the invitations out just this morning. It barely gives people time to respond. This is just awful."

This barrage had been going on for a while. Karina had to find a way to get the reception settled before Tina occupied her entire afternoon. Karina cleared her throat. "I can order deboned baby backs cut in bite-sized pieces. It wouldn't be quite as messy that way." Karina had a perfect view of the foyer from her seat. Patrick came in bearing a beautiful sculpture, which he planted on the empty table. Robert approached him, admiring it and talked animatedly to him before both of them left, and then returned with two more sculptures. Karina wished she could get away to talk to Patrick, but Tina just might drink herself senseless with nothing to do while Karina was away.

"Maybe that would work."

Karina bought her attention back to Tina.

"I just wish I could get them to reconsider. What will our guests think of us serving ribs, potato salad, and corn on the cob? Imagine guests talking with corn stuck between their teeth."

Karina couldn't stop a smile.

"His parents are from Texas. I think that's where Veronica got this ridiculous idea. She and her fiancé are always debating which are better, the southern pork barbecue or the Texas beef variety. Now she's determined to settle the debate at the reception." Tina put her hand to her head as if warding off a tremendous headache. "What difference does it make anyway? Can't they settle it at their leisure? It doesn't have to be served at the wedding reception of my only daughter!"

At the rate she was going, in thirty minutes Tina would be far too inebriated to plan anything.

"I can serve potato salad and asparagus spears with the ribs. In small pieces, the ribs won't be too bad. And the sauce will be grilled into the meat. They won't necessarily have to be dripping. However, we will set a container of warmed sauce on each table for those who like to have extra. The flavor should be perfectly satisfying without the extra sauce though."

"I should count my blessings. She could have eloped. Thank *God* she didn't do that." The woman acted as if she hadn't heard a word Karina uttered.

"The flowers on the grounds will provide the perfect backdrop and I think the setting will be more than satisfactory by the river."

Her glass clinked on the table as Tina set it down for the first time. "Think of the mosquitoes. And what if it rains?" Her voice rose to a shrill crescendo. Several diners looked in their direction.

"With the lanterns we'll put out, your party won't be bothered by insects. I don't have anything else scheduled for that day. If the forecast calls for rain, we can hold the party inside."

"But . . ."

"Now, will you like for us to take care of the cake, or will you have someone else bake it? And would you like another desert to go with it? Maybe a chocolate mousse."

"You take care of it," she said with a wave of her hand. "The less I have to worry about, the better. And I want the *best* of everything. Her father's paying for the wedding. And I'm certainly going to get my money's worth out of him. He's got a girlfriend younger than his own daughter. And he's spending all the money I struggled for on her!"

"You'll want to order champagne for each table."

"Yes. The most expensive brand you can find."

The most expensive brand Harland would be willing to pay for anyway, Karina thought.

"And for hors d'ouevres."

"Salmon pâté for sure. Money is no object."

Karina jotted that down. "And you might want to consider little quiches—maybe ham or asparagus."

"Harland and I should be celebrating the wedding together. But, no, he had to go through a midlife crisis at fifty-five." Frantically, Tina sipped again. "Now that Veronica's grown up, we'd have the time to travel and do the things we talked about when she was younger and we were struggling. But what happens? His stupid macho ego kicks in and he thinks sticking it into a twenty-five-year-old will make him younger." The drink pounded on the table again and Tina took a furtive look around. "I hope to hell she wears his behind out!"

"Well . . ."

"And you know what I mean. At least *your* husband didn't leave you for a younger woman and there's still some youth left in you to make a new start with someone."

Karina cleared her throat.

"If nothing else, my brother saw to it I got my share of money out of him. Do you know that scoundrel tried to get away with paying me a pittance. I struggled through that marriage, too." Another swallow of drink and she was maudlin. "We could be traveling in Europe now."

Karina reached over and patted the woman's hand. "You can still go to Europe. Didn't I see the mayor casting his eyes your way the other week?"

Tina blushed. "Well, he has been asking me out, but I don't even know how to date anymore. What will I do?"

"To tell you the truth, I feel the same way. Just take it a step at a time. Maybe dinner or a visit to a museum and let things progress from there." Ever the businesswoman, Karina gently led Tina back to the details of the reception and they worked on the plans for another hour before Tina signed the contract and Veronica arrived to escort her slightly tipsy mother home.

For all their problems, at least she and Victor had parted on somewhat amicable grounds. Yes, there was pain, but they endured it without hating each other. Karina was grateful for that.

Things could have been so much worse.

The object of Karina's thoughts walked in soon after Tina left. She had not seen Victor since his last broken promise.

"Hello, Victor."

"Karina. How's business?" His voice had the tone she remembered he used when he was unsure of himself.

"It's doing well, thank you."

"Good. Good." He paced, agitated.

"Can I get you something to drink?" she asked.

"Yeah. Scotch and soda will be nice," he said and squared his shoulders.

"I'll get the bartender to bring it." Karina started to get up.

"Forget it. I don't really want anything. I need to talk to you." He shoved his hands in his pocket found his handkerchief and took it out to wipe his brow.

"Are you here for lunch?" Karina asked.

"Can we talk in your office?"

"Sure. This way." Victor spoke to several employees as they passed through the bustling kitchen. She closed her office door behind them for privacy. "Have a seat."

"I need a loan," he said without preamble, and without sitting.

Karina reached for her purse in the bottom desk drawer. "How much?"

"Ten thousand." He spit the words out like bullets.

"Dollars?"

"Yeah." He paced.

"I don't have that kind of money, Victor. I spent everything on the restaurant. I can barely afford a salary."

"The restaurant's doing good. You just said so."

"Not that well. The margin is less than five percent. And the money goes into paying off the mortgage, expenses, and salaries. I don't have anything left."

"Oh, damn." He scratched his head and leaned forward. "Can't you borrow it from Jonathan?"

Karina shook her head. "No, I can't. I'm living on my resources. He's done so much for me. I can't go to him."

"What about me? I've done plenty for you, too."

Karina reached over and touched his hand. "I know. And I can never repay you for it. That's why I thought it only fair to split half my inheritance with you. It was wonderful of you to marry me when I became pregnant."

"Karina, I don't need praise. I need money. You can swallow your pride and get it from Jonathan. I'll pay it back as soon as the shopping center gets going good." He was using his "please, honey" voice now.

"What happened to the settlement you got when we split?" she asked.

"It's gone." He couldn't meet her shocked stare.

Karina sighed. That was thousands of dollars. "I really wish I could help you. Why do you need that much money?"

"This group of people are renovating the shopping center in Petersburg that closed. There're more people living around there now. We've got a committment from a grocery store to open up there if we can get two thirds of the rest of the place committed."

"I think that's a wonderful idea. You know that if I had the money, I'd give it to you."

"Why don't you get it from your new boyfriend?" he said with a sneer.

"What boyfriend? I don't date. Don't have the time."

"The new sheriff. The talks going around town that he's spending a lot of time with you and the children." He looked as belligerent as one of the kids when they didn't get their way.

"The triplets. Not me. There's nothing between us." That was true enough since Karina didn't plan a repeat performance of their lovemaking.

"Does he know?" His lips tightened.

"No, I haven't told him." Uncomfortable with the conversation, Karina had to stop herself from tapping on the desk.

"Well, he's due to pay his share for neglecting the triplets all these years."

Was that jealousy she heard in his voice? "Don't do this, Victor. You were never cruel before. They miss you."

"Our marriage didn't work because you loved him. You couldn't let him go," Victor accused through clenched teeth.

"That's not true." Karina realized her voice had risen. In an effort to maintain some sense of control and privacy, she lowered the pitch. "I tried to be a good wife to you. And we were happy most of our marriage."

"You tricked yourself into believing you cared for me, but you never loved me like you loved him."

"I wasn't pining away for him all those years we were together."

"You tried to block him out of your mind, but you loved him. A man knows when you don't love him."

"Why, now? I tried everything I knew to keep our marriage together. To be a good wife to you," Karina said, tired of an argument that had been fought before, many times. If he was trying to make her feel guilty, he was doing a darn good job of it. She did not neglect Victor's needs throughout their marriage and she knew it. Phoenix's lovemaking came to mind, and with it a sense of remorse.

He waved his hand as if to brush his statement aside. "There's no sense in talking about it now. I need that money. If you don't get it from Jonathan, I'm talking to the sheriff. It's time he paid up."

Karina stood. "You wouldn't do that. I thought you loved the triplets. Why would you want to hurt them?"

"I wouldn't hurt them. You're the one who should worry." Silence hovered in the air. "You just get the money."

"I ca . . ." she began, but he walked off, slamming the

door behind them. Several heads turned in her direction. No one dared approach her.

Karina sighed. She was counting on Victor's love for the children to make him see reason. He wouldn't really do anything to harm them. Would he? He didn't actually mean what he said. As soon as he calmed down, he'd be more reasonable. Karina was sure of that.

Had it been that apparent that she'd loved Phoenix? After a while, she could almost have forgotten her time with him. At least as time passed it wasn't in the forefront of her mind. Which was exactly what he'd said, Karina realized. She hadn't loved him as she'd loved Phoenix. But she'd tried to compensate by keeping the house spotless, and at times when house work was the last thing she wanted to do. She'd paid the bills so he wouldn't have that worry after a full day's work. She'd seen that the grass was mowed so that he could fish or watch his favorite sports without the worry of additional chores. But in the end, none of that had mattered because he'd sensed she didn't really love him.

And now that the divorce was over and finally the antipathy between Phoenix and herself had abated, she couldn't stir the pot again and upset his life by telling him he had children she'd failed to inform him about.

And she would not get the money from Jonathan.

Maybe if she went through the books again, with the added bonus of the banquets, she'd find a portion of the funds.

She tuned out the rattle of pots and pans and raised voices of the staff as she pulled open her ledger to see if she could scrape together something for Victor. After all, when she'd been desperate all those years ago, he'd been a lifesaver for her.

Karina scanned the pages. Her books were always kept up to date and it wasn't long before she realized she was wasting time. The ledger confirmed what she already knew.

There was barely enough for her to pinch out a salary. No extras. Certainly not anything near ten thousand dollars.

Involving Jonathan was out of the question. He'd paid a hefty down payment on their house. Even though Victor was employed, Jonathan had hired him and more than tripled his wages so that he'd have enough to take care of the children and her.

God, she owed so many people. Elbows on the desk, she dropped her face in her hands. Could she swallow her pride and go to Jonathan again for a handout? She'd pledged that she'd be responsible for herself. She'd always been taken care of. And Karina didn't want to be taken care of any longer. The interest carried too high a price.

She didn't regret giving Victor a share of her inheritance, but why hadn't he used the money wisely? How could he have spent what had amounted to more than most people ever got in a lump sum so soon? Then she remembered the new car Victor drove and the spiffy clothes. However, that wouldn't account for all of it. They'd lived frugally when they were married, by her budgeting. And while they didn't live like kings and queens, they weren't paupers either. But then, Karina had always taken care of the finances.

She knew times were tough and he was now working for lower wages. After they parted, he'd left his position at Jonathan's company even though Jonathan wouldn't have fired him. Victor worked hard at his job.

Karina straightened her spine. Victor was an adult and fully capable of caring for himself. The triplets were her first priority. She wouldn't go to Jonathan to bail her out.

Victor would recant his threat.

"Karina?" came a voice over the intercom.

She pressed a button. "Yes?"

"Call for you on line one," came the reply.

"This is Karina Wallace. How may I help you?"

"Mrs. Wallace, Thornton Sterns here."

"How are you, Mr. Sterns."

"I'm calling to discuss the annual picnic. We're doing something a little different this year. All the local bank branches will be having the affair together. I mentioned this before at one of the ball games, I believe."

"How many people are we talking about?" Karina was elated at the sudden burst in business.

"Somewhere in the range of three hundred people. We'd also like to have room for entertainment for children and adult activities as well."

"Because of the river nearby, children must be closely supervised. I don't have the staff for that, but I could hire someone if you like."

"We can take care of that."

"I believe the area around the river will be more than adequate for your needs."

"Wonderful. Towanna Jordan will get with you on the particulars."

"I'll look forward to her call." Karina disconnected with a lighter mood.

Phoenix watched Karina approach the ball diamond wearing an orange top with black, hip-hugging jeans. Miss Drucilla and Luke walked with her, the three talking animatedly. The boys had also talked Mrs. Jones into attending and she'd arrived five minutes earlier.

Phoenix couldn't look at her without thinking of how well those hips had fit beneath his palms. How they melded beneath his fingertips. And he still hadn't determined where he wanted to go from here or if he could consider trusting her again. Her excuse seemed lame to him. Especially for someone as intelligent as Karina. Still, she'd led a protected life, first by her parents then by Jonathan. Her first real taste of life had been with him—while Jonathan was away.

Mrs. Bright called out to him and he waved to the older woman.

As the game started, Phoenix concentrated on the team's plays and not making a play for Karina.

A huge crowd turned out for the Running Kites' first game. The games had turned into much more than children's sport. Grandparents, aunts, uncles, as well as parents and friends, sat comfortably in their beach chairs.

Patrick was the unlucky umpire. The audience was more than happy to give him lots of help with the rules of the game. Many a grandparent had instructions for him.

"That wasn't out and you know it," Mrs. Bright called out. "See if you get a piece of my blackberry pie when you stop by my house again, Patrick Stone. I'll fix you." She shook an arthritic finger at him.

"That's not playing fair, Mrs. Bright. That's blackmail. What happened to teaching the children good sportsmanship?" someone shouted. "That's torture."

"Humph," Mrs. Bright snorted before dropping back into her chair and crossing her arms. "He's still not going to get my pie!"

And the game went on with one gastronomic threat after the other.

Patrick looked at Phoenix more than once with a How-the-hell-did-I-get-myself-talked-into-this look.

At one point Phoenix noticed Victor Wallace's arrival. His sons left the bull pen, happy to see their dad. In his tan slacks and navy-blue shirt that had a few of the top buttons undone to show off his chest, Victor looked equally exuberant—Karina looked anything but.

Karina waited for the boys to return to the bull pen before saying anything.

"I hope you didn't come here just to raise their hopes and then not show up for another three or four months."

"I don't have as much time to spend with them as I used to. You know I care about them. I've got to get this business going." He took his shades off, perching them on top of his head.

Karina remained silent, made both nervous and hopeful by his appearance. Hopeful he'd apologize for his actions yet frightened that he wouldn't.

"Have you talked to Jonathan yet?"

All hope vanished and a nervous queasiness gathered in her stomach. "I told you before I couldn't go to him." Karina clutched her purse tightly in her hands.

"Then I'll talk to Phoenix."

Karina reached out to touch his arm. "Please, don't do that. He doesn't know." She looked toward the field at Phoenix. His eyes were on her instead of the game. Karina looked away.

"Then get me the money. I really need it," he said urgently though quietly so people nearby couldn't hear.

She let her hand drop. This cold man didn't sound like the man she'd married. He'd changed. "Victor, you're not into drugs or anything are you?"

"No. I'd never get involved with that, but that doesn't lessen my need for that money." Karlton hit a home run and bought in three basemen. Then he clapped and whooped. "Way to go, son."

Karina missed the hit, but forced a cheer when she saw her son slide into home.

"You have until a week from Tuesday." Victor slid his shades back on.

Karina reached out to him again but he turned and walked off the field.

When Karina looked back toward the field, she saw that Phoenix was watching her intently, as if he had a sixth sense whispering that something was up. She would not be helpless! It was Saturday and she had three days to make some serious decisions.

Independence meant taking the bad along with the good.

*   *   *

"I wonder what that was all about?" Patrick asked Phoenix after the game. Someone handed him a soda. He popped the cap and took a long swallow.

"I don't know," Phoenix answered, anxious to talk to Karina and wondering at the same time how much he should intrude. Their newly found peace didn't necessarily mean she'd want him involved.

"Karina is really upset."

Phoenix held the suspicion that Karina was still very much in love with Victor, which meant she hadn't loved Phoenix at all. She'd looked very upset when he'd left. So where did that leave them?

They turned in Karina's direction when Karl asked her, "Where's Daddy?"

"He couldn't stay, honey. He had to get back to Petersburg." Her hand trembled. Phoenix was sure that demonstrated her unrequited feelings for Victor.

"But, I thought he was coming to the house," Karl said.

"Maybe another time," she said with a false smile.

"That's what he always says," Karlton dropped his snack back into the bag. Karina looked as if her heart had twisted and she was at the end of her rope when the boys walked dejectedly toward the car.

"Don't you want your snacks? It's your favorite," she asked as if on the verge of tears she couldn't shed.

"No, thank you." They walked on.

"Let me do that." Mrs. Jones gently tugged Karina to the side and took over the duty of handing out the hot dogs, apples, and drinks.

Karina followed the boys.

Phoenix grabbed two boxes and ran after them. "I'll talk to them," he said as he passed Karina. "Hey, fellows, you can't leave before we celebrate. Besides, we have a short meeting while you eat. You played a great game today."

"Do we have to stay?" Karlton asked.

"Yes, you do. It's part of being on the team."

They took the boxes and went to the bleachers to sit with the other boys where Phoenix gave his spiel and tried to humor the boys out of their laconic mood.

It didn't work.

Humor couldn't wash away what amounted to the loss of a father.

Chapter 9

The kids were still upset and quiet when they returned home. After they had showered and dressed for bed, Karina called them into her bedroom and patted a space by her on the bed. "Okay, let's talk." They sat facing her, eager and needing every scrap of love they could capture.

"Mom, why isn't Daddy ever around?" Kara asked, slumped with elbows on her knees.

"Yeah, why doesn't he come see us?" Karlton wanted to know. He reclined on his back, hands behind his head in contemplation as Phoenix often did.

"You know it's hard on your father. He's trying to get a business together." She stroked Kara's hair, squeezed Karlton's hand, patted Karl's knee. "Remember when I first opened the restaurant? I had to spend time away from you. When you don't have much money, you have to do everything yourself."

"But, Mom, we still saw you."

"Well, I had to come home to see about you all." Karina rubbed Karl's head.

"Then why doesn't he come see us? He doesn't love us," Karl said.

"No, honey, he still thinks about you. That's why he's trying to get the business together. For you all."

"How long is it going to take?" Karl asked. "Baseball season will be over with soon. He never stayed to see me go up to bat."

"Well, just give him time. When things get better, he'll spend more time with you."

"Oh, all right."

"Come on. Let's get in bed. Get a good night's sleep. You've got church tomorrow. We'll talk more later." She kissed and hugged them and sent them off. She wanted to tuck them in, but they keep telling her they were way too big to have their mom tuck them in at night.

Phoenix looked up from his papers as Emmanuel entered his office. "Tell me about Ernie's Construction Company? They're new in the area, aren't they?" He tossed the papers on the desk, frustrated at the absence of information.

"Came about a year ago. Not much business so far. Don't know how he can stay with the little that they do get."

Phoenix steepled his fingers under his chin, thoughtfully. "A construction company uses heavy equipment, doesn't it?"

Emmanuel straightened in his chair as his interest peaked. "I didn't think of that."

"Make a check between his employees and the club's construction crew. See if there's a connection."

"Will do." Emmanuel left.

It was Friday and Phoenix had arranged with Karina to take the boys to practice. He didn't mind. Of course, they still gave hints that it would be all right with them if he were to date their mom.

What would he do about Karina? Her kids could come up with a better excuse for marrying Victor so soon after their summer together than she couldn't reach him. Her love for Victor was certainly apparent. It could certainly explain why she was so distraught by his departure from the game. But upon further speculation, he recalled their argument while Victor was there. Perhaps she was taking Phoenix's advice and requesting child support.

At any rate, Phoenix knew they weren't dating. And where did that leave him? Wanting more of what they'd shared in bed. He'd been more than satisfied. He'd been sated. It bought back memories of their closeness of before. Memories he didn't want, memories long buried. They'd been pretense, anyway.

He knew he'd seemed cold and distant after their love-making. Like he'd used her for a quick lay. Never would she know how difficult it was to tear himself away from her that afternoon. He'd wanted to spend the entire night with her in his arms. And he'd disappeared before letting himself settle for more than he could ever expect.

Karina languished on the porch, a rare treat, as she waited for Jonathan's visit. The boys had baseball practice with Phoenix and Kara was at soccer practice.

Karina had taken a half day off and used the time to clean the house and cook dinner, the first she'd done for Jonathan since his vacation.

Car lights beamed up the lane warning her of his approach.

Upon his arrival, by his pleased and jovial spirits, Jonathan seemed to almost float up the steps.

"Need I ask you how the deal with the Kramers went?" Karina asked from a quiet corner on the swing. "Judging by your exuberance, I'd say it went very well."

"You'd be right," Jonathan said, hands in pockets and a Cheshire cat grin on his face. "Using his supplies will

144 Candice Poarch

cut my cost in half. It'll leave more revenue for expansion."
He moved toward her.

"That's impressive." Karina was elated and proud of her brother's success. "Where are they staying?" Karina hugged him and Jonathan joined her on the swing. She started it in motion. The chains creaked in cadence with the movement.

"They left for North Carolina. Their son is taking over most of the business. Harry's easing his way out. But since the larger clients aren't familiar with the son yet, he's turning them over to him one by one."

"That always takes time," Karina said.

"He'll do a fantastic job. He's smart, quick, and eager to please the customers. A chip off the old block." He looked around and listened. "Where are the kids, running through the neighborhood?"

"Actually, the boys are at baseball practice and Kara is at soccer practice. They'll be home in an hour."

"I talked to them this week."

"Oh?" Karina stiffened.

"They're upset about Victor. It seems now that he doesn't have the time to spend with them, they're wondering if I could keep them for a while." Jonathan's mouth twitched at one corner, which Karina didn't miss.

Immediately suspicious as to what they were up to now, and certain that they wanted to leave her, Karina asked with great reluctance, "Why did they want to move in with you?"

"To give you more time to find a husband. Hopefully Phoenix, according to Karlton. He's already broken in."

Karina sighed. "I thought they understood. I had a long talk with them Saturday night."

"I haven't been spending enough time with them lately. I'd like to keep them this weekend." He shook his head. "I actually missed the tykes."

"Jonathan . . . you need to use your time on other things. Not the triplets."

"I want to see them, too. It's good for them to have a man's influence."

"You need children of your own. You're so good with them." Karina had thought they were temporarily satisfied. Jonathan wasn't the answer.

"Well, I don't have any of my own. Let them spend the weekend."

"I can use the breather. And it will be good for them. Thanks."

Jonathan changed the topic. "I hear you have a new friend."

"Who?" Karina asked, knowing the triplets matchmaking schemes with Phoenix.

"Mr. Wilkens."

"Don't you dare laugh." The incident was too new to be humorous. "That man called me for days after they set up that dinner with him. He actually believed I would go out with him."

"Wilkens should have known better." Jonathan clutched his side in merriment. Karina hit him. He held up both hands against her, too full of humor to protect himself. "Okay, okay. Want me to talk to him?" He sobered, wiping his eyes.

"No, he finally got the message." She tittered a little herself in the aftermath.

"How do you feel about Phoenix's return?"

Karina sobered. "It's nothing to me."

"This is big brother here." He picked his way as if he wasn't quiet sure how to approach the topic. "You never told me and I never pressured you because you were so distraught after he left. The triplets are his. The boys favor him. It's only a matter of time before he finds out." Then Jonathan said quietly, "He has a right to know."

"I had hoped he'd never know." Karina thought of her troubles. If she were to approach Jonathan, now was the perfect time. However, she wouldn't.

"He's their father. I would want to know."

Karina sighed, tired of one too many burdens to contemplate. "What good will it do? He'd never settle down here. And then the children will have to suffer through his abandonment just like they're suffering through Victor's. I've thought this through . . . long and hard. Victor came to the game the other evening and didn't even stay around long enough to talk to them." Karina sighed. "I don't know. I try my best, but I'm not their father. They need him. When . . . if . . . they ever get over Victor, I'm certainly not going to have them going through that suffering all over again when Phoenix decides to leave." The antipathy between Karina and Phoenix was gone, but she needed to use extreme caution in deciding her children's fate. "The children are upset enough with Victor's abandonment. I won't put them through that twice."

"Maybe he won't leave. He seems to be pretty stable. Why didn't you tell him you were pregnant? Why did you marry Victor? You certainly didn't love him."

"I couldn't find Phoenix. Then a few days ago, he tells me he was on a special assignment where I couldn't reach him. We spent so much time together that summer and I didn't even know anything about his job." Karina thought of the summer when she and Phoenix were so in love that they didn't take the time to really share their feelings and views. Sex and surface love got in the way.

"If I had been around that summer, this wouldn't have happened."

"Don't you dare blame yourself. I was twenty-one years old, only a year younger than you when you started your business and became my guardian." He should be the last one to feel remorse.

"Still, I shouldn't have gone away that month. I should have waited until you went back to school. You still needed supervision."

"Mrs. Perch lived at the house. Besides you would have missed your chance for expanding. The timing was right for it."

"You were more important."

Karina took her brother's hand. Squeezed it. "Jonathan, you did everything right. Being here wouldn't have stopped what happened. I . . . " she stumbled. "I was in love with Phoenix. Blindly in love. If he'd trusted me more, we may have ended up together. Or if I'd waited . . . Well, hindsight won't help matters. I love the triplets. I don't regret them one second . . . only the pain they're suffering now."

Jonathan lamented. "And how do you feel about him now?"

Karina was silent a moment, contemplating. Then she answered him in a soft voice that seemed far away. "I got over him a long time ago." It was too late to believe anything different.

Jonathan pressed a thumb under one of her eyes and peered at her in the light coming from inside the house. "His being here is bothering you. You've got circles under your eyes. What are you worrying about?"

"I guess I'm so used to working night and day that I can't relax now that I have the extra time."

"How's the restaurant going?"

"Couldn't be better . . . much better, anyway. Business is booming."

He grasped her right hand in his, a hand that wasn't as soft as it was a year ago. "If there was a problem, don't make the same mistake you made by marrying Victor. Come and talk to me. That's what big brothers are for." He squeezed her hand.

"I just didn't want to shame you. I owe you so much for taking care of me and giving up your own dreams after Mom and Dad died."

"You don't owe me anything," he said in a tense voice. "I just started the business I'd dreamed of a few years earlier, that's all. Besides you were never a problem, ever."

"Yes, I was. I remember you being at every game when I was a cheerleader. Taking me places."

"That was to keep the young boys at bay," he said lightly, half serious.

"See. You should have been chasing young ladies yourself."

"I chased enough." He let her hands go, always uncomfortable with the direction of the conversation.

Karina frowned. It was his time for happiness. "When are you going to get over Sheryl?" Sheryl had died a week before Jonathan and she were to marry. And he hadn't looked seriously at another woman since.

"I'm over her. It's just that good women are hard to find."

"Oh, come on. There are several women to every man in this town and you know it."

"And you have a long list for me, I'm sure," he said lightly. He had a way of regarding a person to make them think they were the most special person alive—the reason he was such a special father figure for her and so special for the triplets. All that love to offer was wasted. But she couldn't choose for him.

Knowing his feelings, Karina shook her head. "Far be it from me to choose one for you."

"Sheryl and I were right together. You know, that special someone who as soon as you meet, you know she's the one. When I find a woman like that, I'll marry her. Anything less wouldn't be fair to her or me." He tapped Karina's nose with a long finger. "It will all come in due time. You promised me dinner. I'm hungry. When are you going to feed me?"

"Subject closed. Come on." She grabbed his hand and pulled him up. They went into the kitchen for dinner.

"Mom, we're home."

The sweaty and dirt-streaked boys bounded into the kitchen full of energy, as always. Phoenix followed close behind looking parched, and immediately marched to the fridge for the beer she kept there ever since she'd discovered how he liked one after practice.

"Hi, Uncle Jonathan. We're the best players on the team." The statement was made with the confidence of youth.

"Hi, sports. I wonder if your coach will agree."

Phoenix laughed. "They're good." He rubbed Karlton's head affectionately.

"Phoenix," Jonathan said in greeting. He shook the man's hand.

Jonathan looked at the boys. "How does spending the weekend with me sound?"

"Great!" they answered in unison.

"Pack your bags and we'll be on our way."

"But first you need a shower," Karina intercepted.

"Now?" Karlton stopped, swiveled in his tracks.

"We're hungry." Karl plunked into the nearest chair.

"They can take showers at my house. We're stopping by the Ice Cream Parlor on our way, so make it quick. Your mom's fixed plates."

"All right!" Karlton said looking at Phoenix before turning to Jonathan. "Should we pack all our clothes?"

"No! You're coming home Sunday," Karina said, irked.

They threw a sly glance to Jonathan before, in a dash, they ran down the corridor to pack.

"Jonathan, they're so dirty. They aren't fit to be seen in public."

"Boys are going to get dirty, Karina. Don't worry so."

Karina threw her arms in the air in resignation and turned to Phoenix. "Thanks for bringing them home, Phoenix. It's certainly saves me from having to rush from the restaurant."

"Anytime." He leaned against the sink.

"Well, I'll go and pack a bag for Kara. You can pick her up at soccer practice." She left the men alone.

"How does it feel to be back?" Jonathan resumed his seat. "Have a seat."

Phoenix ambled over to the table and sat across from Jonathan. He put his half-filled can on the table. "It's different. Slower paced, but I like it."

"The boys are certainly taken with you. Karlton even wants to be a sheriff one day."

"They're good kids . . ."

"We're ready." The boys were followed close by Karina.

"You must have packed in record time. Let's go." Jonathan took the bag from Karina and went over to shake Phoenix's hand. "Good seeing you again." He followed the boys. Karina followed close behind.

"Be good and obey your uncle." She gave them each hugs. "See you in church Sunday!"

"Bye, Mom!"

Karina watched the car disappear down the lane. A sense of loneliness and dread swept óver her. Reluctantly she returned to the house. Phoenix was sitting at the kitchen table. "Tea, coffee?"

He shook his head, no. "Coffee will keep me up half the night."

"Milk?"

They shared a smile of memory. "That was your favorite drink," he choked out.

"In college, they drilled into Jonathan how important milk was for women. Osteoporosis. And he drilled it into me. How is the investigation going with Patrick?"

Remembering his conversation with Patrick and of his penchant for keeping information to himself, Phoenix decided to give her a smidgen of information. Though she really didn't have a need to know, she was a concerned friend to Patrick's. "I have a couple of leads. Nothing solid yet. Enough to prove he may not have done it, but not enough to identify the culprit."

"At least that's something . . ." She jumped at the ringing of the telephone. Her friendly, calm mood left immediately. Phoenix sensed that she was tremendously nervous tonight.

Reluctantly, Karina got up to answer it.

"Hello?"

She looked at Phoenix then turned her back to him.

"I told you I couldn't get it!" she said in a whisper.

"Wait!" Hand trembling, she held the instrument away from her ear and looked at it before hanging it up. She smoothed her damp hands on her jeans. Her eyes were downcast, her shoulders drooped with worry as she approached her seat.

"Is something wrong?"

She didn't say anything for a moment. "I think we're going to need that coffee after all." She refilled her cup and poured one for Phoenix.

The cup rattled in its saucer as she handed it to him. Karina wiped sweaty palms on her jeans. "I don't know how to tell you this."

He reached across the table and gathered her hand in his. "It's easier to come right out with it," he encouraged.

"Not this time. I . . ." she cleared her throat and started again. "I'm being blackmailed."

"By whom? And what are they holding over you?" When she didn't respond, he said, "I'll help you regardless of what it is." Phoenix's calm demeanor belied the rage pouring through him at the thought of anyone putting Karina and the children in danger. "Do I need to put protection on the children?"

"No, no. Nothing like that. Just . . . sit down." Karina inhaled deeply. "First, the triplets . . ."

He lightly squeezed her hand for encouragement, gave her a reassuring smile.

". . . the triplets are your children."

Chapter 10

From all that Phoenix had experienced, he'd never been more shocked, hurt, or enraged as he was at this moment when one emotion spilled over into the next. Yet those inadequate words failed to explain his inner turmoil. "Say that again?" he asked quietly. Too quietly.

With a stoic expression, bearing up to impart bad news, Karina elaborated. "After you left I missed my period. The pregnancy test was positive."

Phoenix's head reeled. His stomach heaved. Dizziness washed over him. Taking a swallow of the coffee, he realized the intense heat from the hot liquid was no more painful than the mental anguish from her confession. Looking at the woman across from him and remembering how he'd agonized over her betrayal, he knew that she not only did not love him, she must have *hated* him to keep his children from him. Pulling from the deep resources of his professional training, he tried to stay calm.

But he roared, "The triplet's are mine? And you're just telling me? You kept my children from me for *ten* years?"

"I couldn't find you . . . at first," Karina said quickly. "And then I stopped trying."

While a volcano erupted in him, she sat so calmly, so serenely, explaining to him as if she were describing the weather. It only enraged him more. He wanted her to be as upset as he.

"I knew you didn't love me but how could you keep my children away from me!" Phoenix paced around the table, then snatched her up, holding her tightly by the arms, and shook her.

"Stop it!" She pushed at him but he didn't budge. "I couldn't find you. I tried!"

He shook her again.

"Let me go! You have no right!"

He let her go and she dropped to her seat. He leaned close to her face. "No right! You kept the most important event in my life from me and you dare tell me *I have no right?*"

"No, you don't." Karina pushed him out of her face and stood, her own anger springing forth. "I tried and tried to find you. I called you and all I got was that your phone had been disconnected with no forwarding number. I mailed you two letters. Do you want to know what happened? I'll tell you what. They were returned with no forwarding address! Do you have any idea of what I went through? I was pregnant with your baby and I didn't know how to find you!" Karina glared at him. "I realized I didn't know anything about you. What was I to think?"

"That I would be here for Christmas and I'd marry you." Phoenix's voice was hoarse. How could she have doubted him? "I loved you. You knew I planned to marry you."

"You also gave me your address and your phone number. You said nothing about dropping off the face of the earth. If I had heard from you once in the month before I married . . . just once." She pointed a shaky finger at him. "I would have waited."

His shoulders slumped. "You didn't have to marry the

first thing in pants that came along," he sneered. "That is, if you'd loved me at all."

Phoenix's head twisted with the impact of Karina's smack across his face. He stood there glaring at her for a full minute, wanting to strangle her, before he stalked out, got into his car, and sped down the lane to his house.

The door slammed as he got out and paced and paced in his yard. It wouldn't do any good to go inside the house.

A crushing weight pounded in his chest. He felt like crying, or yelling his outrage. But he didn't do either. Men didn't cry.

His children. His precious, darling children. He'd looked at their faces as they ran to Victor Wallace calling *him* Daddy at the ball game when it should have been him, Phoenix. They hurt when Victor promised to see them, but failed to show up. He'd never do that to his children. Never!

What would it have been like to hold his babies in his arms as newborns? Tiny feet kicking, miniature fingers wrapping around his. She'd denied him the chance to see them take their first steps, to witness their first teeth peep through their gums, to soothe their pain, to hear them say their first words. Had they said dada or mamma first?

How could she have taken so much from him if she'd loved him? He did everything that summer to let her know how important she was to him. How much he loved her. There was no question of him marrying her. He would have. Immediately. *And she knew it.*

Phoenix wanted to go to his children, hold them, tell them how much he loved them, because in the last few weeks, he *had* grown to love them. At ten, the pain . . .

Danger. She said she was being blackmailed. He didn't wait long enough to find out who was blackmailing her and why.

Phoenix was too agitated to get back into his car. He

walked to her house, and in no time he was pounding on Karina's door.

Her eyes were red when she answered. Maybe she could shed the tears he held in check, express the pain he couldn't let surface. He wished he could allow himself some release, but Phoenix Dye didn't let emotions over-power him. With the help of peer pressure, he'd learned that the hard way years ago.

"Who's blackmailing you and why?" He stepped over the threshold.

She sniffed and dabbed a tissue at her eyes. "Victor."

"What does he want?" Phoenix asked impatiently.

"Ten thousand dollars. He threatened to tell you about the triplets if I didn't give him the money."

Phoenix digested that. "If he hadn't threatened you, you'd never have told me, would you?"

Karina lowered her eyes. "Not right away anyway, no. I don't know what I'd have done eventually. What good would it have done to tell you when you'd only take off in a year or so and they would have to suffer again?" She turned away from him looking both angry and hopeless at once.

"Don't you throw the blame on me. I wouldn't have hurt my own children. You certainly don't carry the only license on feelings and love." Pain throbbed in his head as muscles tensed. He looked at the ceiling to lessen the impact and gather his thoughts. "Where does the bastard live? I'll take care of it."

"He's supposed to come here Tuesday morning," Karina said.

"What time?"

"Around ten."

"I'll meet him. You don't need to be here. Just leave the door unlocked." That'd give him time to get to the bank and think about how he would deal with this.

"What are you going to do?" Her red eyes met his.

"I said, I'll take care of it." Phoenix looked away because

he couldn't deal with her pain. He could barely hold himself together.

"I have a right . . ." she began.

"I had some rights, too," he said sharply. "Did you consider them?"

She ignored that but dealt with the present problem. "I'm not leaving. You can't send me away like an insignificant fly." Her jaw was set in that stubborn angle he knew so well.

"I can find him without you."

"I repeat, what are you going to do to him?"

Why was she so protective of the bastard? "What are you afraid of? I'm not going to kill him, if that's what you're thinking. Hell, I should thank him. If not for him, I still wouldn't know about my children."

"I didn't say that you were going to harm him," she said, willing herself not to shout.

"Yeah, it's obvious you have an extremely high opinion of me," he sneered. "You don't think I'm a fit father, so you marry some other man . . . who's worse."

"You're twisting everything. It's not all my fault. You could have let me know where you were. Or at least you could have sneaked in one phone call in a month's time. Last I heard, they have telephones all over the country. And prophylactics don't always work. You didn't care enough to check and see if I was pregnant."

"I trusted you to wait or contact Luke or my mom if something went wrong."

"Your mom left town two weeks after you did. I was married by the time she returned." Karina took a breath to diffuse the rancor. "This isn't getting us anywhere. Maybe my hormones were taking over. I would have wanted to have you there. It wasn't an easy pregnancy. And it got worse once they were born. Miss Drucilla and Mrs. Jones came over every day to help out. Other neighbors came by during the night as well because the children never slept at the same time. And regardless of what you think of Victor, he was a tremendous support. I owe him. You try dealing with three helpless babies at one time. I've done my part."

Phoenix tightened his lips. "And denied me a chance to do mine. If you know what's good for you, don't throw that man's name in my face."

"Don't threaten me. I don't scare so easily," she shouted.

"I'm not threatening you."

"Sounds like it to me."

Phoenix's cheek still smarted from Karina's slap. No way could he hit a woman, much less a five-foot-three-inch little thing like Karina. How did such a small woman bear three babies at once? It must have been a terrible ordeal for her. Looking at her now with her hands placed firmly on her hips and her chin thrust in the air, Phoenix felt a mixture of pride and anger.

"Given the chance, I would have been here." It irritated him that he owed that bastard, Victor, for taking care of his children. Phoenix needed a reason to punch him in the face. If he hadn't been there to bail Karina out, she would have waited for him as she should have. "I don't even know their birthday."

"February 14."

Phoenix was the first one in line when the bank opened. He'd thought it over and decided he wasn't paying Victor off. Even though it tore at his gut because Victor experienced the joys of Karina and his children Phoenix would have loved to share. He had to admit that Victor could have been a bad stepfather, and he hadn't been. Paying him the money was the least he could do.

Phoenix handed the teller the completed withdrawal slip and asked for the balance on his account. When she handed the slip of paper with the figure penciled in, he cleared his throat. "There's an error here. The account is forty thousand over what should be here. Are you sure you activated the proper account?"

The woman hit some keys and shook her head. "I wrote the correct balance. It is your account, Sheriff Dye. I didn't subtract the amount you withdrew today."

"That would make it thirty thousand over," Phoenix said impatiently. He had to get to Karina's house before Victor arrived. "Check the account number again, please."

She checked again. "This is your account. If you feel there's an error, you can talk to Ms. Jordan. Have a seat over there and she'll be right with you." The woman had pointed to a chair in the miniature seating area in the bank before she called for the next customer to come forward. Two of the three seats were occupied.

Phoenix sat beside a woman with one child in a stroller that looked to be around three and a newborn in her arms. He spoke to her and smiled at the children. With the shocking amount of hair on the baby's head, he determined the newborn to be a girl. With dark circles around her eyes, the woman covered a delicate yawn.

"She looks to be a handful."

"It's a he. And he is. He's colicky right now and keeps me up nights." The baby opened his mouth and let out a screech and the woman placed him on her shoulder and patted his back.

"At this age, I can't tell the boys from the girls."

"All blue usually indicates a boy. Pink, girls."

Phoenix nodded his head eyeing the dark blue outfit on the child. That did make sense. What sane parent would put pink on a boy?

He'd never held a baby, except for the one he'd delivered years back. And that was so quick. The ambulance crew had arrived to take over the situation as soon as the little girl slipped out. He wondered if the woman had actually named the girl after him as promised. Some strange name like Pheona to match with Phoenix. He hoped not. He'd sent her flowers in the hospital and yearned for weeks for fatherhood. Soon after, he'd immersed himself in his work and babies were pushed to the back of his subconscious.

"Phoenix!"

"Hi, Towanna." He stood as she approached him.

"How are you?" Her perky heels slowed. Dressed in her navy suit, she looked the perfect bank executive.

"Having a problem with my bank balance."

"Come with me to my office and we'll discuss it."

Phoenix left the seating area, following Towanna to a small office. After offering coffee which he declined, she sat behind a sparsely covered desk in a burgundy leather chair. Phoenix sat in the striped chair across from her. The gold name plate matched the pen and message holder. Subdued paintings hung in discrete intervals on her wall.

"I understand you have thirty thousand more dollars than you should have."

"I have. It isn't often that happens, I imagine."

"You're right. I've a printout of your recent activities." She handed the printout to him. "It covers your activity since the account was activated." She handed him a copy of his transactions.

Phoenix scanned the pages. Six transactions for five thousand dollar deposits each were not deposits he'd made. He put a check mark by each. "These aren't mine." He took a pen out his pocket and circled them.

Towanna looked at the figures. "These are all bank transfers."

"Well, they were transferred into the wrong account. Someone's missing some money."

"Do you have copies of your bills and deposit slips to augment our reconciliation of this?"

"Yes, I do. Granted, I've been so busy the last couple of months, I haven't gone over my records as I usually do. But, I have them."

"Good. I'll trace those records and we can get together . . . let's see . . . will Wednesday work for you?"

WE HAVE 4 FREE BOOKS FOR YOU!

ARABESQUE

(If the certificate is missing below, write to:
Zebra Home Subscription Service, Inc.,
120 Brighton Road, P.O. Box 5214, Clifton, New Jersey 07015-5214)

FREE BOOK CERTIFICATE

Yes! Please send me 4 *Arabesque* Contemporary Romances without cost or obligation, billing me just $1.50 to help cover postage and handling. I understand that each month, I will be able to preview 4 brand-new *Arabesque* Contemporary Romances FREE for 10 days. Then, if I decide to keep them, I will pay the money-saving preferred subscriber's price of just $16.00 for all 4…that's a savings of almost $4 off the publisher's price + $1.50 for shipping and handling. I may return any shipment within 10 days and owe nothing, and I may cancel this subscription at any time. My 4 FREE books will be mine to keep in any case.

Name _____

Address _____ Apt. _____

City _____ State _____ Zip _____

Telephone (____) _____

Signature _____
(If under 18, parent or guardian must sign.)

AR0299

Terms and prices subject to change. Orders subject to acceptance by Zebra Home Subscription Service, Inc. . Zebra Home Subscription Service, Inc. reserves the right to reject or cancel any subscription.

AFFIX
STAMP
HERE

ZEBRA HOME SUBSCRIPTION SERVICE, INC.

120 BRIGHTON ROAD

P.O. BOX 5214

CLIFTON, NEW JERSEY 07015-5214

"No. I've got meetings all week. Why don't we try for Monday, next week."

Towanna marked it on her calendar. "Good."

Phoenix looked at his watch. "Thanks, Towanna. I'll see you in a week." He had twenty-five minutes to get to Karina's. He hoped Victor wasn't early.

He arrived barely three minutes before Victor. The atmosphere quickly grew so tense it could have been cut with a knife. Phoenix threw the packs of crisp bills on the table. "There's your money." He placed his hands on his hips, leaned forward in an intimidating manner. "Don't try that trick again."

Victor paused before snatching up the money and looking at it. "I'll pay you back."

"I don't want it back." Phoenix spat.

Offended, Victor raised his head, eyes glinting. "Don't get all righteous with me. Where were you when I was taking care of your kids?" he asked defensively.

Phoenix looked at Karina then back at Victor. "You have your money. Now, get out."

"This was my home. Don't be telling me to get out."

Phoenix stepped closer. "It's not your home any longer. If you need help leaving, I'll be happy to oblige," Phoenix gritted from between clenched teeth.

"Now, you think you're gonna take up with Karina where I left off." He turned to Karina. "Is that the way it's going to be, Karina?"

"This has nothing to do with us, Victor." Karina was weary and unnerved by the whole ordeal.

"It has everything to do with us." As if spoiling for a fight, he said to Phoenix, "You wouldn't be so smug if I told those kids that you deserted them . . ."

Phoenix punched him.

"Stop it! Stop it you two," Karina shouted.

When Phoenix drew back to hit Victor again, the back of his hand connected with Karina's jaw.

"Oh!" she yelled, clutching her face.

Both men stopped and turned to her.

"See what you did?" One of Victor's hands was covering his nose.

Phoenix went to her instantly. "Karina. Let me see." Phoenix pried her hand off her cheek where a bruise was already starting.

"Both of you just get out!" She waved them away with her free hand.

"I'm not leaving until I know you're okay," Phoenix insisted.

"Me either. At least I've never hit her."

Phoenix's voice rose. "This is the last time I'll tell you to get out. And stay away from my children!" Phoenix turned back to Karina.

"Karina . . ."

"Go." Jabbing a finger in the air, she pointed to the door. "Just go." When no one left she added, "Please."

Indecision crossed Victor's countenance before he sighed and left.

"Let me see your face." Tilting it, Phoenix let out an expletive. "I'm sorry, Karina. Can you move your jaw?"

She gingerly tried moving it and winced.

"I don't think it's broken." Phoenix pulled out a chair and guided her into it, strode to the freezer and grabbed a package of frozen peas. "This will stop the swelling."

Phoenix held it in place and she took it from him.

"You can leave, now. I've had enough of you and Victor," she mumbled through the pain. The peas slipped.

"Stop talking and let the pack work. I'm not leaving you." He pressed the makeshift pack back into place.

She rolled her eyes and she turned her back to him.

"I didn't mean to hit you." He didn't know whether to hug her or what he wanted. He was so confused by so many new developments.

Karina ignored him, then relented. "I know you didn't."

"If you had done like I said and stayed away, this wouldn't have happened."

Just like a man. "So now it's my fault. You and Victor would have destroyed my kitchen. Look what happened with me here." The peas slipped again.

"Stop talking and leave the peas in place," Phoenix said with helpless ire at the situation.

Karina moved the pack. "Get out. Then I won't have an excuse to talk." She plopped the peas back in place.

Phoenix called Robert, asked him to take both shifts that day, and hung around for another two hours to assure himself Karina was really all right before he left under due protest.

"I ran everything perfectly fine before you came here," she reminded him.

"Isn't it a good thing you have some help now?" came Phoenix's curt rejoinder.

"Quite frankly, no. If you hadn't hit me, I wouldn't have needed any help," she replied helplessly.

"Like it or not, you've got it." He slipped a check out of his pocket. "Here's something for the triplets expenses."

"I don't need your money."

"They are my children," he warned. "I will take care of them."

"You're not taking them from me," she shot back like a banty hen protecting her chicks, frozen peas forgotten.

He was weary of the whole ordeal. "I'm not taking them away. But I will take part in rearing them."

"We can't tell them you're their father. They're too young to understand."

"I do have some sense. They spend time with me anyway. They won't think it unusual if I take a more active role in their lives." Boy, she was giving him no credit whatsoever.

"All right." Karina put the check on the table. It was more than she made in a month's time. "This is too much."

"They're worth more." With that he left.

* * *

"Wow!" Phoenix observed Kara's wide-open mouth as she took in the scene in the den. The boys had similar expressions of awe. It wasn't often one could make the three speechless.

He'd bought the latest in computer technology that included a CD-ROM, a sound blaster, scanner, color printer, and loads of software, from math and science programs to the latest in games.

"Gosh, you bought everything. None of our friends have this much." Karl picked up the baseball CD-ROM.

"You even have Detector Mania." Karlton continued to flip through the various boxes Phoenix had piled on the desk.

Phoenix had spent most of the weekend loading and playing some of the games he'd purchased after he'd talked to one of the deputies who had children. The man had a list of programs to choose from. Even said he could name more if needed.

All three kids fought for position at the keyboard.

"It's not going anyplace," Phoenix laughed. "Each of you will get a turn." He stroked Kara's hair. For once she didn't complain. His children. He wanted to do so much for them.

"This is even better than ours. It's got everything."

Kara looked at Phoenix thoughtfully. "Mom's not going to let us play that often. How come you hate Mom?"

"I don't hate your mother," Phoenix answered. He hadn't realized his anger was apparent to the children. "As a matter of fact, we can plan an outing with her Sunday after church. The temperature will be in the eighties."

"A family picnic," Karlton said.

"He's not in our family," Kara informed him.

"How about a picnic with a family friend." It took everything Phoenix had not to snap, *I'm your father.* Winning Kara over would not be an easy task.

"Can I invite a friend?"

"Sure, but first you have to get permission from your mom."

"She won't agree. All she does is work. She doesn't have time for fun stuff anymore," Karl said.

"Yeah, we miss her," Karlton replied.

"Let me worry about that," Phoenix said.

"It'll be a miracle if you pull it off," Karlton told him.

The doorbell chimed. "I'll make the arrangements," Phoenix said impatiently sure it was Karina on the other side. Didn't she trust him with his own children anymore? "Why don't you try out the games while I see who's at the door?"

Phoenix opened the door to Miss Drucilla and Luke who was laden down with bags.

"We won't be but a minute." Miss Drucilla bustled through the door first. "I just bought you some food by so you won't have to eat out every night. Eating out is expensive and it's not as good as home-cooked meals."

"You shouldn't have," Phoenix said. Clarice had left the small freezer in the house saying Miss Drucilla was going to keep it full. She was right.

"I know how you young people are. You'd be eating at burger joints every night if I didn't bring over decent food. A fresh batch of my mutton is in here, too."

"Great, I didn't know what I was going to feed the triplets."

"Karina's working tonight?" Miss Drucilla asked as she tucked the food away.

"Yeah, and Mrs. Jones needed the evening off."

"Lord, but they're quiet. My grandkids are loud enough to raise the dead," Luke said.

"They're trying out my new computer."

"Got you hooked, too. I play with my grandkids' sometimes."

"You all go in there with the children. I'm going to warm up the supper."

"You don't have to do that, Miss Drucilla. I can warm the soup."

"If you're anything like Jonathan, they'll be eating junk. I have enough stew here and it's filling." She shooed them out. "Go on with you. Won't take me but a minute." She took a towel out the closet and tied it around her small waist.

"Heard about those car thefts in Richmond?" Luke said.

"They don't have any leads yet. I hope something breaks soon."

"A sorry state of affairs," Luke commiserated. "How is Patrick holding up?"

"Karina sold some of his sculptures. That keeps him busy and helps financially."

"Boy always did good with his whittling."

"Let's hope he can make a living off it. About time Patrick got a break."

"I hope so. If those partners weren't so stubborn ... I feel bad about having to let him go."

"We're investigating it. We'll see what pans out." Phoenix had always been patient about investigative procedures, but it was hard to maintain that patience when friends were involved.

"Absolutely not. If you want to go on a picnic with the children, that's fine. But don't include me. I have to work," Karina sputtered.

"It's not for you or me. It's for the children. You haven't been spending enough time with them," Phoenix reasoned.

The hair on Karina's neck rose. "I've spent every spare moment with them. I'm the one who's been there."

"We won't get into why," Phoenix added without missing a beat. "They want a picnic with both of us tomorrow. There's no reason you can't accommodate them."

"Like the fact that I run a business and I need to work.

Plus, Robert burned his hand." A picnic with the children was fine. One with the children and Phoenix was not.

"He doesn't cook. He greets the guests. Let him take a painkiller and supervise."

"He's been doing a lot of that lately. Don't try to make me feel guilty about the children. I spend every spare minute I can with them. They aren't neglected." No matter how much time she carved out, for the last few months, it just wasn't enough.

"They need even more of your time. It won't hurt you to give up a Sunday afternoon. The picnic will be at two thirty."

He made it sound as if she complained about missing a relaxing evening at the movie instead of securing a future for her family. Men. When they made decisions, they thought everyone should drop whatever they were doing to accommodate them.

Karina sighed. It was worth putting up with the obnoxious man for her children's happiness. "There's something we need to discuss."

"What is it?" His stance was not accommodating for bearing confidences at all.

Karina plowed ahead anyway. "Was our lovemaking a one time affair? To get me out of your system, so to speak?"

Phoenix looked at her without speaking then put his hat on the table and dropped into his seat. "I don't know what it was. It seemed right at the time."

"And now?"

"What do you want, Karina?"

It was her turn to squirm. "I'm not sure."

"Neither do I. We . . . I need time to sort my feelings. So much has happened so fast. I trusted you once. I don't know if I could ever trust so completely again."

"I guess that's fair enough. Because with your secrets, I don't feel I could trust you either."

Chapter 11

Karina had second, third, and fourth thoughts about the merits of the outing midway through the picnic.

How much longer would this drag on? It was a torturous afternoon, both in the ninety percent humidity and the atmosphere, which was thick with tension. The only thing that saved Karina from complete misery was the steady breeze that floated across the lake and the shade tree where they placed their picnic. Which wasn't much consolation when the tree happened to be the same tree of her many picnics with Phoenix. In the end, it scattered thoughts and only added more apprehension.

On the flip side, it reminded her of a time when she'd been so full of hope, so full of love and optimism for the future. Thoughts of moving to Northern Virginia and decorating their apartment had run through her mind.

How life changed in only moments. Phoenix now resented her for keeping his children from him.

Karina tried not to let the realization that he was a natural father, one who immediately fell into the roll of a loving parent, bring on remorse. They both were responsible for the debacle in which they found themselves.

Her eyes wandered to his attractive shoulder muscles as he leaned over to pick up a strawberry from the bowl. Under the eager eyes of the children, Phoenix held a strawberry dipped in whipped cream to her lips. They had insisted she pack the dreaded fruit.

"Mom doesn't like strawberries dipped in whipped cream," Kara informed him. "But I do."

"I remember a time when they were her favorite," Phoenix said and smiled.

She'd been on edge all afternoon from such comments. Now he stubbornly refused to budge until she bit into the succulent fruit. To end the war of wills, Karina took a quick bite.

"Does that mean you're courting Mom now?" Kara wanted to know.

"No!" Karina answered with more force than she'd intended as she watched him dip another one and feed it to Kara.

"Then why is he feeding you? Robert said that's what grown-ups do when they're in love." That comment was followed by giggles as she chewed on her own delicacy.

"Robert doesn't know everything. And don't you get any ideas about my love life or you're in big trouble, young lady."

She looked at the eager faces of her children and remorse ate at her for wanting the afternoon to end when they were enjoying themselves so.

And Phoenix had been solicitous in helping her with everything. It had been a day off for her. He'd used his charm on her chef in packing the picnic so she wouldn't have to cook. He wasn't supposed to be solicitous. Had he been cold and angry, she could find fault with him. Instead, with him at his charming best, the old, not so dormant, feelings peeked through—unwanted feelings.

"I still don't see why you and Phoenix can't date," Kara

said stubbornly, which was a complete turn around of her earlier assessment.

"That's Mr. Dye or Sheriff Dye, young lady." Drilling proper manners into her child was a mother's duty, especially when it was the perfect distraction.

"He said we could call him Phoenix."

"I'm with them so often it doesn't make sense to be so formal," Phoenix defended easily.

"You can use the familiar address when you're alone, but when you are around other people, address him formally."

"All right, Mom. Genie and I want to go for a swim. It's hot." Genie was Luke's granddaughter.

"Your mom and I will take a dip, too," Phoenix called out to the boys who had walked farther away. "Karlton, Karl, ready for a swim?"

"Yeah," they agreed immediately.

"You go on. I'll watch from here," Karina said slowly.

"Oh, no you don't." Phoenix picked her up, ran to the lake, and dropped her into the cold water amid her shrieking and sputtering. When she came up for air and cleared her face, the kids were beside her laughing.

The boys attacked the girls as Karina pushed Phoenix under for all of five seconds before he caught her legs and dragged her down. And before long she realized she was enjoying herself for the first time that day.

Phoenix slammed the car door, ignored the crowd, and trekked over to second base to confront Patrick who was cleaning it. "What was all that, 'spend more time with Karina's children' about?"

Patrick stood and scratched his head. "What are you talking about?"

"Cut the crap." Phoenix's hand sliced the air. "Did you know they were mine?"

"Oh, that." He shrugged. "I had a feeling."

"Then why the hell didn't you tell me? I thought you

were my friend." They were alone on the baseball diamond. Curious eyes watched them, but Phoenix didn't care. They were too far away to hear.

"Hell I didn't know for sure. I just counted months and assumed." He shrugged as if the matter held little import.

"Would it have been too much for you to have told me?" Phoenix nearly shouted.

"I only recognized it two years ago. And then I wasn't sure because you and Victor have the same build and coloring. Besides, Karina was married." Patrick bent, brushed dirt off the base, then tapped the sand out of the brush and looked back at Phoenix. "What good would it have done at that late date? It would only have served to destroy her marriage or make you miserable about not being able to claim your children. How did you find out?"

"The son of a—was blackmailing her," Phoenix spat.

"Hell. I thought he was in love with her."

"Yeah. It seems he needed the money more." His voice was laced with sarcasm.

"At least now you can take an active part in the kids' lives. Hell, you do anyway," Patrick said in his usual easygoing tone of one who never fretted about anything.

"If I'd known, I would have come here and confronted her. And I would have taken care of my children," Phoenix added with banked fury.

"You shouldn't have waited this long to come back anyway." That assessment tilted Phoenix over the edge.

How was it that Patrick knew how to push all the wrong buttons? "There was a time when you wouldn't have kept secrets from me." Phoenix strained to keep his pitch normal, though his blood pressure shot to the stratosphere.

"Karina was five years younger than you. I'd think you'd have had sense enough to use protection and if you didn't, you should have checked to see if you left any little packages behind. You expect me to have gone to Washington and browbeaten you back here to take care of your responsibilities when you never even mentioned Karina's name to me?"

"It's what I would have done." Phoenix strolled back to his team, clipped out last minute instructions before they started the game. The boys must have sensed something was up because they didn't give him any trouble or the regular ribbing.

After the game, Phoenix approached Thornton Sterns who was standing near Mrs. Bright. The woman conversed while Thornton looked on.

"Have you discovered how the extra money got into my account?" Phoenix asked.

"I thought you suddenly had a lucrative source of income coming in," he joked.

"Working here?" Phoenix raised an eyebrow.

"That's why I keep my money in a safe little place in my house," Mrs. Bright intervened as he gave a half smile. "You will never catch me putting my money in a slippery bank."

"Now, Mrs. Bright, look at all the interest you're losing by keeping your money under the mattress," he said and laughed.

She eyed him sternly. "You been snooping around my place?"

"No! No. It's just a euphemism. An old saying, so to speak."

She sniffed. "I used to keep it there. Now, I've found someplace safer."

"Still you're losing an awful lot of interest. Especially if you put it into one of our CDs."

"I remember the thirties. At least my dollar will still be a dollar when I'm ready to use it and not ten cents." She clutched her purse tightly under her arm.

"You aren't including the cost of inflation. A dollar ten years ago is worth a lot less than a dollar now."

"That's okay. At least I won't go to the poor house as long as I keep my hands on my own money." She elevated her chin and walked off, her little legs looking like sticks poking out of her walking shoes.

Phoenix had to smile. The depression had left a mark to last a lifetime for those who'd lived through it. And nothing was likely to change their perception of financial institutions. With this latest development with his account, their beliefs seemed to have merit. Except he was getting more instead of less. Maybe he should have his friend at the FBI check into it. Especially if the people in town weren't computer savvy enough to handle the problem.

"Towanna is still researching your problem. Hopefully we'll find something soon." Thornton smiled and patted him on the back.

Phoenix hated that gesture. It always seemed insincere. "Good," he said uneasily. He never trusted a banker's smile either. But he trusted Towanna.

"The team's looking good. They'll be playing in the tournament if they keep it up."

"They're aiming for it. Great bunch of players."

"The town's mighty proud of them and you for your devotion to them."

"We couldn't have done it without the help of people like you who were generous with funding."

"Glad to do our part." The perfect banker's rejoinder.

Tylan Chance brought the small cooler, the sodas, and snacks his grandma had asked him to bring from the store into her kitchen.

"You having a party or something? What do you need a cooler for, Grandma?" He kissed her on her weathered cheek and set the cooler on the kitchen counter.

"Luke and I are going to see that gospel music show everyone's raving about in Richmond and spend the night in that new hotel." She opened the cooler to air it out and started unpacking the bags. "You know how expensive sodas and snacks are in those hotels."

His grandma spending the night in Richmond? With Luke? Red hot fury exploded through Tylan. He faced her with his hands on his hips. "You and Luke are staying overnight in Richmond?" he said in a deceptively quiet tone. Wrapped up in what she was doing, she didn't catch the warning in his voice.

"Uh-huh."

"I don't see why you have to stay the night. Take in the early show and come back afterward." That was a reasonable enough solution.

"We're going to see the late afternoon show. Luke doesn't like to do a lot of driving at night on the highway. The gospel show should be nice. First time I've seen one in a while."

"What time is it? Maybe Clarice and I can drive you and Luke. He won't have to worry about driving." She was not spending the night in Richmond with Luke Jordan if he could help it. "Or you can take a room with us if you really have to stay overnight. It wouldn't bother me to drive back though."

"I thought you were doing something with the ball team this weekend. And Clarice has papers to grade. She told me so." Miss Drucilla started washing the cooler.

"Clarice can grade papers later." Tylan dismissed the excuse.

"It's up to her. I don't get in her business."

"Grandma . . ."

"I don't need you going on a date with me," she snapped impatiently. "I never went on yours."

Tylan thought of some of his nights in the back seat of Jonathan's car then imagined his grandma and Luke in bed, her skirt tossed . . . Darnit, they were too old for that nonsense. "Forget the trip. Either I go with you or you stay. You don't need to be going to Richmond anyway."

"Boy, you've been working too hard. I think you've lost your doggone mind."

"You're really going to think so when I get my hands

on Luke. I know he hasn't been spending nights here because I see his truck leave at night. But now he's sneaking you away to Richmond to . . ."

"Don't you even *think* about lecturing Luke or me on proper behavior. I have never sullied your grandfather's name and never will. You watch that tongue of yours, young man. I saw you before you saw yourself." She pointed a soapy finger at him. "I'm going to Richmond without you and Clarice. Accept it."

Filled with outrage and regret, Tylan wished he could recant his words. He should have been more subtle. He knew his grandmother was the essence of propriety. But darnit, she had no business spending the night away with Luke Jordan. "Grandma . . ."

"You better think long and hard before you say another word." Her eyes still had the power to shrink him with a look as she glared back at him.

Darn it if Tylan didn't feel like a ten-year-old in trouble receiving the lecture and stare that had always been worse than a spanking. But she was the one out of line this time, not him, he reminded himself. "Grandma . . ."

"We're her . . . ere."

Tylan turned as Mrs. Jones walked into the kitchen, the triplets bringing up the rear.

"I came by to pick up the clothes for the church charity bazaar. Hi, Ty . . ." She stopped short.

The door slammed as he stormed out.

"Well, what in the blazes got him in such a snit?" Mrs. Jones asked.

"You should have asked him." Lips pinched, Miss Drucilla resumed scrubbing the cooler with a bit more vigor than before. "The clothes are in the black garbage bag on the porch."

With a puzzled frown, Mrs. Jones got comfortable in one of the ladder-back kitchen chairs. "I'll get them on my way out."

"Coffee's on the counter if you want some."

"I think I will take a cup." Having been over enough times to know where they were, she got up to get a cup and saucer. "Mrs. Bright been talking about the spaceships over her place again," Mrs. Jones said, Tylan forgotten in the face of juicy gossip.

"That woman is full of foolishness. Probably woke up with sleep in her eyes."

"I don't know, just the other night on 'It's a Small Universe,' they talked about spaceships and the scientific research they were doing on them. Government folks are trying to keep it hush-hush, but you know how you can't keep anything from those reporters nowadays."

"Then, how come I didn't see it on the news?"

"Not much difference. A newsmagazine's close enough. Anyway, they described the spaceships and the people in detail. They said some of the spaceships emitted bright yellow lights." Mrs. Jones took a quick swallow of coffee. "Mrs. Bright said her spaceship had yellow lights, too. I'm not saying she actually saw one, only what she said. Course if she did see one, too bad she didn't get pictures or one of those videos of it. That way she could go on the magazine show and become a millionaire by the time she worked her way around to them all. Then they'd probably write a book about her, too."

Miss Drucilla ignored the silly woman. One was just as batty as the next.

But that didn't deter Mrs. Jones from enjoying her gossip. "Had poor Mrs. Bright scared to death to turn her own lights on in her own home, fearing they'd come and capture her in the dead of night. You know she lives smack in the middle of nowhere with nobody but that batty old man as a neighbor."

Miss Drucilla looked around at the triplets, all three avidly glued to every word Mrs. Jones spoke. "I'll fix you some of my fresh corn pudding and you can eat it out on the porch." She dried her hands and got the pudding out the refrigerator. Miss Drucilla never had much to do with foolish people. She wished the woman had stayed home. She could have had Clarice or Tylan drop off the clothes at church.

"I love your corn pudding," Karl rubbed his small tummy.

"Good. I fixed up a batch especially for my favorite children." She dished up three bowls and microwaved them before handing them to the children. Tylan had given her the microwave three years ago, but she'd never used the blame thing until Luke talked her into it. Said it would give her more time with him and cut down on her work and, doggone it, it had. A sudden sadness enveloped her thinking of the rift with Tylan. He'd never been angry with her before and she didn't quite know what to do about it. Blame it, she was a grown woman. He had no business talking to her in that manner. A child's voice cut into her melancholy.

"We want to hear more about the spaceships," Kara said.

"Nothing but foolishness. Eat your pudding."

"Thanks." They sat at the table, eager eyes and ears waiting for the next tidbit of interesting information.

"Now, go on out back." Miss Drucilla hustled the kids outside. Once they were safely out of hearing, she turned on Mrs. Jones. "You need to be careful what you say around busy ears. They might believe that nonsense," she sniffed.

Mrs. Jones peeped out the door before saying, "You're right about that. Good thing I'm keeping the kids now. They aren't getting into nearly as much mischief as they used to."

"Keep it that way by not telling tales."

She sniffed. "Mrs. Bright doesn't believe they're tales."

Miss Drucilla felt as nervous as a teenager as Luke walked her to her hotel room. His room was down the hall from hers. "The show was just beautiful and the dinner delicious. I still think you spent too much. You could have taken me to a cheaper restaurant," she said.

Luke opened her hotel room door and handed the key to her. "You're worth every penny. I'm glad you enjoyed it." Quite frankly, he wanted time away from curious eyes. Time to spend alone with his lady.

She preceded him into the room. "Have a seat." Two chairs graced the small table by the window. "Can I get you a soda?"

"Yes, thank you."

Miss Drucilla eagerly jumped up to fix the drink. Luke had filled the ice bucket for her before they left.

"The ice is probably melted by now. I'll get you some more."

While he was gone, she poured his favorite soda and put it on the table. She had enough time left to run her hand down her dress to make sure it was neat.

When he entered, he put the ice bucket near the sink and went over to where Miss Drucilla was fidgeting with the curtains. "You sure are pretty in that dress." He ran a callused hand along her collar, barely touching her neck. "I've waited a long time for you. Sixty years." He pressed a gentle kiss on her lips and gathered her close. "I know you don't believe in sex without marriage." He reached into his pocket and brought out something and gathered her hand. "I love you. Marry me, Drucilla. Lord knows we've lived a good long life. I don't want to waste what's left tiptoeing around you, waiting for Tylan to bash my skull in if I make the wrong move. I'm too old to be supervised like a teenager." He slipped the diamond on her finger.

She looked at the huge sparkling gem. "Oh, Luke. It's so beautiful."

"And before you tell me I shouldn't have, let me tell you when a man waits this long, he can damn well buy his woman what he wants." A world of possessiveness laced his tones as his proprietary gaze swept over her.

Her knees were as shaky as jelly. She didn't know why he was attracted to her and wondered how he would see all the wrinkles on her body. She was long past the stage of fresh youth and had never thought to seek the affection of a man at her age. But it was so nice having him paying court to her the way he was. Lord, but what was a woman her age doing getting butterflies in her stomach? She was too old for her heart to be pitter-pattering the way it did when she thought of him. Just the other day, she was picking a dish of Kale from her garden to cook for dinner. She was daydreaming of him sitting at the table eating with her that very evening and how he stretched those long legs out when he read the evening paper. She'd gotten hot all over and she was well past the stage of menopause and hot flashes. She looked up at him.

"Here I am older than you and I feel so unsure. Where's that little boy I used to baby-sit?"

"He grew up. When you get to be as old as we are, age doesn't matter."

"I guess you're right. I'll marry you Luke Jordan. It certainly took you long enough to get around to asking."

"I was ready years ago." He sealed their engagement with a long joyous kiss.

Luke was still a handsome man to Miss Drucilla's way of thinking. And he still had all his teeth. Strong muscles still firm from farm work. Although his sons and grandsons ran the farm, he still helped out. Miss Drucilla liked a productive man. One who didn't sit around with a lot of idle time on his hands. She was always busy and couldn't stand having somebody under foot twenty-four hours a day.

Yes, they would get along just fine.

He tasted Miss Drucilla one last time. "I better get on down the hall to my own room before Tylan really has a reason to punch out my lights."

* * *

"Phoenix, I can't find the triplets." Karina's frantic voice quivered over the phone. "I checked their rooms and they weren't there. I looked outside and called them just in case they were up to something. They weren't there, either. Do you think Victor would snatch them. Oh, God. I don't know what I'll do if something's happened to them. But Victor wouldn't harm them. He loves them."

"Calm down." His own heart beat had picked up. His precious children ... "Did you have an argument with them? Could they have run away?" he asked trying to think like a professional, not a father.

"No. I checked their things. Their bags and clothes are here. They've never run away before, even when I've chastised them."

"Were there indications of forced entry?"

"No!" she yelled. "You're wasting time asking questions. We've got to do something!"

"I'll check the area around here."

"I'm coming with you."

"Karina, I don't want you driv—" She had disconnected. Phoenix slammed down the phone and pulled on the jeans he'd left on the chair, slipped his feet in his sneakers and ran down the stairs while pulling a T-shirt over his head. As he ran outside, Karina's car sputtered to a screeching halt, half off the sidewalk, and barely missed swiping his car.

"You've got no business driving—"

"I don't have time for one of your lectures. I've got to find my babies."

Phoenix grabbed a flashlight out of his glove compartment. "First, we'll walk around on foot."

Karina almost had to run to keep up with Phoenix's long strides. They walked toward Miss Drucilla's house. She was away with Luke for the night. The night was bright with the full moon in its glory. Twigs snapped under their feet. The thick forest with its cover of trees would conceal the low beam of a flashlight until one was relatively close to it. Then with the neighborhood lights, it would be diffi-cult to detect anyway. But Phoenix and Karina walked on. They'd seen no signs of the triplets by the time they reached Miss Drucilla's house. It was dark in Tylan's house.

A little more than a week ago Phoenix discovered he had children. The possibilities for their disappearance were endless. Someone from his past may have come back to harm anyone close to him. Phoenix held onto the thin hope that no one knew, since Karina and he still hadn't made the information public. But the criminal mind of today . . . God, let his children be safe, he prayed. Hope-fully, the three were together planning some mischief. He didn't ever think he'd wish for such. He quickened his pace until he realized Karina was out of breath. "You should have stayed at home," he snapped impatiently.

"Don't worry about me. I can keep up." She trod on with him.

"I think I see a light over there. I'm going to turn off my flashlight," Phoenix whispered knowing sound carried at night.

He and Karina moved stealthily through the forest. Just before they cleared the trees adjacent to the lake, they heard Karlton say, "We've searched for spaceships long enough tonight. I'm ready to go home."

"Just a little longer," Kara insisted. "We don't want to miss anything. The last time they came, it was a Saturday night. Maybe they'll come again and we'll video it. Then we'll be on 'It's a Small Universe' and we'll be overnight celebrities."

"Miss Drucilla said there weren't any spaceships."

"But it was on TV," Karl said. "And Mrs. Bright and Mrs. Jones said they exist."

"Maybe Miss Drucilla just hasn't seen one yet. They probably zoomed in first and spotted her shotgun and were afraid they'd get shot if they tried landing near her."

"You're in big trouble." All three stumbled and screeched when they heard their mother's voice. "What were you thinking coming out here in the middle of the night? I want you back at home. Right now! Had me frightened out of my mind."

"But, Mom, we want to film the spaceships!" Kara said.

"That's another thing we're going to talk about," she shouted furiously.

"Do you kids realize how dangerous it is? What if you were injured? Your mother had no idea of where you were. You're grounded for a week. And no Nintendo while you're grounded."

"You're not our father. We didn't break the law," Kara said.

How hard it was not to blurt out *Oh, yes, I am.*

"Nevertheless, you're still grounded," Karina said. "And don't use that tone of voice with an adult. I've taught you better. Now, move it!"

They walked past Karina and Phoenix and trouped up the path toward the house.

"Thanks for helping me. I was so frightened," Karina whispered to Phoenix as they followed the children.

"Are you okay, now?"

Tight lipped, Karina nodded, yes. She didn't want to blow up at the kids in front of him because she knew he'd accuse her of overreacting.

Phoenix remembered late night excursions with Patrick. His mom was a heavy sleeper and once she succumbed to sleep, there was no waking her. In contrast, Karina was a light sleeper. The least little noise would disturb her.

Phoenix felt like a hypocrite having to chastise the children for the same stunts he'd pulled as a child.

As they trudged on in the cool night temperature, pain sliced through him. He'd thought Kara was on the verge of accepting him. But now as she marched ahead of her brothers, snapping fallen twigs as she stepped on them, he wondered if she'd ever come to love him. Or if he'd get the opportunity to spoil his daughter as a father would love to.

Chapter 12

The scolding had been delivered and the children tucked into bed when Karina walked outside with Phoenix.

"You're firing that woman," Phoenix said as he closed the screen door behind him.

"What are you talking about, Phoenix?" Karina was tired and only wanted to go to bed now that her babies were safe and snugly tucked away. And this time, she felt the damp coolness of the night.

"Mrs. Jones is not keeping *my* children any longer. She's a bad influence. Look at what happened tonight."

Karina ran a hand up and down her arms to ward off the chill. He would have to hash this out now instead of waiting until tomorrow. "Do you know how difficult it is to find a competent baby-sitter?" she asked, resigned to letting the newness of parenthood settle in.

"You still haven't found one."

"I know she tends to be somewhat . . . eccentric," Karina said soothingly. "But even if I had another sitter, they'll come in contact with Mrs. Bright and her in church, at games, stores. They can't avoid them. It's a small town."

"Eccentric hell! They're as nutty as a fruitcake. And I will keep my children away from them."

"But Mrs. Jones is good to the children. She cares about them and she takes very good care of them. I'm racking my brain trying to determine who's going to keep them while she's out of town for three weeks. Her daughter's baby is due in two months and she'll be spending three weeks with her when the baby arrives."

"Good, in the meantime we can find someone else," he said with finality. "I've had enough of their silliness. I even get phone calls from Mrs. Bright in the middle of the night."

"So speaks the man who's never had to search for a day care provider." Karina looked up at the stars. "Take it from me, we've got it good."

"That's debatable. Another thing. We need to get married."

"Married!" Karina had trouble following the gist of the conversation. At the same time, elation shot through her that he still loved her. Despite that, she wondered what on earth brought that on so suddenly.

"The kids get into too much mischief. They need a full-time father around. One they can feel comfortable with leading their lives. As long as I'm a neighbor, they don't see me as a parent figure. At least in the role as stepfather, it would give me more credibility."

So much for love. "I'm not going into another marriage of convenience. I've tried that route once. It doesn't work." Karina didn't want to deal with the feelings she was already having about Phoenix. She was not going to complicate matters with a one-sided love situation.

"We have to get married. For the children," he insisted.

"You live next door. You can guide them from there. If there's discord within a home, it will make the situation worse instead of better. I don't want them to live in a tense atmosphere."

"We can get along for their sake. Stop thinking of us and think of what they need."

"You can't exclude us. They know how a husband and wife are supposed to live. They can tell when something's wrong. They aren't stupid. I'm not doing it, Phoenix. I'm not putting them through that." She shook her head. "Besides, how long will you be here? You'll get another plumb of a project and be off to some other exciting place and I'll be left here to pick up the pieces. No, thank you."

"I'm not leaving my children. I'll be here," he entreated.

Had he said he loved her, then she'd have married him in a minute.

"We're not through with this subject."

"We may as well be, because I'm not changing my mind. I took care of the triplets just fine alone."

"You're not alone anymore." He pressed a kiss to her lips and left.

Karina watched the distance increase between them as he walked under the full moon–lit night bright with stars. A sudden sadness enveloped her. Would the time ever be right for them? Sometimes, like now, she felt alone. It would be so nice for him to wrap his arms around her and walk her back inside the house and prepare for bed together. She could have all of that if she said yes to his proposal that hadn't felt like a proposal.

Could she really consider marrying him for the children's benefit? All of her actions so far had been for her children's well-being. Was it selfish to want something for herself for a change? A marriage with a man who loved her, whom she loved in return?

She wondered lately how their marriage would have survived had he not disappeared or if she had waited. Would the blind love they had for that short summer have survived? Or would it have fizzled with the problems of most couples today?

That, Karina would never know. She could consider marrying him and hope that one day he would grow to love her. Except, it wasn't just her to consider now. She had the triplets and she couldn't afford to experiment. No, she'd never marry again without love between both parties.

After a cholesterol-raising breakfast of three-egg omelets, hash browns, and fresh baked biscuits that weren't quite as good as hers, Luke and Miss Drucilla checked out of the hotel. The bellman loaded their luggage onto a cart and started out the door ahead of them.

Luke grasped her hand. "Did Tylan give you any trouble about the weekend? I swear he's watching at night to see when I leave your house."

"I can handle Tylan." The dreamy smile on her face evaporated with the thought of the unsettled dispute with Tylan.

"You sure about that? Just say the word and I'll have a talk with him." She looked so pretty, Luke was speechless for a spell.

"Don't worry about him. I've been handling him since he was knee-high to a grasshopper," Luke heard through a tunnel. He had to shake his head to clear his thoughts and focus on her words. He put his arm around her petite shoulders.

Recalling how well she'd fared in the fifties after her husband died, he knew she could handle just about anything life threw her. He was glad he'd be there to take some of the strain off her shoulders. Fragile shoulders they looked, but looks were deceptive when it came to his Drucilla Chance. Soon to be Mrs. Drucilla Jordan.

Drucilla Jordan. How he'd waited for that day. He squeezed her hand and took it in his. Her's weren't soft office worker's hands. Her palms were rough with the calluses of raising the gardens, canning, and the neat-as-a-pin house she kept.

She'd said yes to his proposal. Finally, this woman whom he'd loved a lifetime would be his.

As they ventured outside, the sun seemed brighter, the grass greener. Nothing could interfere with this beautiful day. Because he was walking with—he was going to marry—the love of his life.

"Let's not have a long engagement, Drucilla."

She smiled shyly at him. "We won't."

They stopped at the spot where the car was supposed to be.

It wasn't there.

"Maybe I parked it someplace else."

"No, it was right here," Miss Drucilla insisted.

Luke walked around the parking lot to make sure. "Yeah, it was here."

About twenty feet away another hotel guest shouted, "My car's gone!"

"Oh, Lord," the bellman said and backtracked with some very distressed and angry guests. The hotel manager escorted them into his office and he called the police. It was three hours before everything was done and Tylan arrived to get them.

He was still tight lipped and Miss Drucilla and Luke had argued long before Luke finally concurred and let Tylan come for them.

"We should have waited until I could reach one of my grandchildren," he whispered.

"They weren't in and I wasn't waiting all day. Don't worry about Tylan. I'm some kinda upset about your car. And him."

"Well, it's gone now. No sense crying over spilled milk. At least it's insured."

"You never get back the full value though, Luke." She touched his arm in a rare soothing manner. "You work so hard. It just isn't right that somebody stole it right out from under you. What they need is a good switch."

Tylan was still reeling from the argument with his grandmother. Clarice had insisted on riding with him, ostensibly to keep him in line. She jumped out of the car immediately after they arrived at the hotel.

"Are you two all right?" she asked.

"We're fine. Just spitting mad, is all," Miss Drucilla answered.

"At least you weren't in the car when it happened."

"Humph. Spoiled my outing. We had a lovely time before this."

By that time Tylan had loaded the luggage in the car and joined them. When he did no more than speak, Clarice jabbed him in the side.

"So, what did the police say, Luke?" Tylan managed, rubbing the now-tender spot.

"They've had several calls from hotels this morning. It's the same as the previous thefts. They wait long enough for the authorities to relax before they hit again. Thanks for coming."

Tylan relented. "Anytime. This mess is a darn shame."

They were soon on their way.

"Lord, I needed this," Towanna Jordan said as she kept casting shy looks in Robert's direction. For the ladies' luncheon, she'd dressed especially well in her red suit, the skirt stopping a scant three inches above her knees.

"So did I," Karina rubbed her forehead.

"Girl, you are working much too hard." Towanna scanned the menu. "And Clarice, if you get any bigger you're going to burst."

"I feel like I'm ready to burst. I can't wait for this baby to come." She slipped the chair back to give her girth more room and placed a delicate hand on the protrusion. "I can't imagine what it was like for you, Karina."

"Let's just say I was glad when it was over." They laughed.

"I think we all feel that way. So, Towanna, anything interesting with your love life?"

"What love life?" She sneaked another look as Robert seated a late lunch guest.

"You always have something interesting going on."

Towanna shrugged. "Not anymore. I haven't had a date in months."

Karina noticed that Robert's gaze lingered on Towanna each time he passed.

"What about you, Karina?"

She focused on Clarice. "I don't have time for it." She sipped on her glass of water. "Although Charles asked me out, but I put him off. You know, I think it's time I started dating again."

"Good for you. But couldn't you find someone other than Charles?" Towanna turned up her nose.

"He's really nice," Karina defended.

"He's a nerd. You'd have to lead him around if you can get him out of the coroner's office long enough. He'd never be adventurous." Towanna turned up her nose again. "And how you can stand to kiss a man who smells like formaldehyde?"

"I need someone peaceful. What I don't need is a live volcano." By the name of Phoenix, Karina thought.

"Give me the volcano any day. Tell her Clarice. I know Tylan isn't tame."

"You can say that again. But there's nothing wrong with Charles. His nephew is in my class. He's very intelligent and doesn't give me a minute's trouble. A teacher can really appreciate that."

"Like I said. A nerd."

"I don't care what you say. I'm accepting Charles's date." With that settled, Karina snapped her menu open before she realized she knew every item on the blasted thing. Charles would take her mind off Phoenix. So what if her conscience worried her that she was probably using Charles? There was no law against two people who were somewhat attracted to each other going out on a date for companionship, was there?

"Oh, Towanna, it was awful that your father's car was stolen," Clarice said.

"His car was stolen?" Karina asked. It was odd that the restaurant wasn't buzzing with the news.

Clarice filled her in. "You know Miss Drucilla and he stayed overnight after the gospel show at the colosseum. When they were ready to leave this morning, it was gone."

"That's horrible."

"Richmond has had a wave of car thefts the last few weeks and the police don't have the first lead. I know Luke talked to Phoenix about it this morning. You know how he likes that Lincoln."

Karina shook her head.

"His pride and joy," Towanna said. "At least he's not taking it too hard. He was hard at work with farm business when I left the house."

"That man works harder than someone a third of his age," Karina said.

"Granddaddy will never completely retire. Miss Drucilla won't either. She's always busy with something."

"Keeps them young at heart," Clarice added. "But Tylan is fit to be tied. Every night when Mr. Jordan comes over, he walks the carpet peeking out the window until his truck leaves." She stroked her abdomen lovingly. "If this is a girl, I'll have my work cut out for me when she starts to date. Do you know he wanted to go to Richmond with them? Came to the house fussing about Luke taking advantage of Miss Drucilla by spending the night. Now you know she would get an extra room. She doesn't believe in shacking. But you can't tell Tylan that. God, that man. Had words with her just before they left. He tossed and turned that entire night. Kept waking me up."

"Granddad is put out with him, too. Now that they're engaged, Tylan shouldn't have anything to fuss about."

"They're engaged," Karina crowed. "That's fabulous!"

"Then maybe I could get some sleep," Clarice said.

"I think they're cute," Karina added. "She's so small and he's tall and handsome. They make a lovely couple."

"Like Karina and Phoenix," Towanna said. "Speaking of Phoenix, I don't see why you don't set your sights on him. He's a much better catch than Charles," Towanna said.

"That's all relative. I need something soothing in my life. I have three live volcanos running around my house every day."

"Are you ladies ready to order lunch?" Robert came out of nowhere.

"Yes, we are." Clarice said, and Robert signaled to a waitress.

"Towanna, do you remember Robert? I think he was a few years ahead of us."

"I remember him."

"I kept thinking I remembered you from somewhere." Robert had a teasing glint in his eye. "Weren't you the little girl who used to wear red bobby socks and blue bows on your hair regardless of what color your clothes were?"

"It's impolite to mention that," Towanna said, embarrassed he remembered that particular stage in her life.

"I especially remember a striking yellow dress you wore with blood red socks one bright spring day."

Karina knew Robert had been grilling Towanna's brother on some of her childhood quirks.

"I was teased so much, it cured me of my red craze."

"Except her apartment has plenty of red all over," Clarice added.

After the meal, Robert quirked an eyebrow before he handed a desert dish to Clarice. "I bought your favorite. Just don't let Tylan know. And I have some more packed in the back for you to take home."

Clarice took a peek. "Bless you. Tylan lectures me about the sweets, but I can't get enough raspberry trifle. Thank you, thank you." She hefted herself out the chair and kissed Robert, who was thoroughly embarrassed at the show of affection.

Karina had long ago determined that all his talk about disliking children was a ruse. The triplets adored Robert and he them.

While sitting at her desk putting the finishing touches on the junior-senior prom breakfast, Karina pondered her planned date with Charles. He'd been speechless when she'd accepted. It took him a minute to stammer a reply. She was more amused than enamored. And she waited for the adrenaline to rush. Why didn't her heart go pitter-patter when she thought of him, the way it did with Phoenix?

Maybe she'd buy a new dress tomorrow for the occasion. It had been ages since she even thought about buying something new for herself, except the usual wardrobe for the restaurant. She wanted something different for her date, more daring.

"Karina?"

"Yes, Robert?

"Telephone, line two."

"This is Karina, how may I help you?"

"Phoenix. How would you like to see the new movie tomorrow night?"

"Thanks, but I have plans." He was keeping the triplets for her tonight.

"Doing what?"

"None of your business." She bristled at his proprietary tone.

"Everything you do is my business."

That possessive statement didn't warrant an answer. He wouldn't ruffle her feathers. She needed a diversion. She made a notation, reminding herself she had to get cereal.

"What about the children?"

"They're staying at Jonathan's. Towanna told me about Luke's car. Have they found anything yet?"

He sighed. "No. You're evading the question. What are you doing tomorrow night?"

"Phoenix, you can share the responsibility for the children, but what I do has nothing to do with you."

"What you do reflects on the children. So it's very much my business."

That didn't warrant a response either. "I've got to go. Goodbye." Karina hung up. The nerve of the man. Acting as if he owned her or had a right to know her every move now that he knew they shared children.

So what if her heartbeat was still accelerated from hearing his voice? She'd get over it quickly with his attitude.

"The sheriff's spending plenty of time with you these days," Robert said from the door. He wore a sports jacket and dress slacks.

"On your way out?" she asked, deftly avoiding the question.

"Yeah." He sat on the edge of her desk as if he had all the time in the world.

"It wasn't very nice of you to tease Towanna."

"I couldn't resist." One leg swung back and forth against her desk. "How was the lunch?"

"Wonderful. It's been a while since we've been together. Clarice will probably name her son after you. Trifle is her favorite."

"Please. I don't want any little urchins named after me. Towanna certainly looked pretty. Can that woman cut a style in her clothes. I'd like to see her without them."

"Robert!"

"A guy can wish, can't he? I bet Phoenix is thinking the same thing about you, and you about him."

Karina's face heated. She already knew what he looked like under his clothes. Striking.

"So what did the good sheriff want?" Robert obviously missed her reaction.

"He asked me out tomorrow night."

"You accepted, right?"

"I already have a date," she said, impatient with everyone trying to match her with Phoenix.

"With whom?" Robert dared to ask.

Karina sighed. "Charles."

"You've got to be kidding." The incredulous look on his face would have been funny if she didn't halfway agree.

Karina straightened her shoulders. "Charles is a perfectly respectable coroner."

"Who works with Phoenix."

"So?"

"You're asking for trouble if the sheriff's after you, too."

Chapter 13

"Sheriff," said Mrs. Bright as she strutted over at the end of the ball game and flagged him down by waving a pristine handkerchief. Phoenix escorted her to a chair. Winded, she gasped for breath when she reached him. With barely enough energy left she whispered, "Sheriff, I wasn't sure, so I didn't call you but I think I saw that spaceship leaving last Saturday night." She looked around assuring herself no one else was in hearing distance for fear someone would hear the juicy tid-bits before she had the opportunity to spread the gossip herself.

Thank you, God, Phoenix thought. A 2 A.M. wake up about spaceships after he'd lost sleep in search of the triplets who'd been looking for the very same spaceships wouldn't have boded well for the woman. Phoenix got angry again at the thought of his children being out alone in the middle of the night because of the gossip this woman indulged herself. He didn't mind her unusual pastimes, except when it concerned his children. Other than that, it was harmless enough. But one look at her kind eyes stilled his hostility.

She must have detected his irritation because her next words were hesitant. "I . . . I saw the lights just as they were leaving. I knew it wouldn't do any good to call you since they'd be gone by the time you got there."

"You did the right thing. If you see them, just call the office and someone will check it out."

It was Sunday afternoon and the Nottoway Running Kites had just won another game. Clarice was working and Phoenix was in charge of the triplets. Mrs. Jones had the evening off. And good riddance. He'd been discretely searching for another sitter. It wasn't long before he discovered most of the eligible women worked now and Mrs. Bright was certainly out of the question. All he needed to do was get her and Mrs. Jones together and the kids would be building spaceships instead of searching for them.

He had made progress in one area! Phoenix knew Karina had a date with Charles. He'd see that Charles was otherwise occupied Friday night. Karina was the mother of his children. She had no business dating another man. They *were* getting married and the quicker she realized that, the better.

After a meeting with the boys, Phoenix and the triplets were headed home. "What would you like for supper tonight?"

"We could go by the restaurant and pick up some take out," Karlton suggested.

"Or we could fix dinner," Kara added.

"You can cook?" Phoenix asked.

"Of course we can. Our mom owns a restaurant." She rolled her eyes toward the ceiling as if she were talking to a simple adult.

"What will you fix?"

"Taco salad."

"Tell you what. I'll operate the stove and you can do everything else. Deal?"

"Deal!"

"Mr. Chance has everything we need in his store."

"We'll stop there on our way home."

Tylan came up behind them while they were searching for taco sauce. "So they've talked you into spending money in my store. You're as big a pushover as Jonathan."

"They're cooking dinner. What're you doing here so late? I thought you left early now that you're an expectant father."

"Clarice had a craving for sherbet. Although we have several flavors, they wouldn't do. So here I am." He held out the box of rainbow sherbet in his hand. "What's with Luke's car? Have they heard anything in Richmond?"

"The gang has been at it for two months now. They never know when the robbers are going to hit. And they take three to four cars when they do. Too sporadic for them to pin down anything. And just when the hotels take the extra security off, they strike again."

"Damn. Grandma and Luke had no business over there anyway," Tylan said irritated again.

"They have a right to enjoy the theater without mishap, you know. From what Luke says, they had a wonderful time. Even got engaged."

"About time, too. Especially if they're going to be spending nights out of town."

"Don't tell me, after all the skirts you've chased, you're turning into a prude. Clarice's pregnancy must be scrambling your brain. Besides, if Luke got out of line, Miss Drucilla would bop him over the head with a skillet."

"That is something. I came close a time or two lately myself."

"Now that they're getting married, you should be pleased."

"It's taking some getting used to. I'm not accustomed to seeing Grandma with anyone. But, it's about time. I guess she could do worse."

"A lot worse. She's got the added advantage of marrying a man madly in love with her. It's lasted through the decades."

"You're right. I was a little ticked off by them staying in Richmond. But I've come to terms with it."

"We have everything, Sheriff Dye," Kara said as she came over with a bag of corn chips.

"I've got to get going. Clarice will wonder what happened to me," Tylan said and left.

After they purchased the items, Phoenix took the children to their home to cook. Karina had said she would be out late and didn't want the children up. Everyone got busy with chores. Phoenix felt a certain tranquility working with his children. At one point he stood back and just watched them, enjoying their presence and reflecting on the years he'd missed out of their lives. And Karina thought she was actually going to bring another man into their lives. In essence, dating someone would make that person part of the children's lives. No way. He'd spent too many years without them to be a neighbor dad or "friend" as his children considered him. Or worse, an uncle. He wanted them to sleep down the hall from him at night. He wanted to be the last one they saw at night before closing their eyes. And he wanted to fall asleep, then wake with Karina in his arms.

After filling up on taco salads, Phoenix said, "Now we get to do the dishes."

"Do we have to?" Karl asked.

"Yes, we do. We can't make a mess and leave it for your mom. She'll be tired when she gets in. You have to help her out around here." Phoenix took his plate and utensils to the sink, rinsed it and stacked it into the dishwasher.

"All right. But I thought we'd get a break tonight since it's Sunday."

"Your mom doesn't get a break."

Phoenix assigned duties to everyone and soon the kitchen was spotless.

"I wish you were our dad. I don't like doing dishes, but you're fun. How come you spend more time with us then he does?" Karlton asked.

Phoenix almost choked on his emotions. "I think he wants to see you, but he's busy." That sounded lame even to Phoenix. He shouldn't have to make excuses. Victor should never have married Karina. "How would you feel if I dated your mom?"

The three looked at each other. "We'd have to talk it over first," Kara replied.

"You do that and let me know. Okay, it's time for showers. School's tomorrow."

"Can't we play one game before getting ready for bed?"

Phoenix relented, knowing he was a pushover. "One hour, then you shower."

In the end, they played Scrabble and then went off to get ready for bed. Phoenix went to his car to get some paperwork.

When he settled down, the kids were talking in Kara's bedroom. He knew he shouldn't eavesdrop but they were talking about him. He could tell the boy's voices apart now.

"I think it's too soon to trust him," Kara said.

"No, it's not. Mrs. Jones said Mom needs a man. He

likes us and we like him. It'll work out perfectly.'' Karlton was always his champion.

"I like him, too," Karl added. "He does things with us. Even when Dad was here, he didn't go to our ball games."

"I still think we should give them more time. What if he leaves us like Dad did?"

"I don't think he will. And he doesn't have to do things with us," Karlton said.

"That's right. It's not like he's our uncle or anything," Karl said.

"Maybe we'll try him out. But, I'm keeping my eyes on him."

"It's time for bed," Phoenix said quietly.

"Good night," they replied one by one as the boys left for their room.

Phoenix went into the family room and started to go through the casebook he always kept. He liked to look through it to stay abreast of the different cases in the department. Make sure he hadn't missed anything. But as he sat he saw a photo album on a side table. He picked the book up. They were baby pictures of the triplets, Karina, and Victor.

The book was entitled "Our Growing Stages." On the front page, pictures of the triplets were shown with their names listed below each photo. The babies looked so tiny. In Karina's neat little handwriting, she'd printed that each child hovered around three pounds. Incubators could be seen in the background and various tubes were attached to the children.

The second page held pictures of the children with Karina and Victor. They were still in the neonatal unit. Farther on were photos of their first day home. In one particular photo, Karina was half asleep on the couch with Victor's arm around her while they held the children. The pose was so intimate that anguish lanced through Phoenix. He had to close the book at that point because of the ache that settled in his chest from his loss of his children and Karina. He should have been holding his children and wife.

At that time the bitter wound of losing Karina had been sharp and staggering. He took the most dangerous of assignments, not purposely trying to get killed, but needing something that would take all of his concentration. And because of the results of his previous assignments, his supervisor was more than happy for him to handle them. If only they'd known . . . he would have been assigned to desk duty.

Unwilling to dwell on the pictures any longer, Phoenix pulled out his casebook.

He'd learned long ago to write everything, even if it seemed insignificant. It was the odd little trivial things that usually paid off in catching the inventive criminal. It took a while before he could concentrate fully on work, but once he did, he became completely engrossed.

He chuckled when he ran across the first recording of Mrs. Bright's spaceships. She'd seemed to have been around forever. He remembered her when he was a kid— always baking something good for one church function or another. Even now, she was actively involved. Thank goodness, she had enough children and grandchildren to take her anyplace she needed to go. They all loved their eccentric grandmother.

As Phoenix delved farther into the theft recordings, he realized some of the dates seemed familiar. He flipped back through the book and, indeed, the spaceship dates coincided with the car thefts. He flipped through his book again, then picked up the phone and dialed. "Emmanuel, I want you to check out Mr. Harold's barn tomorrow morning and see if there's anything unusual. In the meantime, if you hear of any car thefts tonight, have a couple of cars discretely drive by there."

"Sure, what's up?"

"It may not be anything, but Mrs. Bright's spaceship sightings coincide with the thefts."

The barn was a perfect place. Mr. Harold was hard of hearing and refused to wear a hearing aid. He no longer used the old barn. With only two senior citizens in the immediate area, it would be easy to strip a vehicle in that location and dump the remains at some out-of-the-way place in Petersburg, which is what they must have been doing.

Phoenix also looked at his notes on the construction theft hoping he could tie something to that. There wasn't anything.

Having gone through his notes, Phoenix lifted the photo album from the table again and continued to peruse its contents. Pictures of each birthday as well as the first day of school were present. There were Easter egg hunts, Christmas pictures, ballet recitals for Kara, soccer for her and the boys. School pictures, their first attempt at sitting in a high chair. Their first steps, their first crawl. Daisy, Brownie, and scouts pictures. Miss Drucilla's barbecues, piano recitals. Phoenix couldn't get enough of looking at them. Even as he nodded off, the last face he saw was Karina playing a circle game with them. And he was determined to take back what was his.

When Karina arrived home from work, Phoenix was sleeping on the couch with the photo album opened on his stomach. He looked vulnerable somehow, not the stern sheriff wrecking havoc in her life. She padded over and picked up the album. She was so accustomed to the album's presence in the family room, she hadn't thought of the pictures being there. Nevertheless, she should have thought to give him pictures of the children. How selfish of her not to realize that he'd want to experience that part of their lives. She made a mental note to herself to put together an album for Phoenix.

Suddenly he was alert and his eyes opened. Though he hadn't moved another muscle.

"You're home," he said rubbing a hand across his face.

"How did the children behave?" Karina put the album on the table and sat in a chair across from him.

"They were fine. They even cooked dinner for me." He sat up in the chair and stretched.

"Kara loves to cook. She assures me she will run the restaurant after college and she will boss her brothers." Karina took her shoes off and massaged her aching feet.

"Except Karlton wouldn't want to run the restaurant. He wants to be sheriff."

"Like his dad," she said quietly. He was silent for a moment and Karina wished she'd kept her mouth shut.

"Have you given any thought to my proposal?"

"I can't deal with that just now. Let's give it a few months."

"The children need me now."

"And you're here."

Phoenix decided to let that rest. He got up and sat on the ottoman in front of her and lifted her feet in his lap. He massaged the balls of her feet and worked his way up her legs. "What about tomorrow night? That will give us a chance to get to know each other again."

Karina tried to pull her feet away, but he held firm. She could barely think with hot emotions going through her. "I've made other plans."

Phoenix nodded his head. "All right." He worked a hand up her calf. "We'll let you call the shots. For now."

With the tingling going through her, his words barely registered, but as his words penetrated she became instantly alert. Phoenix had never let her call the shots. She'd always had her say, but he never gave up. His tenacity was what had made him so good as an FBI agent. She tried to pull her feet back again, but his touch sent such fiery sensations through her that when he held firm, she gave up the fight and reveled in his touch.

"Did you eat dinner?" he asked softly.

Her eyes were closed. "Earlier tonight. I'm just exhausted now."

Phoenix wished he could run a hot tub for her and wrap her with a warm fluffy towel when she was through. Then snuggle up with her in bed. One of the things he missed most was their quiet time together. Each doing their own thing, without pressure—enjoying each other's company. "Want me to run a tub for you?"

"No." She cleared her throat and opened her eyes. "Thank you. I'll take a shower." She looked away from him, probably remembering times when he'd stroked her after a long day of work. He'd been on vacation, so his days were free while she'd worked at Jonathan's firm during her summer vacation.

First thing the next morning, Phoenix met with Emmanuel and went to Mr. Harold's house. He was away visiting with his grandson but gave them permission to search the premises. They looked around the barn and found evidence of vehicular traffic. The door wasn't locked and they went inside. They could see a little grease spill, but not much on the cement floor.

"They're using this place to strip the cars," Phoenix said.

"You don't think Harold is renting the space to them, do you? Not knowing what they're actually doing with it?"

"No. Too dangerous. He could identify them if they'd asked him for permission first. Besides, a hurricane could come through without him knowing. And Mrs. Bright thinks she's seeing alien ships when she sees the lights. She's too far away to see what's actually going on." Phoenix opened his car door. "Let's keep the information quiet.

We don't want anyone to realize we know the location. I'll call Richmond and have them call me the minute they hear of another hotel car theft."

"I wonder who could be doing it?"

"No telling. They haven't left many traces behind. Except for the grease spill, the place is as clean as a whistle.

Chapter 14

"That was low, even for you, Phoenix Dye. How dare you get the children involved with us?" Eyes blazing, Karina glared at him.

"A man's got to use everything at his disposal."

Wearing a mauve silk blouse which outlined gently rounded breasts that invited a man to want to reach out and stroke, and the miniature print skirt that kissed high up her thighs, that had the gall to have a split in the side, she was damn lucky Charles was busy tonight. "Is this impromptu visit for my benefit?" From behind his office desk, Phoenix's facade expressed all innocence. He wore slacks with a sports jacket. May as well be on hand when she discovered her precious Charles was unavailable.

"I'm waiting for Charles. Even though the triplets gave me a fit about not going out on a date without you," she huffed.

"I'm crushed that you don't think I'm a terrific guy. At least the children think I am. That's some consolation." He tapped a pen on the desk. "Is he your hot date for the evening?" he asked, already knowing the answer.

Karina straightened, "Yes, he is." Her tone bordered on defensive. "I would appreciate if you wouldn't encourage the children."

"In what way?" he asked, all innocence.

"About us."

"And you're in love with Charles?" His hooded eyes didn't allow her to read his feelings. She was too agitated to even try.

"Dating will give us a chance to get to know each other."

"My thoughts exactly. Instead of wasting time with Charles, who you know you don't love, you could be giving us a chance."

"You don't know who I do and don't love."

"I did learn a few things about you when we dated, and Charles definitely isn't your type. I hope you don't play your silly games with him and end up hurting him while trying to spite me."

"This may be news to you, but my life doesn't revolve around you," Karina replied hotly.

He was silent for a moment. "I'll go along with your games for a while, Karina. But the day will come when I'll tire of it." His eyes narrowed. "In the future, you need my approval before you go out. Any male in your life affects my children."

Karina slammed her purse on his desk and leaned over toward him. He'd gone too far. "It will be a cold day in hell before I ask you for approval of my dates. I am an adult and quite capable of running my own life, thank you."

"I didn't say your weren't. My concern lies with my children, I will have a say."

"Do I get a say in your dates?"

"Certainly. I'm willing to take you out tonight."

"Too bad."

"I'm crushed, Karina." He leaned back in his chair tapping his pen on the desk, the clicking noise irritating her. "Just to show you what a wonderful guy I am, I hope your evening is everything you want it to be."

She looked at him uncertainly. "How gallant of you."

Charles's timid knock sounded at the door.

"Hi, Phoenix." He grasped Karina's hand as he walked in, eyes bulging when he saw Karina's outfit. Phoenix wanted to rip them out for Charles casting them on his woman. He noticed that Charles had even picked out some decent clothing for a change. Yet his hair was slicked back and he looked every bit the nerd. "Karina, I'm sorry, but I have to work tonight." He'd lowered his voice to a whisper.

"I thought you had the evening off." Irritation crept into her voice. And he did smell like formaldehyde.

"I did, but something came up. A body came in from Dinwiddie. It's been dead for a while and I've got to determine how long and how it died. I'm really sorry about that." He stopped and looked at her as though he really saw her for the first time, or he had memorized some line for his perfect date, Phoenix thought. "You sure do look pretty tonight." He had yet to take his eyes off Karina.

"Thank you." Karina smiled at him.

Someone called Charles from the back room. "Hold your horses," he yelled back. He turned to Karina. "Hate to leave you, but I've got to go." He stood as if uncertain whether he should kiss her or not. Someone called to him again.

"Better get going or they'll drag you out of here." If he put his lips on Karina, Phoenix would bash them in.

"You're right." Charles settled on kissing the knuckles of her hand that he still held, never taking his eyes off her as he backed out the door.

Phoenix put down his stack of papers he held just for show. "I'm available."

She gave him a withering look that had no effect at all. "I'm going home to a good book." She picked up her purse off his desk.

"Now, aren't you being a little stuffy? You're free for

the evening, I'm free. We may as well see a movie or something together. Charles won't mind." And he added as an afterthought, "What's wrong with me?"

"There aren't enough hours in the day to enumerate, besides, I thought you were working."

"I came in because I had nothing else to do. It's lonely sitting at that house all alone. I don't even have the kids to keep me entertained."

God, but he sounded pitiful. And Phoenix Dye had never been pitiful. Karina was instantly suspicious. "Did you have anything to do with Charles having to work?" Her eyes narrowed.

"Me? I don't make his schedule." Phoenix was all innocence. "He sets his own hours and quite frankly I don't care when he works as long as the job gets done." He learned long ago eliminating information wasn't really lying, Phoenix decided. "The body didn't come from Nottoway. He works for several counties."

Karina wavered, indecisive.

Phoenix decided not to give her too much time to ponder. "I'll follow you home and then we can go someplace. You name it." He put his hand on the small of her back to urge her out the door. "Have you had dinner?"

"Actually, no. We were going out to dinner. Anyway, I don't think this will be a good idea. We'd just irritate each other."

"I'll be on my best behavior. Promise." He held his hands up in supplication. "We can start with dinner and go on from there."

In the end, Karina wanted to stay in and they ordered takeout from her restaurant. Phoenix picked it up on his way. By the time he arrived, Karina had changed into comfortable jeans but she kept on the bright blouse. She really didn't want to spend the evening alone.

"Thanks for understanding I needed to stay in. I just wanted some time at home."

"I aim to please."

After a meal of chicken picatta with a salad, broccoli, and rice, Phoenix put on some oldies and they went outside to sit on the porch and enjoy the evening breeze as they listened to the music. The mellow songs were the perfect backdrop for the clear, bright night. Stars outlining the big dipper stood out in stark relief.

Phoenix sat next to Karina, a bit too close she felt. "Do you miss the agency?" she asked to cover her unease. "How did you like working there?"

"Pretty tough at times, but I wasn't under the illusion that I could go in and solve the problems of the world. With enough of us out there, I thought we could make some difference. But I soon discovered it was like pushing sand against the tide. As soon as you solve one case, there are a hundred more to take its place." He adjusted his position and turned toward Karina. "I don't miss it."

"Is that why you left?"

"In a sense. I was just . . . burned-out. Saw too many people who didn't have positive influences early enough in life or who wanted to take what they thought was the easy way out. In the long run, there is no easy way. We've all got to pay our dues in this world. Here, I can reach the children while they're still young. Most of the people know each other. I'm not naive enough to believe I can wipe out crime, but at least I will be able to see my results." His face lit as he talked about the career he loved. Phoenix was involved in so many programs and instigated others he couldn't participate in. He would make a difference.

Karlton was like him. He wanted to right the wrongs. Her children were lucky to have a father who would always be there with a helping hand regardless of what life spewed fourth.

Suddenly, Karina found his arm around her shoulder. With just a little tug, he bought her up against him.

"Come here, Karina. I'm tired of waiting for what I really want." He tilted her head back and his lips met hers. This was no tentative kiss, seeking a path, charting untried waters. This was a kiss of a man who'd covered that ground before and knew what to expect, knew what he wanted.

The suppressed passion in Karina sought release. She responded as she'd never thought to respond to him again. Her body knew, if not her consciousness, the delights to behold in his arms.

Callused, but gentle, masculine hands stroked her neck, soothing her as he would an anxious kitten, building roaring fires of desire spiraling from her core, sending out hot electric flashes all over her body. He adjusted his position until she was flat on the carpeted porch, his weight upon her while sure hands busily unbuttoned her blouse.

Karina felt the cool air hit her upper body. Her nipples harden with the combination of hot kisses streaming down her, and even more when he captured one chocolate bud between his lips, all the while caressing the other one with his hand. The contrast of his hot tongue and the cold air excited her even more.

Karina's hand tore at his clothes and he quickened the pace of their lovemaking. When the last stitch had left, bodies that were battling with the cool dampness of the night and the fire built within, Phoenix bought her to a fever pitch, then using the requisite protection, he gently but surely entered into her. Karina legs wrapped tightly around him and they rocked to the old drumbeat until, under the cover of the bright stars and the crescent moon, an explosion shattered them.

In the aftermath, Phoenix kissed her, stroked her softly. "I've waited so long for this. We're a perfect fit."

What had she done? She shivered.

"Here." Phoenix wrapped his shirt around her, misinterpreting her reaction now that their bodies were cooling rapidly from the glistening sweat. "You're cold." He laughed. "I didn't realize how cool it was."

"Thanks." Karina sat up and buttoned the shirt as Phoenix pulled on his pants. Karina felt around for her underwear and quickly slipped them on.

Phoenix pulled Karina back into his arms. "Can't you see we belong together?"

She remained silent.

"Karina, marry me."

She pushed away from him. "Is marriage what this was about?"

He bought her back close to him. "No, but it makes no sense for us to stay separate. We belong together."

"Why, because of the triplets or good sex. You can go anywhere for good sex."

For the first time that evening his anger stirred. "What we just experienced was more than good sex and don't you deny it."

"I can deny anything I want." She sounded like a five-year-old, Karina thought.

"We're just delaying marriage. Our separation eleven years ago was due to a misunderstanding. Had it not been for that, we'd be married now. We're just doing it a little later, that's all."

"Time didn't stand still during those eleven years. Both of us changed. I don't know you anymore, you don't know me."

He squeezed her tenderly. "You know me well enough to make love to me. That's enough as far as I'm concerned. Our basic values and views on life haven't changed."

"Our perception on life has. I felt the world was mine for the taking in college. Now, I know life isn't so easy. There's a price to pay for what you do and dues to pay for dreams."

"Ah, Karina, why do you have to make it so difficult? As long as we trust each other, everything else will fall into place." He tightened his arms around her. "Calm down. I'm not going to rush you into anything."

"That's exactly the reason I don't want to date you. Because you bulldoze your way into getting your way. It's not going to be that easy this time. Sex and the children aren't going to make me change my mind." Karina sighed.

"I made one mistake, I'm not making a second one, Phoenix."

"You were quick enough to do it before," he sneered.

"Sure, when I had babies to consider. I'm strong enough to stand on my own two feet now, which is what I should have done eleven years ago. I'm not that young, impressionable college student any longer." Retrieving her own clothing, she unbuttoned his shirt and tossed it to him.

"We can't let what we once had disappear again with silly misunderstandings. We played that tune once." Phoenix put his arm through the sleeve. It held a touch of Karina's perfume. "I'm not giving up on us. Give me a chance to get to know the new you and you'll discover the new me. You may discover that we haven't changed that much after all." Phoenix kissed her quickly on the nose and walked away.

"I don't want to know the new you," Karina yelled after him.

Phoenix smiled after he heard the door slam. She's running away from her feelings just as he did for so long. He ignored the little voice in his brain that said she hadn't agreed to marry him. He could work around that. Sooner or later she'd come over to his way of thinking.

Phoenix continued to analyze the situation as he walked down the path to his home. He looked up and saw the evening star, and made his wish.

At 3 A.M. Phoenix got a call from his contact in Richmond. "We've had another wave of car thefts, in Petersburg this time."

"What time?"

"Half hour ago. Someone saw them leaving but by the time we got there, the scent was cold. We think they were traveling south in a blue Mercedes. License plate number Charlie Able Charlie 1–2–3."

Phoenix disconnected and called Emmanuel who had the night off. Phoenix only hoped he was home.

"Meet me at the intersection of Carson and Taylor. I don't know how many people are involved." Phoenix made the necessary calls while he dressed. There were ten cars at the intersection when he arrived.

This might be the break they were waiting for. It wouldn't do Luke any good. By now his car was striped and distributed.

He quickly explained the situation to the officers and they surrounded the area. Upon their arrival, they were drawn to the barn by the lights shining there. As Phoenix's officers got into position, he heard drilling sounds and muffled noises from inside. Someone yelled out, "You've got five minutes, then we leave. Carter, time for you to get that car down to South Carolina. Paint's dry," a deep husky voice called out.

"See you guys tomorrow." Phoenix presumed the voice was from Carter.

"And damnit, don't drive above the speed limit. Your car is a different color and you have a new license plate. No need for anyone to be suspicious of you. So don't do anything to attract attention."

"Yeah, yeah," was the quick reply.

"Damn young whelps," the disembodied voice rang out. Someone opened the barn door. Phoenix signaled his officers.

"This is the police. You are surrounded. Place your hands above your head . . ." The car roared back.

"One coming your way, Emmanuel." Phoenix shouted through his radio.

People were chased and arrests made. When the men were on their way to the station, the officers took inventory. Tow trucks carted off the cars to the impound.

* * *

"I want my guys out of there, now," Tom Snyder demanded. The very fact that these guys could afford such a prestigious lawyer meant that they were working for power and money. "There will be an investigation. It's your sheriff who should be behind bars. He's been feeding these guys information."

At the belligerent voice, Phoenix went to investigate what was going on. "Are you accusing me of something?"

"Damn, right I am. Now that you've gotten all the kickbacks you need, you're making a big bust to make yourself look good. You won't get away with it." The attorney snapped his briefcase closed.

"Your guys are going to stay in jail where they belong. They aren't going to get off by making stupid accusations they can't substantiate. If you have a problem, then you can press charges." Phoenix charged back into his office. Where the hell did they get off making accusations against him? But a nervous quiver skittered through his stomach. This didn't feel quite right. What the hell was going on here? He'd never taken a kickback for anything. And they damn well knew it.

"It couldn't have been better had I planned it myself. Our dear sheriff is getting his comeuppance. And I'm going to add a little spice to it." Einstein took a puff from his cigar. "You can trust your men, can't you?"

"Sure," Casey answered.

"And they won't identify you?"

"Nope. Only one of them has met me. The others don't know what I look like. And Randy won't talk. He's got too much to lose and the people in South Carolina will take care of matters should he decide to talk. He's aware of that."

"Good, good." Einstein tapped a finger against his cigar. "Ordinarily, I don't like working with outsiders or too many people for that matter. Things have a tendency to go wrong. But as long as they don't lead the police in our direction, then we can live with it. Besides, they'll get a lenient sentence and be out on the street in no time. After all, there are far more hardened criminals out there." Einstein flicked his lighter to relight his cigar. "Let's see how this works out before we proceed, shall we? I'll work on some things from my end. Keep a low profile in Richmond."

Phoenix sat in his office listing to the mayor.

"We're looking into the allegations," Warren said. "We won't take the word of a criminal alone. They can't identify you. They've never met you. They can only say their leader said that you were giving him inside information." The mayor was the perfect politician, always trying to remain distant but still wanting to turn any occasion to his advantage. "It's not enough to arrest you. Just make sure there isn't any evidence for them to prove you actually did tip them off."

"Hell, anybody can *say* I was giving them leads. But the crime didn't occur here. Why don't you just give me the lie detector test?"

"No sense in being too hasty. At this point we don't need to take those measures. I hope you can find out the root of all this so it can be over quickly. The town doesn't need another problem with the sheriff. In the meantime, perhaps you should keep a low profile until some of this clears." As Warren left, Emmanuel came in and closed the door.

"We're behind you, man," he said. "We know you weren't involved. Man, you care too much."

"Thanks." Phoenix got up to stare out the window. He'd worked so hard to do what was right. And now, slowly things were happening around him. First Stump and his safe. Patrick, and last, the robberies. All in some way involving people close to him. He didn't believe in coincidences. Each crime was connected to him. Why?

And he had an extra thirty thousand in his bank he couldn't account for.

Chapter 15

Once at home, Phoenix turned on his computer and dialed out. It was only a matter of time before they uncovered where the extra money came from. He should have been more suspicious and made the traces when he first discovered the funds. It was up to him to trace its origin. No one in Nottoway was going to help. Especially the mayor. But he could only get so far on his own, since he wasn't a computer genius. He kept a list of the names of several computer forensic experts who could break into just about anything. Tim Malloy always said he could trace anyplace he wanted, given the time—which was why Phoenix had called him as soon as he returned home.

Phoenix thought of his options. Even if he wanted to go back to the agency, at this point he couldn't. Not with this cloud over his head.

He was tapping into his old cases when Emmanuel arrived. Phoenix poured the iced tea Miss Drucilla had made earlier.

"We found out a man named Casey planned the thefts,"

Emmanuel sat on the porch steps. "We miss you man. You really know how to conduct those investigations. You need to be working from the inside, not from here."

"Casey who?"

"They only knew the name Casey. They've never met him. Casey works through Sticker Jones who's skipped town."

"Casey . . . Casey. I remember that name from somewhere." Phoenix got up and hastened into the house. He was back in a minute with his trusty casebook. He flipped through pages. "Aha. I never forget a face or a name. Casey convinced Stump to rob Tylan's store."

"Wasn't that guy in the witness protection program?"

"Still is." Phoenix closed the book. "This is more than a regular car theft ring. This has something to do with my work in the agency."

"Wow," Emmanuel said.

"I've got phone calls to make," he said jumping up, almost forgetting about Emmanuel in his haste.

"Sure, I can't stay. I'll see you later."

"Thanks again." Phoenix said to Emmanuel as he left. He dialed Grady's number.

He needed a break and this just might be it. "Hey, Grady, Phoenix here. I need a favor. Can you search the computer for any case that I worked on that had some connection with a Casey?"

"You've had nothing but trouble since you moved to that town. Maybe you need to come back here?" Grady's gravelly voice came over the line.

"It's crossed my mind." In truth, Phoenix liked it here. He never wanted to return to the agency.

"Your job is waiting for you."

"I have to clear my name, you know that. I don't care what I've done in the past, this kind of blemish will tarnish my reputation." Phoenix heard Mrs. Jones call from the screen door.

"Hold on a minute, Grady." He covered the mouth-piece. "Come in," he yelled. She was probably here to tell him what a terrible job he'd done and it was about time something was done about him. "I'm back." He resumed his conversation.

"If you need anything more, just let me know. Anything. I really liked working with you," Grady offered.

"Thanks, man." He disconnected and greeted Mrs. Jones.

Gearing up for an unpleasant visit, he was jolted when she said, "Sorry about your troubles." Shock must have shown on his face because she waved her hand. "I know I thought Emmanuel should have had the job, but you're doing okay with it. I like the programs you've started and there is a big difference from the last sheriff. It's just not fair this happening to you."

He went over and hugged her. "Thank you, Mrs. Jones. You don't know how much it means to have you say that."

Warm, soft arms encircled him. She patted his back and said, "Oh, go on with you. Your mamma will be proud of you. Well, I can't stay long. Jonathan will be by soon with the children."

"Thanks for stopping by." He walked her to the door.

And that wasn't the last visit he had that day. Mrs. Bright got her grandson to bring her by saying a phone call wouldn't do. She also left a chocolate cake and cookies with the assurance that chocolate would lift his spirits. Her visit certainly did.

Several people stopped by and called before the trip-lets arrived. Phoenix was touched. He didn't realize he had so much support in the community. But confronting his children was another matter. At ten years of age, they wouldn't be able to discern the fact that he could have been set up for the crime. To children, things are right or wrong. Hardest of all was having them disappointed

in him. He could endure anything but their disen-
chantment.

"Mrs. Jones said you were in trouble. Is that true?" Kara
asked, perky as always.

"Yes, it is." Phoenix geared himself for her grilling.

"What happened?"

Phoenix remembered Karina's lecture on how he never
shared with her. So he explained in detail, at least as much
as they could understand, what had happened.

"That's a lie. We know you couldn't have done that."
Karlton's chest poked out in indignation.

"That's true, I didn't. But I have to prove that I didn't."
At least one of his children believed in him. He was choked
at Karlton's unswerving support.

"So, what are we going to do?" Kara asked.

We? It was a moment before he could answer. He cleared
his throat. "I'm going to search for the evidence to clear
my name. I'm using the computer for that."

"What can we do?" Karl asked.

"Just believe in me," Phoenix said quietly.

"We do." All three of them said in agreement.

A huge weight lifted off Phoenix's shoulders, to have
the unqualified trust of his children.

"We know all about computers. We can help a lot with
this," Kara said.

The wedding had gone well as planned. Though Tina
Landrum worried herself, as usual, she was escorted by the
mayor. Her ex wore a perpetual frown on his face. Karina
noticed that Tina had sipped nothing more than the champagne with the bride and groom's toast. She was slim and
in fighting form. Good for her, Karina thought. She was
certainly happy as she threw rice to send the bride and
groom off.

"It's just too bad about Phoenix," one of Karina's
patrons whispered conspiratorially to her as if she hadn't

been spreading rumors about the incident since it happened.

"Yes, it is. But they'll soon find out that he's innocent." Karina dismissed the woman and turned to help another guest. She couldn't wait to leave to offer him moral support. One thing she knew about Phoenix Dye was that he would not commit to any wrong doing—but she wasn't naive enough to believe that truth always wins out either. Many innocent people went to prison because they couldn't prove their innocence. She prayed Phoenix wouldn't be one of them. She tried several times to reach him by phone, but his line had been busy all afternoon.

"The reception was splendid, Karina." Tina was wearing a tan silk taffeta dress with alençon lace. "And the ribs turned out wonderfully. Not as bad as I thought it would be."

Karina noticed a red speck on the mayor's white shirt when she glanced his way. He was playing politician as usual. "I'm glad you enjoyed it. And I see that Warren has finally made his move."

Tina blushed. "I thought it was about time I got out again. I'm just sorry I waited so long." Her hand smoothed the diamonds at her collar.

"Good for you."

"I'm so glad this is done and over with. The weather held up beautifully and the river scene was just breathtaking. We couldn't have chosen a better spot. It was certainly a novel idea for you to have that area cleaned up."

"I just love that river view." Karina dodged a hanging pot on the back porch as she walked with Tina.

"And now my daughter and her husband can fight over Texas and Virginia cooking to their heart's content in their own home without me." Tina frowned. "Warren told me about Phoenix. I was so sorry to hear that."

"He'll be able to clear his name in no time. He has always been a stickler for what's right." Karina didn't know how much longer she'd be able to stand this constant bombardment.

"That's true enough. I don't care what people say, although he was years younger than me, he was always a nice, decent person. He wasn't as bad as people said."

"No, he wasn't."

"I hear the two of you had a date the other night."

"Yes." News certainly traveled quickly.

"I remember you dated a few years ago. I thought you made such a lovely couple. Perhaps you can work it out this time."

"We'll see. And good luck with the mayor."

It seemed Tina wasn't ready to part. "Warren is awfully worried about what has happened. He didn't want to relieve Phoenix of his duties, but had no choice. His political position and all. And he certainly isn't qualified to handle the investigation." Tina looked around to see if any eager ears were in the vicinity. "I think he's going to call for outside help. Although many people on the force didn't like Phoenix when he was appointed, the really good ones have grown to respect and like him and those left aren't qualified for the investigation. It's in Phoenix's favor to get someone good so that they can be sure to gather the evidence to clear him."

"I tell you, this is such a mess," Karina commiserated.

"It is indeed. And Warren knows that if Phoenix was part of it all, he certainly wouldn't have disclosed the information he'd discovered about the barn. It would have been in his best interest not to mention the sight at all. But some stubborn people can't see that." She shook her head. "Nottoway has certainly been dealt more than it's fair share of problems in the last year. This is a small community. I'd hoped we were immune to such. But as with everything else, crime is everywhere. I know divorce certainly is."

"Harland couldn't keep his eyes off you during the reception."

"I didn't look his way once. Did he really?" she asked, excitement ringing in her voice.

"Yes, he did."

With an air of nonchalance, she said, "Well, you know I've heard trouble is brewing between him and his young sweetheart."

"No, I hadn't heard."

"Well, it is. He pulled me aside and said he wanted to talk to me about something before he left. I certainly hope he doesn't think I want any part of him. I've begun to turn my life around and Warren is such a gentlemanly man. I really like him. And he treats me with kindness and respect. By the way, I need to come by and schedule a small dinner meeting with you for Warren. He asked me if I would plan it for him. I think I've found my calling."

"You'll make a lovely mayor's wife."

"Well, things haven't gone quite *that* far yet. But there's always hope." Tina smiled and left. Soon after, Robert arrived to relieve Karina.

"I'm glad you're here." She rushed around completing last-minute chores. "I need to leave. They're cleaning up after the reception now. I may not be in early on Monday, so don't forget to order the extras for the prom breakfast," she called out on her way out the door.

"I won't."

Karina hurried for Phoenix's place.

She was surprised to see the triplets were there with him.

"We're doing detective work helping the sheriff clear his name," Karlton said.

"Well . . . good." Karina sent a questioning look toward Phoenix.

"We're linked into the FBI database," Kara said. "We're seeing all kinds of neat stuff."

"Why are you in the FBI computer? And a better question is . . . isn't this illegal?"

"Extra money showed up in my bank account that I didn't put there. I talked to Towanna a few weeks ago, but she couldn't trace it. I'm trying to find its source before anyone else does."

"Phoenix, what is going on? How will you ever clear yourself?" She gave him a worried frown.

"Don't worry, Mom. We're going to help him," Karlton said. "You'll see."

"I'm sure you will, sweetheart." Karina only wished it could be so easy. But she knew that life wasn't so simple. At least the children weren't too distressed as they eagerly worked to clear their father's name. She knew Phoenix needed their support.

This pleased her. She'd expected to find him distraught over his dilemma, but instead he was upbeat and steadily working at a solution.

"Can I get you something?" he asked.

"Yes, I'd love some . . . whatever you have. I'll help you fix it."

"Can't you fix it yourself, Mom?" Karl asked. "We're busy."

"No, I can't." She patted his head at his impatience.

Phoenix punched some keys. "We haven't found anything significant lately. Play a game or something until I get back."

"Oh, Mom. You're slowing our progress."

"I'm sure you can use a break," was Karina's response.

As she went to the kitchen, Karina looked back to make sure the children stayed in the den. "I talked to Tina Landrum today. You know she's dating the mayor now." She plunked her purse on the counter top. "Anyway, he's talking about bringing someone else in to investigate."

"I expected that."

"Oh, Phoenix." She walked over to him and caressed his arms, distressed. "What if they can't find the evidence?"

"I've got to believe they will." He gathered her in his arms and pressed a kiss to her brow. "I certainly don't plan to wait for them. I'm doing my own investigating."

"This isn't television. You know lots of innocent people go to jail because they can't exonerate themselves."

"You're supposed to be my support. I'll turn over everything until I do clear my name. I've got friends back at the agency helping me, unofficially, of course."

"What can they do from Washington about a crime that takes place here?"

"It's not just a local crime. Names are cropping up from my past. They're trying to track it down for me. And that extra money in my account didn't come from Nottoway. So far it's been traced to several major cities in the States and a bank in Switzerland. Whoever set it up made it virtually impossible to track. But I have contacts who work in computer security." Phoenix pinched the bridge of his nose. "God, it could take just about forever to find it." He sighed. "I'll tell you what really bothers me is that Luke and Miss Drucilla have put their wedding plans on hold until this mess is over. I asked them not to because this could take months to uncover."

"I completely forgot about them."

"I haven't told my mom yet. I hope she doesn't find out. It would just about kill her."

"What a mess." Karina gathered him in her arms and caressed his tense back and shoulders.

"Mom," Kara said from the doorway.

Guiltily, Karina stepped back and turned toward Kara's voice. "Yes?"

"Are . . . are you going to marry the sheriff?"

"She was just giving me a supportive hug. You know, like when you scrape your knee or something. Doesn't it feel good to get a hug?"

"Oh, yeah. Sure." She walked uncertainly toward him. "Well, I can give you a supportive hug, too."

"It'll sure be nice about now." Kara closed the distance between them and hugged him. It felt better than gold, since she was the most reluctant to accept him.

"I've got to go to Ms. Chance's," she said. "The baby

usually kicks this time of day and I get to feel her big stomach. I'm never having babies. I don't want my stomach getting that big."

"You're never going to get a husband if you aren't going to have any babies," Karl said from the doorway.

"I can always be an aunt. Like Uncle Jonathan is an uncle. He gets to be with us and he doesn't have children."

"He's single because his fiancée died."

"Single's not so bad." Kara retorted. "I don't want a man telling me what to do anyway."

"A marriage is sharing. Not one telling the other what to do," Karina added. "Your dad didn't tell me what to do. We shared."

"Another reason not to get married. Dad's not around any more, is he?"

"Honey, you don't have to take on the weight of the world at ten."

"I've got to go before the baby stops kicking."

"We're going, too." Karlton and Karl followed her.

"Oh, Phoenix. I hope I haven't turned her against marriage. It can be a wonderful thing with the right person. My parents' marriage was wonderful. I'd hoped to have one like theirs."

"We will. Kara is coming around. She didn't accept me at all in the beginning. Now she is. I think we're making progress."

Karina wouldn't comment on his taking marrying her for granted. It wasn't the time.

After Karina and the children left, Phoenix reveled in the pleasure of his family—he considered them his family—however, his total enjoyment was marred by his recent problems.

He sat down to review his notes again and studied all of the unusual crimes that had occurred in Nottoway recently. It started with the safe robbery, which had been solved, but also involved the car thefts, since Casey had a hand in both, to the country club robbery where he hadn't been able to find any clues yet.

It puzzled him that he hadn't come up with anything on that. Where were they dumping the parts, he wondered. There was only one salvage yard in Nottoway. He picked up the phone. "Emmanuel, we need to check out the salvage yard again. I know you checked it once. But the heavy trucks have to come from someplace. Let's see if anything was missed."

When they arrived at the yard, the owner was there, and from the looks and smell of him, he'd spent most of the day making inroads into a liquor bottle. He didn't request a warrant, which probably meant he had nothing to hide.

"Whatever you want, go find it yourself. I got a headache to nurse." He staggered back into the shack that served as his office and left Phoenix and Emmanuel on their own.

Cars and parts in various degrees of disrepair were littered throughout the twenty-acre area.

"We're going to have to split up if we're going to make it through this today," Phoenix said to Emmanuel.

"Sure, see you . . . whenever."

Even though it seemed the whole process was helter-skelter, there was a system to the madness. Cars were grouped according to make. Thinking of Luke's Lincoln, Phoenix headed to the Ford section. He walked foot by tortuous foot through the huge area with no success.

Crushed cars were lined up ready to be carted off to the scrap metal plant. Phoenix passed busses and trucks. He inspected those areas to assure himself nothing was hidden behind the huge parts. At one juncture, he passed the forklift that was lifting a car onto the crusher.

After two hours of no success, Phoenix met up with Emmanuel.

"I didn't find anything, how about you?" Emmanuel

asked, dust covering his shoes. He took out a handkerchief and wiped the sweat off his brow.

"Same here." Looking equally bedraggled, Phoenix looked toward the woods. He could see a few odd pieces sticking up. "Let's check that area. It seems to be the only place we didn't cover. Did you check it before?"

"No, it's probably some old car parts, long forgotten about. I've seen more rusted frames and junk here than I've seen in a lifetime."

Phoenix aimed for the debris in the forest and Emmanuel trailed with him. They passed an old electric stove. Other odds and ends filled up the space, patches of grass reaching up around them. Walking farther, he saw a washer and an old cement mixer. Though a road large enough for a truck cut through, the spaces to the right and left were so thick with trees, that cars and large equipment couldn't be stored there. As Phoenix walked along, he turned a corner and came upon a wide area and stopped. "We've hit pay dirt."

"What?" Emmanuel asked from several feet back.

"Look ahead." He heard Emmanuel jog toward him.

"Jeeze! Will you look at that?"

"And what do you see?"

"Compressor, generator, aluminum siding, . . . all going to waste. Why didn't they sell the stuff?"

"Probably waiting for the heat to let up," Phoenix said. "It wouldn't be easy to sell this stuff in this area without suspicion."

"Right under our noses all this time. I can't see old Brimley having anything to do with this."

"He's always too drunk to know what's going on. His nephew runs the place, doesn't he?" Phoenix asked. "You're going to have to charge both of them. But get the construction foreman down here to identify the equipment first."

"I really messed up on this one by not checking everything. The space looked too congested with trees to hide all this stuff.''

"Happens to the best of us," Phoenix said, a smile of triumph splitting his lips.

Chapter 16

"Kara, you can't punch out everybody who says something bad about Phoenix. He wouldn't want that." Karina was proud of her daughter's protective nature toward her father yet appalled at her assertive behavior.

"At least Bobby will keep his mouth shut now. He's not going to call Phoenix a criminal and get away with it." Kara's chin jutted out at that statement, fire blazing in her eyes.

"Honey, we know he's innocent, but everyone doesn't know him like we do. You have to make allowances for their ignorance." There were a few people Karina had also wanted to punch in the mouth, but she didn't have the excuse of being a child. It wouldn't do to let Kara think it was acceptable behavior.

"No, I don't." She crossed her arms.

"Yes, you do." Karina responded. "But to hit somebody in the nose! I had better not get any more calls from school that you've punched anybody else."

"I'll hit him in the stomach next time then."

"You won't hit him anywhere, understood?" She gave

her daughter a stern gaze before clipping her earrings to her lobes.

"Well, what are we supposed to do, let him get away with telling lies?" she countered indignantly.

"Explain to him that, in this country, a person is innocent until proven guilty." She leaned toward the mirror, slid on mauve lipstick.

"Yeah, right, Mom. That'll mean a lot. They'll really shut up and quiver when I say that."

Behind schedule to leave for the restaurant and out of patience, Karina pointed the tube at her belligerent daughter. "I don't care what they say, you keep your hands to yourself, young lady."

A knock sounded at the door, interrupting their debate. Karina looked up to see Jonathan leaning casually against the jam.

"You be good for Uncle Jonathan, you hear? And remember our talk," she called back as she unlocked the screen door.

"We're always good for Uncle Jonathan." Kara hefted her bag and pushed past her mom.

"Try to get a nap before your prom breakfast," Jonathan called back. "I'll pick the boys up after their baseball game."

"Thanks." Karina locked the door after them and rushed to get dressed.

Jonathan started the motor and drove down the drive, sending a questioning glance toward a sulking Kara.

"Uncle Jonathan, who's our real dad?"

Jonathan swerved and almost ran into the ditch. "What makes you think Victor's not your dad?"

"Because when we visited Aunt Flo two weeks ago, she was fussing at Dad about not spending enough time with us. He told her to stop nagging him. He said we weren't his children. Mom was pregnant before he married her. I guess that means she's not our aunt either." Kara took a breath. "She was so mad Dad hadn't told her about that."

Jonathan let out a deep breath. Flo Wallace was Victor's sister and she was very disappointed when Karina married her brother, which was probably why Victor didn't confide in her. She never softened toward Karina. "You have to ask your mom."

"But she's so worried about business and Phoenix. And I got in a little trouble at school. There's never a good time to ask her."

"What kind of trouble?"

"I punched Bobby Joe in the nose when he talked about Phoenix."

Jonathan almost said "good for you," but knew his sister would give his ears a good blistering for his efforts. "Did it work?" he asked instead.

"It sure did. And he didn't say another word, especially when everyone knew a girl bested him."

"Maybe for your mom's sake, you'll try to find another way to settle your disputes." That was diplomatic enough, Jonathan thought. The differences among the triplets were amazing. Karlton would have tried reason. Karl was a charmer, but Kara, the little spitfire, would punch first and ask questions later.

"I'm supposed to tell him how a person is innocent until proven guilty." She mimicked Karina.

She said it so comically, Jonathan burst out laughing and Kara joined him, after casting her eyes heavenly as if wishing for divine intervention.

"Your mom means well," he said.

Dressed in a yellow polo shirt and brown slacks, Warren stood at Phoenix's door. "Well, are you going to make me stay outside all evening?"

Bleary eyed, Phoenix pushed open the screen door and stepped back. "So, what brings you to this neck of the woods?" Phoenix asked as he motioned Warren to a seat. It couldn't be good news.

"I just finished talking to the FBI. It seems they had agents in Petersburg monitoring the car theft ring. They cleared your name." He cleared his throat and reached into his pocket to pull out a sheriff's badge. "We want to reinstate you in your position."

Dressed in everything from subdued pastels to a lavish array of bright and dark colors, the junior and senior ladies arrived in droves, escorted by their handsomely tuxedo-bedecked dates. Some of the males wore shirts that matched their partner's gowns. Beautifully arranged corsages graced gowns and wrists, the males were resplendent in their boutonnieres and subdued hair cuts. Hairstylists must have made a mint if one could determine that by the ladies' stylish coiffures. In her plain black gown, bereft of any adornment, Karina felt dowdy by comparison.

Many conversed in hushed tones in deference to the formal occasion, and adult respect, while others were a bit more free-spirited. But all in all, Karina acknowledged that they were a well-behaved group. At least as well behaved as any teenagers were. A rural area advantage was that all children were taught proper social and moral behavior because everyone mixed in churches as well as regular social activities.

The after-prom breakfast was well chaperoned by parents and adult volunteers, especially on the grounds, which afforded plenty of hidden places for indiscretions. Even Mrs. Jones had volunteered to help out.

The woman in question hustled in an embarrassed couple who immediately went to the breakfast buffet.

"Caught them necking on the bridge, I did. Told them to come in and nibble on that buffet instead of each other." Winded, she hastily sat down in the nearest chair. Mrs. Jones took her post seriously.

The teenagers were pouring in in droves by three-thirty and scattered over the grounds and the restaurant. Many of the girls donning their date's jackets to ward off the early morning chill.

Karina was grateful she didn't have to worry about the whereabouts of the energetic teenagers. Mrs. Jones only sat for five minutes before she was up and at it again.

As a surprise to the prom participants, the parents had arrived to decorate the restaurant around eleven-thirty that evening. A huge banner outside the door welcomed them. Streamers and festive balloons hung inside. The group was pleased with the effort.

Karina went to the speaker's stand to announce the drawing. Several of the local business owners had donated gifts as an incentive for the teens to attend the breakfast instead of other less admirable forms of entertainment. Karina had donated two dinners for two. Representing the bank, Thornton had donated two fifty dollar savings bonds, and Tylan, a free tune-up. The local grocer added a fifty dollar shopping spree. There were tennis balls and rackets, free visits to hair salons, and gallons of ice cream from the Higabothums. The police department had taken up a collection for a savings bond. Luke gave three one-month passes to the country club, which was almost finished. The teenagers had to stay the night to receive the grand prize donated by Jonathan. A pentium computer.

There were games aplenty to keep their interest. Tylan had moved in two of his video game machines for the occasion. There was bingo for prizes, card games, scrabble. And others just enjoyed walking around the flower gardens enjoying their first night out past 12 A.M.

Karina had just finished the 7 A.M. grand prize drawing when Phoenix walked in. Amid the hoops and screams from the winner, Karina had the presence of mind to recognize his easy smile, which indicated something positive had happened about his case.

"Meet me in your office," he whispered and kept walking.

It was five minutes before Karina could get away. Storming through the kitchen, Karina barely noticed the hissing of bacon and sausage sizzling on the industrial stove, the clatter of pots, the whirl of the blender, the hum of conversations, so intent was she to get to Phoenix. She closed the office door behind her. "Well, what happened?"

He observed her from head to toe. "First, let me tell you how beautiful you look tonight."

Unprepared for the compliment, Karina blinked. "Oh, thank you."

He perused the length of her again. The gown's lines were simple, but on her, it was anything but as it caressed her rounded curves. She was stunning. A pearl clip in her hair and tasteful pearl earrings dangling from her ears completed the outfit.

"Well," she squeezed his hands. "What's the hot news?"

It took seconds for him to redirect his thoughts. "You mean besides my wanting to take you home to bed immediately."

"Phoenix!" she laughed.

He relented. "I've been cleared of all charges." He picked her up and swung her around. Darn it felt marvelous holding her. After their first date, they had started to see each other, unofficially.

"That's wonderful." An enormous weight lifted from Karina's chest. As he embraced her, she closed her eyes and said a silent prayer of thanks. As if coming from a tunnel, she heard clapping, wolf whistles, and hails from the kitchen. She faced the glass window. Work had stopped and all the employees stood at the window cheering. They could see everything going on. Phoenix put her on her feet and, cheerfully, everyone went back to work. "Tell me everything?"

Phoenix leaned on her desk while she sat on the edge of her chair.

"Warren called the local FBI in to help him on the case. The agency had a plant in the car theft ring who knew everyone working on the case. He was holding out to find the contact in South Carolina."

"South Carolina? What does that have to do with anything."

"They seem to be transporting cars there. Where, they don't know yet." He told her about the salvage yard. "I've been reinstated."

"Oh, Phoenix. I'm ecstatic."

"Tell me about it." He wiped imaginary sweat from his brow and sat on her desk facing her.

"I was so worried." She squeezed his hand.

"Well, all isn't over yet. We still don't know how Casey ties in to all of this. Earlier this evening, Grady told me Casey was once a cellmate to a man I killed on an assignment two years ago. But Casey always dealt in petty crime. He was never smart enough to execute something this complex. Somebody's behind him. We knew that Jimmy, the guy I killed, had a brother we haven't been able to locate. He's college educated. They had different fathers and he's never been in trouble. Only a matter of time before we find him unless he's under an assumed name." Suddenly he noticed Karina wasn't really listening.

"What's wrong? I've lost you." He tilted her chin. "Am I confusing you by going on and on about this case?"

"I'm not sure. I think Victor mentioned some guy named Casey. Something about him going into a shopping center deal with a Casey. The man was pressuring Victor for the ten thousand dollars. His share of the investment money." At Phoenix's expression, she said, "But it couldn't possibly be the same Casey."

"Do you know Victor's phone number?" He flipped open the pad that Karina had already recognized as his lifeline.

"I'll dial him. Victor wouldn't get into anything illegal.

He may have his faults but he'd never do that . . ." Karina quieted when a recording came on.

"His phone's been turned off."

"Give me his address, I'll pay him a visit."

"I'm going with you." She grasped his arm to detain him.

"No, you aren't. I don't want you involved with this."

"I'm already involved. Besides, Robert came in an hour ago. He can take over now that the last drawing's done. I just want to say a few words to the organizers before I leave."

"Absolutely not," Phoenix snapped. "This is police business. You're not part of it."

"Then I'll go alone." Karina was adamant.

Phoenix raised an eyebrow in preparation for saying something else. Instead he said, "All right. But do exactly what I tell you. Do you understand?"

"I know exactly what Kara meant by not wanting any man telling her what to do."

"This is different. Your life could be at stake. And when you're in danger, I will damn well tell you what to do."

"Save me from dictatorial men." Karina sauntered off to say her goodbyes to the chaperones. That part was well in hand. They thanked her for the spectacular success of the event.

Stopping long enough to grab a light jacket and warn Robert he was on his own, they exited through the kitchen door. Only the muted sounds carried from the restaurant. The clanging of the game machines rang out. Tired laughter from a long night.

The sun had barely made its entrance by the time they reached ninety-five.

They arrived at Victor's apartment twenty minutes later. He rented a duplex in one of the poorer areas in Petersburg but a neighborhood with many senior citizens who kept what they had in good condition. But, Victor wasn't home.

"Darn it." Phoenix looked both ways to make sure no one was about. He pulled out a slim instrument he used in his agency days.

"What are you doing?"

"Picking his lock." He inserted the pick into the key-hole.

"I have a key." She searched through her huge purse.

"What are you doing with his key?" A jogger neared. Phoenix faced the door and pretended he was pressing on the doorbell. As soon as the man passed he held out his hand for the key.

"He gave it to the triplets when he first got the place." She finally located it.

"Give it to me."

"No." Karina pulled the purse strap to her shoulder. "You can't go in his home uninvited."

Phoenix resumed his efforts with the lock.

"You can't do that," she hissed.

"Be quiet before you draw attention. I know I can't use the information for evidence."

"It's not fair to go through his things when he's not around. He's not a criminal."

Phoenix continued with his probing. A blast of music hit them as a car passed. Probably a teenager, Phoenix thought.

"Here." She shoved the key in his hand. "You can't use anything you find against him."

"I know that. I need information. I'm afraid for you and the children. I didn't work with law abiding citizens in the agency." Phoenix shoved the key in the lock. "I don't see why you're so protective of the man. This is the same man who blackmailed you, remember?" Phoenix was unaccountably stung by her protectiveness. No matter what that man did, she still stuck up for him.

"He was there when I needed him."

"Don't make me angry by starting that again." Phoenix unlocked the door, opened it, and went in. Close on his heels, Karina followed him. He closed the door behind her on the dew-drenched morning.

The room was semi-tidy, but didn't look as though Victor planned to stay very long. He had only the bare essentials. A lone sofa graced the living room and a rickety table and two chairs stood in the kitchen. Not one picture hung on the wall.

Phoenix pulled out several drawers in search of papers or anything else useful.

"It's intrusive to go through his things. Why can't you just wait until he gets home to talk to him?"

"If it bothers you, go back to the car and wait for me."

"I will not."

"Then be quiet so I can do what I need to do." He started opening cabinet doors. Only a box of cereal and a handful of cans topped the shelves.

"I am not a child to be spoken to in that manner. What are you looking for anyway?" Karina opened the refrigerator to stale milk which she promptly plucked off the shelf.

"Don't throw that out. Leave everything as it was."

"This is ridiculous. We can't leave stale milk in the fridge. He won't mind."

"He won't know, if you follow instructions." Phoenix sighed and returned to his search. "I won't know what I'm looking for until I find it." The foray downstairs proved fruitless. Phoenix started up the carpeted stairs. The bare, lonely walls seemed more a motel room than a home.

Karina scurried behind.

Doors led to three rooms. One was the bath. A razor and shaving cream were left on the sink. The wash cloth and towel were dry. He hadn't spend the night here.

The next room they reached was empty except for a few cobwebs in the corners and dust on the wooden floor.

The last room was sparsely decorated. Burgundy sheets lay tangled on the unmade bed. A picture of Karina with the triplets adorned the bedside table.

"I feel so sorry for him. This isn't like a home at all. It's so . . . lonely."

Phoenix felt the man was intruding on his family. Victor had no right to a picture of his own family, and Karina shouldn't be feeling remorse for him. Then he thought Victor must still love them to keep a memento for all to see. Especially if he entertained a special woman. Some of his antipathy left at the realization of what Victor was losing and what he, Phoenix, was gaining. After all, the man had taken care of his family for ten years.

Papers scattered on the table near the picture caught his eye. Phoenix walked over and leafed through them.

"What do you have?" Karina asked.

"Some stuff about a shopping center." He flipped a page, scanning easily with the help of the bright light floating through the off-white blinds. "I've got a feeling Victor is either a part of this or he's being used."

"Being used more likely. Despite what you think, Victor wouldn't do anything illegal."

"Then he's been conned out of a lot of money."

"Poor Victor. He thought he'd fallen into the perfect business. And now he's lost everything. This is going to be devastating to him." She went over to the bed.

"I'm more worried about you and the triplets. I'm betting Casey has tied you all to me. Otherwise, why get Victor involved, except to pump him for information. First they got him to trust them. I've got to find him and talk to him." He put the papers back in the space outlined by the dust. "Karina leave the bed alone."

"You don't think Victor knows about all this, do you?" She clutched the sheet. "Oh, Lord, Phoenix, where can he be this time of the morning? He hasn't slept here."

"Probably spending the night with a girlfriend or something. Don't go borrowing trouble." Phoenix took one last, fruitless look around. "We've got to get out of here before we're discovered."

"I think I'll leave a note for him."

"No, you won't. We don't want him to know we've been here. We didn't have a search warrant, after all."

"Oh, all right. I'll talk to him later."

Thoroughly exasperated, Phoenix said, "You'll do no such thing. It could put his life in danger if he knows too much. Let me handle the investigation, will you?"

"We can't just leave him ignorant. He's got to know he's involved with criminals," she argued as they descended the stairs.

"The less he knows, the safer he'll be. Let me and the department do our jobs. That's why you should have stayed at the restaurant."

Phoenix looked cautiously out the front door to make sure he didn't open the door to Victor or a curious neighbor as they left.

Once in the car and driving down ninety-five back to Nottoway, Phoenix thought more about the case. "Karina, I'm going to assign protection to you and the triplets."

"You're going overboard. Nothing's happened to us."

"The very fact that Victor is involved with my old case indicates you're involved. I want you and the triplets protected. I'm putting twenty-four hour protection on the four of you."

"That's ridiculous."

"Humor me. At least they should be okay for now."

"Why is that?"

"They're with Jonathan."

"Meaning it's different when they're with a mere woman."

"Don't pull that women's lib on me. It has no place when you and the kids are in danger."

"They're in just as much danger with Jonathan as they would be with me."

"To show you I'm not a chauvinist, I wouldn't be afraid if they were with Miss Drucilla. I know that if anyone came snooping around her place they'd be greeted with a buckshot up their backsides. The triplets would be perfectly safe there.''

"Touché.''

Phoenix drove on a few miles in silence.

"You need to keep a lower profile at work.''

"I can't do that. I've got too many things going on. Miss Drucilla's engagement party for one. Now that you've been cleared, there's no reason to delay it any longer.''

"I'll put someone on the restaurant too.''

"You don't have enough people working with you for that.''

"I'll do whatever is necessary to protect you.''

"I think you're getting carried away with this cloak and dagger bit, but I won't argue about you having someone watch the children. I won't need anyone because people will always be around me at the restaurant. I'm seldom there alone.''

"Make that not at all.''

"All right.''

Chapter 17

"Your name's being bandied about. It's time for you to skip town." Einstein said. He preferred not to have any surprises occur at inopportune times. It was bad enough that the sheriff got off so easily.

"Not before I get my money," Casey responded. "I can lay low for a few days until I get my payoff. Then I'll leave."

Einstein shook his head. "Can't take the chance. They're looking for you. And I don't want you connected to me."

"Who's going to take care of the sheriff for you? You sure aren't going to do it," he smirked. "Might mess up that Italian suit."

"You'd be surprised at what I have the stomach for," Einstein said sharply. He considered. "Maybe you shouldn't come by here anymore. I know this place is isolated, but you can never tell when bicycle riders may come by and recognize you."

"You know how to reach me."

As Casey left, Einstein felt no pleasure at the latest development. Instead of having Phoenix on the run, Casey's people were scattered, half of them in jail. Matters were working out much too favorably for Phoenix.

Einstein paced the carpet in front of his desk. Nothing brought him solace now. Not his opulent surroundings, his Dominican cigars, his Napoleon brandy. Everything hinged on Dye.

Einstein's fist hit the desk. "If I have to kill the bastard myself, so be it! *I must have satisfaction.*"

Forebodings of danger stirred Phoenix to settle the case quickly. Frustrated with the meager results he'd attained so far, he pulled into his driveway before he recognized a strange car. Three men were on the front porch with duffel bags beside them. It took a moment before he recognized his buddies from the agency. "What are you guys doing here?" he asked as he approached the porch.

"Heard you couldn't make it without us. You leave us and the next thing we know you're running into all kinds of trouble," the one called Grady Taylor said. "We were due some vacation time." Based on their grungy outfits, an ordinary person would never be able to tell that the three men facing him were some of the best agents in the field. They gave the appearance of campers out for a male bonding experience.

"You guys are too much."

"We had a talk with the office in Petersburg. There's quite a racket going on down here." Steve Gross kicked back and rocked in the swing. One could never tell he was one of the best electronic experts in the country.

Phoenix sat on one of the fancy chairs Clarice had left on the porch. It was the first opportunity he'd had to relax all day.

While they updated each other on the case, Phoenix looked at them one by one. Steve, with his baby face resembled a college student more than an agent.

"Have you been able to track down Jimmy's brother?" Phoenix asked.

"He took a six-month sabbatical to Europe."

"That counts him out," Grady declared.

Steve stroked his smooth chin. "Maybe not. There are ways of returning to the country undetected."

"What part of Europe?" Phoenix still tried to digest the fact that these people really cared enough to use their vacation time to help him. He'd been a loner most of his life. It was so good having friends.

"Germany, they say. Why?" Grady asked.

"The excess money in my bank account has been traced to several places in the States and Europe. So far."

"Casey doesn't have the knowledge or the connections," Grady said.

"No way. Hasn't got the brains," Steve agreed.

Tommy Lark spoke for the first time. "The brother is probably behind it."

"I'm setting up surveillance on Karina and the triplets," Phoenix said, more determined than ever. The queasiness was back in his stomach.

"What do they have to do with this?" Grady asked.

"The triplets are mine." He couldn't stop the crooked grin from appearing on his face.

There was silence and then someone whistled.

"You ever hear of starting out small? You've been keeping secrets or what?" Steve said.

"I just found out about them. They're ten. It's a long story." Shivers coursed through him at the possibility of a threat. Thank God these seasoned warriors came.

"Three little Phoenix's running around. Hard to fathom. You never did things the normal way. Girls? Boys?"

"Two boys and one girl. They don't know I'm their father, but I spend a lot of time with them." A smile flirted across his face. "Karlton wants to be a sheriff like his old man and Karl doesn't know what he wants to do yet. Kara was the hardest to win over."

"Man, you've got it bad." Grady slapped his hat on his leg. "We'll never get you back now."

"Tell us about this Karina." Tommy was all business.

"She's their mom."

"This country town has warped your brains. We gathered that much," Grady smirked.

"We'll probably be getting married before too long. She doesn't know that yet."

The men chuckled.

"Anyway, she was exhausted so I left her home. It's the house across from here. I'll go over in a couple of hours. I'll spend the night over there and maybe you guys can watch them tomorrow. Take the kids to school, pick them up."

"Sure."

"Karina owns a restaurant. Darn good food. Someone needs to be there with her all day. May end up with dishwater hands, knowing her."

"For some good southern cooking, I can live with a few dishes. I've done worse." Grady rubbed his muscled stomach.

"Miss Drucilla lives alone in back of me. She pops in and out at her leisure. Don't be surprised if you see her carrying a shotgun now and then, especially if she feels Karina's in danger," Phoenix continued with his drill.

"How old is this Miss Drucilla? She sounds interesting. I just might check her out myself," Steve said.

Phoenix's lips twitched. "You're too late. She's already spoken for. Her fiancé may not take kindly to your trying to snatch his woman out from under him.

"Luke Jordan is Miss Drucilla's fiancée. You'll see him a lot." Phoenix continued to familiarize them with the area. "Mrs. Jones baby-sits the triplets. Anyone other than them will be considered suspicious. Some friends may visit, but we won't take any chances."

"Let's get back to Miss Drucilla. I like a woman who can take care of herself. Did you say she was single?" Steve pushed his glasses up on his nose and leaned forward with interest.

"She is. Her husband's dead. But she's very self-sufficient."

"You can introduce us while we're here. When she meets me, she won't give those country boys the time of day." The glasses gave that pretty twenty-eight-year-old face of his an extra measure of maturity.

"If you insist." Phoenix shrugged.

The woman in question rounded the corner, wearing her blue polka-dot dress, her shotgun at the ready. When she saw Phoenix, she lowered it. "Oh, Phoenix, I didn't know you were home. When I started my walk, I saw these folks and wondered if they were up to no good."

Phoenix got up to help her to a seat. Her sneakered feet barely made a sound on the wooden steps. She put the gun on the floor in back of her chair.

"Miss Drucilla, if something seems out of line, call the police. Don't you try to handle it. You could get hurt."

"Oh, posh. I've been handling trouble all my life."

"Not any longer. Promise me you'll go home next time and call." He gave her a serious look.

She stared right back, but after a while she relented. "Oh, all right. Since you're handling things now."

"Good. These are some of my coworkers from D.C. They came down to vacation for a few days. Guys let me introduce you to Miss Drucilla Chance."

They got up to shake her hand.

"How do you do, Mrs. Chance."

"Everybody calls me Miss Drucilla."

"Steve here's taken a liking to you." Phoenix grinned.

"Well, you wouldn't have a no-account friend, so I'll take a liking to him, too. You going to be here the weekend?"

"Yes . . ." Steve said cautiously. With a sign of nervousness, he touched the bridge of his glasses again.

"Then come on by to my wedding reception. Love to have you. All of you are welcome. And I'll bring some of my barbecue by here for supper."

"Well, thank you," the men said.

She conversed with them a few minutes before Steve took her home and bought back the barbecue.

The phone woke Karina out of a sound sleep. "Karina," Robert asked, "are you going to make it in?"

"Oh, God. I overslept. I'll come right in. Give me forty-five minutes." Karina looked at the clock. Three-thirty. Almost time for Jonathan to bring the kids home. She'd make it in just before the evening rush.

Karina rushed through her shower and preparations. She debated about calling Victor's sister to ask him to contact her. Phoenix wouldn't like it if she talked to Victor, but she felt she needed to. Living with a man for nine years gave her some insight into his character, didn't it? She dialed his sister's number but didn't get an answer. Just as she hung up, she heard a knock at her door. She answered it to Phoenix and a stranger. Since she, at least, had a passing knowledge of everyone in Nottoway, she knew he wasn't a local.

Phoenix gave her a familiar peck on the lips. "Karina, this is Grady Taylor from Washington. He works at the agency."

"Hi, Grady." Karina extended her hand for a shake.

A wide grin split his lips. "Well, I've waited a long time for the woman who bested this old guy." Instead of the proffered shake, unexpectedly he pulled her into his arms for a quick squeeze and a kiss on the cheek. "Welcome to the family."

"Well, thank you . . . I think." She looked questioningly at Phoenix.

"You sure do know how to pick'em, bro." He never took his eyes off her.

"It's nice to meet you, too. I wish I had time for a visit, but I'm on my way to the restaurant. How long will you be visiting, Grady?"

"Grady'll go with you." Phoenix turned to Grady. "I'll relieve you later on. And watch those eyes of yours."

"Phoenix, really." Karina frowned in exasperation before she grasped her purse and keys from the counter top.

He pressed a kiss to her lips. "Humor me, baby."

Phoenix volunteered to talk to Jonathan about keeping the kids for her.

"Chief's pretty taken with you." Grady grasped the dashboard as they rounded a curve.

"How is life in the agency?" she asked instead of commenting on his statement.

"Meaning for him?" He cautiously released the board.

"Yes." Grateful for the opportunity to grill someone about Phoenix's life the last few years.

"He was hard to get to know. A damn good agent. But pretty much kept to himself. Two years ago, we worked on a case together. Let down his hair a little, not much, but when your life's on the line, well ... I can tell you this, I've never seen him happier than he is right now. I hope you make an honest man out of him."

Karina smiled. "I don't know if we could live with each other. He knows what he wants at this moment. But what happens after he gets it? He's got the wanderlust in him."

"He'll take care of the situation." He said it with such certainty, Karina wondered if he thought agents were omnipotent.

"Just maybe he needs taking care of, too," Karina said as she parked the car.

"Maybe he does at that." A strange look flighted across his face.

Casey walked into the restaurant at the busiest time of the evening. Karina Wallace, in her usual friendly manner, darted from place to place greeting guests and making them feel welcome. Casey was dressed in a suit and tie. Although he hated the stuffy attire, Einstein made sure he could wear the uncomfortable clothing as if he were born to it. So when Mrs. Wallace greeted him in the spacious foyer wearing a lovely lavender suit as colorful as springtime flowers, he used the charm that had been pounded into him for months. Einstein would be proud of him.

"Good evening. Welcome." Immediately she had him conquered like a charmed guest.

"And a good evening to you. Your brother, Jonathan, told me what a wonderful restaurant you had and said to be sure to stop by. I must say, I am impressed." He held out his hand as if he wished to shake it, but once she placed her delicate fingers in his, he bought them to his lips and kissed the back of her hand for a European flavor.

"Why, thank you." Karina said. She was sure to seat him at a prime table. Anything to help business for her brother. She escorted him to a window seat overlooking the river. The flowers were in full bloom.

"Tell me," Casey inquired, "what would you recommend?" The hum of dinnertime conversations surrounded them.

"They are all wonderful dinners, but the salmon is our special tonight. It was flown in this morning. It is especially succulent."

"Then I shall try it."

"Your waitress will be right with you. Enjoy your dinner." She swiveled and returned to the foyer chatting to guests along the way.

"I'm sure I shall." Lord, he'd never used such words before.

Before the words were out of Karina's mouth a full minute, a dutiful waitress appeared. After his latest payoff, he could easily become used to such treatment. Unfortunately, he was going to have to involve such a beautiful woman in Phoenix's demise. He hoped he'd find a way to take care of business without hurting her. But, if it became necessary . . . well, business was business. For a moment, Casey entertained the thought of maybe dating Karina himself, consoling her once Phoenix was gone. Now, wouldn't that be justice for you?

Karina passed his table, leading an elderly couple to a seat. Casey scanned her, imagining what she looked like without the fashionable clothes. She was a few inches shorter than the women he usually dated, but he was adaptable.

Karina's opinion wasn't quite as favorable as she pretended. She felt the man's eyes undressing her whenever she passed him. For Jonathan's and her business's sake, she'd tolerate the obnoxious behavior, but the sooner this man left her restaurant the better she'd feel. His polished veneer failed to cover the rough substance beneath. She hated for men to look at her like she was a piece of meat ready to be gobbled up. How would he feel if she returned the look? On second thought she didn't want to know. She was glad Phoenix had insisted that Grady stay at the restaurant. Even now, he was tucked away in the kitchen filling desert cups, secure in the supposition that if anyone attacked, it would be after the rush of guests, when she was about to close for the night.

One of the prep people failed to show up. Grady graciously volunteered to help out. An offer she wasn't about to refuse. As soon as she could spare a moment, she dashed into the kitchen to see if everything was on schedule.

"Everything's just fine. I've got a real knack to this now." Grady wielded the spoon like a pro.

"I wish I could stay back here. I've got a real sleazeball out there." She took a napkin and wiped a smudge off one of the desert cups. The cook took the aromatic potatoes augratin out the oven.

Grady wiped his hand on the apron and started for the door.

"Where are you going?" Karina called out.

"To take care of Mr. Sleaze."

"He hasn't done anything." Karina was almost embarrassed to say, "It's just the way he looks at me. He's one of Jonathan's clients." When she realized she was talking to his back, she rushed after him to impede his exit.

"I'll still handle it."

Karina grabbed his arm. "No, no thank you. If I need help, I'll come get you. Right now, I need you more here."

"At the slightest hint of trouble, you holler. I'll be right there." His aggressive stance reminded her of Phoenix. Did all agents try to take over wherever they were?

"He hasn't done anything out of line. It's just . . ." Feeling foolish, Karina marched back to the dining room leaving the smell of seafood, steak, and onions behind her.

Once Casey had finished his meal, he ordered desert. Karina had delayed revisiting his table. It would be obvious if she didn't stop to chat with him as she'd done with the other guests. "How was your meal?" She pasted a polite smile on her face.

"Wonderful. I bet it was your own special recipe."

"As a matter of fact, it is."

"You southern girls can really cook." His sly eyes over her again.

Just where your kind would think a "girl" should be, Karina thought.

"Where are you from, Mr . . ."

"Potts. James Potts. You can call me James."

"What kind of business are you in?"

"Supplies. I travel around the country selling specialized made-to-order supplies that customers can't find any other place," he answered smoothly.

"Will be you here long?"

"Unfortunately, no," he said with obvious reluctance. "I should be leaving within the week."

"I hope you get a chance to see our lovely countryside."

"And beautiful country it is."

His dessert arrived and Karina parted with, "I hope you'll stop by again when you're in town."

"I wouldn't miss it."

Phoenix came in an hour later. After talking to Grady, he pulled Karina aside.

"Make it quick. I've got a crowd out there."

"Where's the sleezeball?" By now she was familiar with the possessive look he gave her.

Karina sent an irritated look at Grady who only shrugged his shoulders, no regret in his demeanor. "He's gone. You can't arrest a man for looking."

"Describe him," he barked impatiently.

Karina sighed. "You're making too much of this."

"He made you nervous didn't he? It could have been Casey."

"He was one of Jonathan's suppliers. He wore an expensive blue pin-striped suit and Italian leather shoes. His hair was slicked back."

"It could have been a disguise. Have you seen this man with Jonathan before?"

"No, he doesn't always dine with his suppliers."

"I don't like this. Come get me if you see anyone suspicious. Anyone at all," he warned.

"All right. I've got to get back to my guests. Oh, and Grady, get something to eat before you leave. Tell them to fix you anything you want."

"Thanks."

"Thank you. I don't know what we would have done without the extra hands."

The remainder of the evening was uneventful. Around nine, when there was a lull, Karina and Phoenix sat for dinner.

"Grady and Tommy are spending the night over at Jonathan's to protect the triplets. I'm staying with you. I thought it wouldn't look right having the triplets staying in the house with you and me staying there, too. There's no way I'm going to stay outside in a car with the four of you in the house unprotected. At least one of them will be awake at any given time."

"Don't you think you're carrying this too far?"

"A clever enemy always seeks out your weakest point. You and the triplets are mine. The people I know will realize that it would hurt me more by harming you than to kill me."

Karina shivered and rubbed her arms to chase away an invisible chill. Her appetite fled. "You win."

Phoenix cut a piece of steak. "This man has gone to too much trouble to do nothing."

Chapter 18

In the midst of working on the plans for Miss Drucilla's reception, Karina heard a noise. When she looked up into James Potts's face, the first thought that popped into her mind was that the restaurant hadn't opened to guests yet, not even the cook had arrived. And wasn't Potts supposed to be out of town anyway? Even more puzzling, where was Grady, her protection?

"Good morning, Mr. Potts. We don't serve breakfast here." Somehow she knew he already knew that.

He pointed a wicked-looking gun at her.

Karina heart skipped a beat, the pen falling unnoticed from her frozen fingers. She didn't utter a word.

"Now, if you do as I say," he explained in a threatening timbre, "there won't be any trouble. It isn't you that I want anyway." He moved forward. "It's your boyfriend. Your children's father," he added just to be sure she understood the situation.

The only bright side to this equation was that he had captured her, not her children. "You're Casey, aren't you?"

"In the flesh." He waved the gun and in an abrupt shift of demeanor, he said, "Now, if you'd be so kind as to precede me out of the building and into the car, we can get this little show on the road. Boyfriend will do anything to get his little mamma back." He nodded his head, and stepped back.

Karina shuddered. Shaky legs pushed her to her feet to do as he requested. "What do you have against Phoenix?"

"He killed my best friend." All pretense gone, his face hardened as he urged her on by jerking the gun.

"Your friend probably would have killed him."

"That's the breaks you get when you're in this kind of business."

"Are you really that callous? If you really felt that way, why are you upset about your friend?"

"I don't call it callous when you're avenging a friend's death. Jimmy was like a brother to me. I couldn't have asked for a better one. As long as you do as you're told, you've got nothing to worry about." The amicable, charming veneer of the previous night had disappeared. "Now move it and don't try anything stupid because I know how to take care of anybody that crosses me."

Karina now knew she should have been more careful as Phoenix had asked. But she needed to come in early to make sure the special orders were put in. She stumbled over Grady as she walked out the door. "Oh, my God! What have you done?" She bent to feel his pulse. Thank God he was alive.

"I just tapped him on the head. He won't be out too long."

"We can't just leave him here," Karina said. "At least let me get him in the building."

Casey motioned to her with the gun. "I don't have time for that."

"I'm not leaving until he's taken care of," Karina said stubbornly. She reminded herself of Kara.

Casey immediately stooped and pulled her up none too

gently by both arms. "I can shoot him and you wouldn't have him to worry about him anymore, would you? I said, we will leave now. I mean now."

The green of his eyes was deadly. Karina knew she was looking into the eyes of a man who could kill . . . who had killed without compunction.

He released one of her arms and pointed toward the car. "Move it."

Lips tight and nerves crawling in her stomach, Karina moved to the car. "You drive," he said and took her chin in his hand. "I don't want to have to kill you. And in case you watch too much TV, don't even think about diving into a ditch or driving too fast. Because I'll beat the living hell out of you if you do. Not even your mamma will be able to recognize you." He released her chin and the peppermint from his breath still floated in the air as he handed her into the car.

Karina shivered as she watched him walk around to the passenger side, the gun still pointing at her. He handed her the key and, with shaky fingers, she started the motor. She knew she might not live to see tomorrow. To see her children grow up. He couldn't let her live. She could identify him. He gave her directions to a house in Petersburg. Taking inventory of the surroundings, she saw the neighborhood was a nice, middle-class area. Azaleas were in bloom and one of the neighbors was picking aphids off the rose petals. A child was skating up the sidewalk. Karina lingered to let the child get farther away from them. When she got out, the gun hidden in the small of her back kept her from calling out to his neighbors for help.

The house was cool but as sparsely decorated as Victor's. "Does Victor know anything about this?"

"No, your ex is still too enamored to get you involved. He doesn't have the stomach for real crime anyhow." He grasped her arm and pushed her into a chair. Then he took a rope and tied her hands and feet to it.

Karina had never realized how uncomfortable being tied with your arms stretched taunt behind you could be.

"I hope you're not in love with your sheriff. It might be better if he's in love with you. Now, we wait for the sheriff. He ran the gun barrel down her cheek, then replaced it with his hand.

"Don't touch me." Karina twisted her head to the side. His hand continued it's path down her neck. In revulsion, she shuddered.

"You and I are going to have lots of fun when this is all over with. I can't wait." Voicing the threat, he swiveled and walked away.

Karina shuddered again. But as soon as Casey left the house, she tried her hands to see if she could loosen the rope, but it only seemed to make the strands rub her skin more. Her arm became chafed and raw. He'd remembered to tie a bandana across her mouth, so yelling would do no good. She looked around the room with hopes that she could scoot the chair someplace and slice the rope. Driven to free herself, she endured the pain and renewed her struggled. If she didn't do something she and Phoenix wouldn't survive. And her children would be left with no parent at all, just like Jonathan and her. Karina struggled with the chair with renewed vigor. She took a deep breath, moved her fingers until they finally touched the rope and discovered Casey really wasn't too particular in tying the rope. Her arm stung, but she clawed and twisted at the rope until it began to loosen. One hand was all she needed. She worked and worked. At least a half hour passed, and by the time she untangled herself, she was sweating in the cool room.

Phoenix read the fax he just received from the FBI.

"Phoenix?" the dispatcher called out to him.

"Yeah?" Impatiently, Phoenix looked up from the pages.

"Got a call for you on line two."

"Who is it?" he asked as he marched to his office.

"He won't say. Said it's something about Karina Wallace."

Phoenix dropped the papers on the desk and snatched the phone. "Sheriff Dye here."

"This is Casey."

He tensed. "Yeah?" Phoenix motioned for one of the officers to have the call traced.

"Have you talked to Karina lately?"

"You son of a bitch." Fear pounded in Phoenix.

"Let's not be hasty, now. You haven't heard me out yet." The menacing voice laughed, a grating sound over the wire.

"If you hurt one hair on her head, you're going to regret the day your mother delivered you," Phoenix barked.

"I had a lot of time behind bars regretting being born. Now, my days are more fruitful, shall I say? There are a few things I'd like to talk over with you. Meet me in three hours at Nottoway Park. You should find it easily. It's the only park in town." He laughed at his own humor. The annoying sound cut through Phoenix. "Oh, and come alone. If I just see one police car, I'll kill her. And you know I won't hesitate to do it. By the way. How is your friend? You know the one you sent to protect her?" Phoenix heard him slam the phone down.

"Did you get the location?"

"Yeah, it's a phone booth in Petersburg. He's long gone by now."

"Where exactly in Petersburg?"

"On the east side."

"Check out the area," he said and then shouted, "Get an ambulance to the Riverview Restaurant, pronto. Emmanuel!" Phoenix yelled out.

"Yeah?" Emmanuel ran to his office.

"I need to borrow your car."

Emmanuel dug the keys out his pocket and threw them to Phoenix.

Phoenix tossed them back to him, deciding to take Emmanuel with him. "Karina Wallace has been kidnapped and it needs to be kept quiet. Drive me to Victor's house first and hope he knows where this Casey lives. I don't want to use my car in case he can identify it."

Emmanuel gunned the motor and left a layer of rubber from the tires in the parking lot when he pulled off. He stepped on it all the way to Petersburg and made the distance in thirteen minutes.

Phoenix was out the car before it settled to a complete stop and banged on Victor's door loud enough to wake the dead. The only person he knew who could possibly know Casey's whereabouts was Victor.

Sleepily, Victor answered his summons in red stripped pajamas.

Phoenix grabbed him by the collar and backed him against the wall. "The slime you've been associating with has kidnapped Karina."

Victor tugged at Phoenix's hand. "Let me go. If she's kidnapped, it's because of you and your work, not me."

Phoenix let the man go, not taking the time to access that he was right. But Victor was still at fault for blabbing.

"I'm hoping you have at least an ounce of decency," Phoenix said, trying for calm. "Do you know where Casey may have taken her?" It took all his will power not to take out his frustration on the man.

"Well, he's real secretive about where he's living. But one night I was too drunk to drive home and he took me. He stopped by his place before taking me."

"Where?" Phoenix asked impatient.

Victor gave him directions to the house. "But, I want to come with you."

"Just stay out of my way." That would be too easy, Phoenix thought. But it was all he had to go on. He didn't wait for Victor to dress.

It took five minutes to reach the tree-lined neighborhood. He walked around the ranch-style house listening for voices and trying to peep in windows, but with no success since the curtains were closed.

Emmanuel knocked on the door on the pretext of selling something. When no one answered, Phoenix picked the lock as quickly as he could. As soon as he stepped into the room, he had barely a second to deflect an apparition descending toward his head. Instead it hit his shoulder.

"What the . . ." He turned to punch Casey out.

"Phoenix!" Karina barely escaped a black eye. "Did I hurt you?"

"Oh, baby." He grabbed her in a bone gripping hug. "Lord, I've never said so many prayers. What the hell happened?" Phoenix rubbed his smarting shoulder.

"Oh, I've hurt your shoulder. I'm so happy to see you." Karina began to massage it for him. "Casey knocked out Grady and came into the restaurant for me. He tied me up. It took me forever to get lose. I thought you were him coming back." She looked around to see Emmanuel on the phone and whispered. "I was so afraid he would kill both of us and the children wouldn't have either one of us. I'm so glad you're all right." She shuddered and Phoenix took her in his good arm. "I'm so sorry about your shoulder."

"I've had worse. I'm proud of you, woman. That was quick thinking."

"The local police are on their way. In unmarked cars," Emmanuel said from behind them as he hung up the phone.

"Good. We're going to take you to the hospital as soon as they arrive. I want to make sure you're okay."

"Don't be ridiculous. I can put some ointment on my arms. They're barely scratched."

"You need to be checked out anyway."

"My biggest problem was getting the rope loose. I think he was so impatient to get out, that he only half tied it."

"Are you sure, baby?"

"I've had worse," she mimicked him and then kissed him for reassurance.

Impatiently, Phoenix looked at his watch. He hoped the officers would be quick. He wanted to get Karina to safety and set things up at the park.

Emmanuel kept a lookout at the front door. "They're here."

"Great." Phoenix went out to talk to the officers and left with Karina and Emmanuel.

Emmanuel drove. He looked at Karina in the rearview mirror and asked, "How are you holding up?"

"Fine."

Before they could set up the stakeout in the park, the Petersburg police apprehended Casey at his home. However, he wasn't talking and insisted that he was working alone.

From Karina's house Phoenix first called the hospital about Grady. "He's just fine, considering. Since he was knocked unconscious, they're keeping him overnight," he told Karina. The second call he made was to his office to tell them he'd be in later.

The adrenaline was still pumping from the fright. He pulled Karina in his arms and kissed her hard, almost afraid that he would hurt her and yet thankful she was safe with him. "I haven't been so frightened in my entire life and I've been in some terrifying situations." He kissed her again while pulling her clothes off, careful not to injure her wrists. He needed to touch her all over, to be inside. . . . With trembling fingers he unclasped the front closure of her bra and nibbled on her sweet chocolate breasts, all the while backing her down the hall toward her bedroom, scattering clothes along the way. By the time she fell back on the bed, the only item left was her panties. He hooked a finger along the edge, caressing her.

"Oh, Phoenix, honey, I . . . Ohhh . . . !"

Phoenix slipped a finger inside her sweet, wet passage, stroking her back and forth. But when she was almost at the edge, he wanted her to enjoy his touch longer. To the tune of her sighs and moans, he kissed her thighs, caressed her calves, kissed her ankles, abdomen, shoulders, back.

There wasn't a spot starving for attention by the time she'd half ripped his clothing off him and he had buried himself in her.

"Sweet . . . sweet mercy," he said in the midst of extraordinary sensations of such closeness with her. "Baby . . . southern cooking doesn't get better than this," he gasped as he followed her over the edge.

After the enervating day, they promptly fell asleep.

"Luke and Miss Drucilla's reception can go as scheduled," Karina said as she prepared dinner. The children were outside playing.

"The reception's fine but you still need protection. I'm sure others are involved."

"I can't live in limbo forever. Victor never met anyone else. If others were involved, he would have said so by now." Karina looked out at the kids who had arrived with Luke's grandchildren. Grady was on the back porch with an ice pack, nursing his smarting head. The other agents guarded the kids in the backyard.

"I trust your judgment, but Casey's in jail and I know you will get the truth out of him, eventually. You're good at your job." Karina sauntered over and rubbed against him, put her arms around him, and kissed him. "I know I'd tell all."

"Casey doesn't look anything like you, sweetheart." Phoenix set his glass of wine on the table and slid his hands over her backside, nuzzling her neck in the process.

Chapter 19

Luke was so impatient to marry Miss Drucilla before
something else happened that they skipped the engagement party and planned a quick wedding instead. It was
scheduled late that very afternoon. Now, Phoenix sat in
back of a room at the rec center listening as Thornton
talked about banks and the benefits of saving to nine- and
ten-year-olds. The triplets were part of the wedding party,
so they would have to make a quick dash home to change
after the hour-long talk.

During Thornton's discussion of certificates of deposit,
Phoenix's mind drifted to the information he'd gathered
so far. First, Stump robbed Tylan's store at Casey's urging.
Next Mrs. Bright's strange lights turned out to be lights
the men from the car theft ring used in the deserted barn;
the country club robberies; money planted in his bank
account; and Jimmy's brother was reported to be in
Europe.

Phoenix had worked on several cases within the last year
including a sting operation involving computer pentium
chips. To think that something smaller than a fingernail

could sell for over eight hundred dollars boggled the mind. His latest involved a lunatic stalking a senator. Casey's name, however, narrowed his suspects to Jimmy's brother.

Since Karina had already ordered everything for the engagement festivities, changing it into a wedding reception wasn't difficult. But how a florist could create the mountain of floral arrangements in the church with such a short notice, Phoenix didn't know. Baskets of ferns, carnations, lilies, and roses were positioned perfectly for the affair. Bright candles cast a warm glow over the scene.

It was a huge affair, with Kara and one of Luke's granddaughters as flower girls in their pretty white dresses with peach trimmings. Karl and Karlton as ring bearers, who weren't very pleased with the prospect, were handsome in their black tuxes and peach cummerbunds. They argued they were much too old for their roles. Phoenix and Karina threatened them to silence so as not to insult Miss Drucilla and Luke. Reluctantly, they marched down the aisle between the five hundred guests. As many people lingered outside, unable to fit inside the church.

There was something special about a couple marrying at that age. Even more, knowing Luke had loved Miss Drucilla for over half a century.

Phoenix was one of the groomsmen in the ceremony. The thought of having to wait as long for Karina was daunting.

When the minister offered a prayer for the couple, Phoenix added his own with an addendum asking God to bless him with Karina and his children. Although things hadn't quite worked out yet, he was a lucky man. There was hope for him yet, Phoenix thought as he watched the bride march down the aisle on her son's arm.

So much had changed since he'd returned home. He'd come home as a loner and now he was a father. Not with one child but three. God had blessed him. He only hoped that Karina would recapture the love that she'd had for him so many years ago. Because, God help him, he loved her even more.

After the prayer, Luke helped Miss Drucilla stand up and swiped a hand down the beautiful pale peach gown to straighten the folds. In his nervousness, he almost knocked the matching wide-brimmed summer hat off her head.

A fetching smile full of love graced the face nearly hidden behind the fragile lace. But before long, Luke eagerly lifted that veil for the first husband and wife kiss. Joyful sighs resounded throughout the church.

Thrilled, the wedding party marched out of the building amid cheers. Phoenix was happy for the couple. After a few robust congratulations they all returned for photographs. In the interim, most of the guests traveled on to the Riverview for the reception where the whole restaurant was used. The children were supervised in the picnic area near the river and veranda to allow enough room inside for the adults. And of course, Tylan had hastily barbecued five hogs for the festive occasion. There was enough of the tasty meat for everyone's palate.

"You country folks sure know how to throw a party, don't you?" Steve said after stuffing himself with the savory fare.

"That we do," Phoenix said. He'd come outside to make sure the triplets were on their best behavior. Karina and her entire staff were working today and she didn't have a minute to spare.

When Steve returned to the restaurant, Jonathan joined Phoenix. Even though he and Jonathan had attended the same schools, Jonathan was older than Phoenix and they had never traveled in the same circles.

"I'm happy for Miss Drucilla and Luke. They deserve each other," Phoenix said.

"I agree." Jonathan had a way of scrutinizing people as he conversed with them. Phoenix felt like a insect being observed under a microscope. But Phoenix was a master at waiting, a trait that had irritated many in the past. They continued to make small talk until Jonathan broached the subject closest to his heart. And when it came, it was a thought that startled even him.

"Kara asked me who their real father was a while back." With emotionless eyes, Jonathan merely clasped his hands in back of him as he waited for Phoenix's response.

For once, Phoenix couldn't channel his response before reacting. "What?" he asked, flabbergasted.

"It seems they overheard Victor telling his sister that he wasn't their natural father, and they wanted to know who was."

"Does Karina know about this?"

"I haven't told her yet. And the children were afraid of upsetting her because she's been so busy and on edge lately."

"Too busy," Phoenix said, thinking of her at this very moment hustling back and forth in the restaurant.

"She seems driven to make a success of this place."

"She has made a success of it." The enormity of his children knowing his true identity thrilled him. "If you don't mind, I'd like to talk to Karina about it," Phoenix said.

"I don't mind at all." Jonathan looked Phoenix squarely in the eye, arms folded across his chest. "I'm not pleased about the way things turned out eleven years ago. I should have been more aware of Karina's distress and her youth. However, this time, both your eyes are wide open. And you're old enough to know what you're doing. If you continue to see her, I expect a marriage to result from it."

Phoenix couldn't remember the last time he'd been reprimanded by a parent. Ostensibly, Jonathan was as much her parent as he was her brother. Before he could clear his outrage enough to respond, Jonathan continued.

"The children need stability. They know Victor isn't their father and that he doesn't care about them. They love you. It's time their lives settled down. And Karina should have help raising them.''

Phoenix wasn't tongue-tied for long. He was livid at being dressed down like a teenager, but he chose his words carefully. "I can appreciate what you're saying, but I'm thirty-seven years old, and quite capable of taking care of Karina and my children. I'm old enough to make my own decisions without interference from an older brother."

"You were a grown man eleven years ago also—and look at the results. Karina's been through some very painful times as a result of that affair. There are responsibilities that go along with lovemaking. Responsibilities you didn't take care of. I want to make sure that doesn't happen again."

"The last thing you have to worry about is a repeat performance. It's not me who's against marriage."

"Then do something about it."

"Believe me, I will," Phoenix said.

Karina looked in horror at the petition for joint custody. What on earth was Phoenix trying to do? Dialing with trembling fingers, she called his house immediately. He wasn't home. She called his office, but he wasn't there, either. She was shaking all over by the time she hung up the phone. Next she started to dial Jonathan's number, her anchor in the sea. After the first three digits she stopped abruptly. "I can handle this," she said to the empty room. What would Jonathan do in this situation? She called her lawyer who explained to her that, as the father of the children, Phoenix was petitioning for equal access to the triplets. Also, after he explained that since Karina had kept their identity from him, it seemed that he had even more grounds to sue her. But when Karina explained his unavailability back then, the lawyer said she had a few options.

"He doesn't need to do this. He already has equal access. I don't keep them from him," Karina said frantically. "Do you think he'll try to take them from me? No court of the land would take my children away from me, would they?"

"Don't jump the gun; he isn't trying to take them from you at this point," he said in a voice designed to soothe. "If he wins, it only gives him legal access to them. Let's fight one battle at a time, okay?" came the perfect lawyer's reply.

Karina hung up feeling just as panicked as when she started. The lawyer had asked her not to contact Phoenix, except through him.

When she reached the stage of almost pulling out her hair, Phoenix knocked on her back door, grinning as if he didn't have a care in the world.

"What do you think you're doing?" She shouted at him as she unlocked the screen door.

Phoenix didn't play dumb for a minute. "It's just a little technicality. Nothing to worry about."

"A court petition is not a 'little technicality.'" She snatched up the paper and shook it at him. He backed up a step hands raised.

"I just want to make sure the children are legally mine," he said amicably as though he hadn't so completely disrupted her life.

"Phoenix, they don't know yet." She threw the paper on the table as if it were a coiled poisonous snake. "If you go on with this, the word will get around town that they're yours. They're much too young to understand. I hope I can appeal to your sense of decency."

"They aren't too young to understand. And I don't think they'll have a problem with it. Besides, the word won't get out. It's against the law for the clerks to talk about it."

"You've got to be kidding. A juicy tidbit like that will spread like wildfire. This isn't the big city where no one knows each other."

"I just want some fatherly rights," he appealed, coming over to touch her shoulder.

Karina evaded his touch and crossed her arms. "I let

you see them whenever you want. We don't need the courts involved," Karina said with her hands on her hips.

"What if you remarried and he decided to take you away? I wouldn't have any rights to my children."

"I'm not even thinking about remarrying," Karina said with a mixture of exasperation and fear. "What are you going on about?"

"Well, you had a date with Charles. What if you fell in love with him, got married, and then decided to work in another county in . . . say, New York. I couldn't see them every day as I do now."

"I'm not marrying Charles. We haven't even talked since that date. Phoenix this is a bunch of nonsense. Why don't you reclaim your petition?"

"No way." He took her trembling hand in his. "Honey, you're getting all worked up for nothing."

"Don't patronize me. My children mean everything to me and you're trying to take them away." She snatched her hand away.

"They mean everything to me, too, and you've kept them from me." A touch of anger surfaced for the first time.

"You know why!"

"Listen," he rubbed his forehead and regrouped, trying to reason with her. "There's no sense crying over spilled milk. I just want legal access to my children."

"You're doing this to hurt me, aren't you?" She crossed her hands across her nervous stomach.

Phoenix sighed. "It's not personal."

"When you're taking my kids away from me, it *is* personal. I'll see you in court." Karina pushed him out the door. "Don't think we'll go on as usual while you're suing me."

Karina left the children in the seating area in the bank while she took care of business with Towanna. The children's parentage had been the talk of the restaurant. She and Phoenix had to talk to the children before they discovered the news from someone else.

"Girlfriend, you've got bags under your eyes." As soon as she closed the office door, Towanna led her to a chair before she collapsed.

"If it isn't one worry, it's two," Karina said. "This business with Phoenix is driving me crazy. And now everybody's talking about it. They're calling me a loose woman. Towanna if they declare me an unfit mother and take the children away, I don't know what I'll do."

Towanna jumped up and came around to Karina to try to comfort her. "They'll do no such thing. I think you're blowing this out of proportion."

"You know he's not going to stay in one place very long. He'll be back in D.C. taking my children with him."

"I don't think he's leaving the area. His family is here. And he loves his job."

Not wanting to take up her friend's time with her problems, Karina broached the business she'd come for. Before she left, Towanna gave her a parting warning not to worry about the triplets. When Karina went downstairs to retrieve her children, they each had an adult male, interrogating them.

"Mr. Sales," Kara said. "What is your favorite food?"

"Well, let's see." Mr. Sales stroked his chin. "I've got to say, chicken fried steak."

Kara recorded that on her sheet of paper.

"What are you doing?" Karina asked.

The children jumped and swiveled to face her.

"Oh . . ." For the first time, Kara was speechless.

"We're doing this for a school project," Karlton said.

"I haven't heard about this project," Karina said.

"It was just assigned to us. We wanted to get a head start in front of the rest of the class," Kara said.

"We'll talk about it at home. You can't hold up the line. The bank's closing soon."

Reluctantly, letting the people go, they gathered their notes and followed her.

Mrs. Bright tottered into Phoenix's office. He jumped up to assist her to a seat.

"I don't need any help," she insisted as he guided her.

"Now, you wouldn't deny me the pleasure of escorting a lady, would you?"

She blushed and tottered on without complaint. There was no telling what bought her in this time. Phoenix thought the episode with the spaceships had been solved. Possibly she was seeing new ones or something.

"Well, I guess I won't be submitting an article to the magazine about the spaceships after all," she said.

"But you did something even more important by leading us to the biggest car theft ring in this area. You'll be getting a hefty reward for your discoveries."

"Oh, my. That's wonderful! Social security doesn't pay enough for me to live off of. Even though I have some savings tucked away, I could always use a little more."

"The insurance companies have offered rewards as well as the hotels. You'll be getting checks from several sources."

"Well, I have to say I'm pleased with that." She shifted in her seat. "I'm quite pleased that you have decided to do the right thing by your children, too. Although, I don't quite condone your leaving Karina all those years ago. I think it's commendable that you're taking steps to play an active part in their lives now."

Phoenix was taken aback, but he managed to stammer, "Why, thank you, Mrs. Bright. I can't tell you how much it means to me that I have your support."

"But I'd think it would be even better if you married her."

"Believe me, we're working on it."

"Karina couldn't find a finer person than you to marry. And the father of her children, no less."

"Thanks for the vote of confidence."

"I knew you were no good and this proves it." Gladys Jones carried her considerable bulk into Phoenix's office, not ten minutes later. "Left that woman high and dry with three children to raise the best she could." She waved a finger at him. "I knew they never should have made you sheriff in the first place. How are you going to talk to young men about not fornicating as teenagers and to take care of their responsibilities when you didn't take care of your own?"

"Mrs. Jones, this is a personal matter between Karina and me."

"Humph. Just planted your seed and went your merry way without a thought to what you may have left behind. What Karina ever saw in you, I don't know," she said on a parting note and slammed the door behind her. "You certainly aren't fit for sheriff of this town," she yelled loud enough for everyone to hear. Her precious good opinion of him certainly didn't last.

Phoenix had been getting calls and visits all day. He now realized his decision may not have been the best one he'd ever made. He had no idea it would spread all over town. And now Karina wouldn't even talk to him, except through her lawyer. The case seemed to have split the town in half. Some of them thought he was making the right move by taking steps for fatherhood. Others thought it was much too late. At least Karina had agreed to talk with the triplets with him as soon as school was out. He hoped they'd reach the children before someone at school mentioned it.

When he arrived at her house, she was tense and wouldn't look directly at him. They all sat around the kitchen table, the children with glasses of milk, and Phoenix, coffee. Karina sipped on a cup of hot tea, lips trembling. Phoenix wanted to reach over and hug her, offer the moral support she needed, but she didn't want to have a thing to do with him.

"What's wrong, Mom?" Karlton asked. "You look so sad."

She gave him a wavering smile. "I'm not sad, honey. But Phoenix and I would like to talk to you about something." She took a breath. "Jonathan said you overheard Victor telling Flo that he wasn't your natural father. Well, he isn't."

How do you tell your children you've lied to them all their lives? And expect them to believe in you in the future?

"Who is?" Kara asked.

"Phoenix is."

Silence reigned. "How come you didn't marry him, like other moms do?"

"You know I worked for the FBI. Well they would send me away on special assignments where no one could reach me. When your mother discovered that she was going to have you, she didn't know how to reach me."

They looked at Karina for confirmation. "That's true. And Victor said that he loved you and me and he wanted to be your father."

"Then how come he left us?"

"It had nothing to do with you. He and I had problems we couldn't resolve. He loved you as babies and he still does."

"I don't think so. Uncle Jonathan loves us. He's always there. Dad . . . what are we supposed to call him?" Kara asked.

"You can call him Dad if you like. He was a father to you."

"Then what do we call Phoenix?" Karlton asked.

Karina deferred to Phoenix to answer that.

"You can call me whatever makes you comfortable."

"Why didn't you tell us when you came here?"

"He didn't know. He only recently found out he had children," Karina answered.

"Why didn't you tell us, Mom? Why did you act like you didn't like him?"

"Phoenix and I had some misunderstandings to work out."

"What kind of misunderstandings?"

Karina explained to them . . . the abridged version, on a ten-year-old level, what happened after Phoenix and she parted that summer.

"Is that why Dad left?"

"Your father and I had problems we couldn't work out. We grew apart. It had nothing to do with you. We explained all that when we parted."

The children asked dozens of questions and Phoenix and she fielded them as best they could. Karina rubbed her throbbing temples after they told her why they were questioning the men in the bank.

"Honey, you should have told me."

"We didn't know how," Kara said.

God, what a mess she'd made of their lives. And how would they ever straighten it out.

She still didn't have much to say to Phoenix by the time he left.

The children prepared for bed in somber moods. Later on, she heard them conversing in Kara's room. She didn't interfere in their private conversation. They needed time to adjust to the news. And they liked to talk things over among themselves. As she passed their door she heard them making plans for one of them to always be around to make sure that they didn't get lied to again. Hurt, Karina put a hand to her chest and continued on down the corridor, reminding herself that they needed the time to adjust to the news.

God, would they ever trust her again? Would they believe

her when she told them bad things about drugs, alcohol, and whatever? It took everything she had not to invade their privacy. She'd talk to them again tomorrow. But tonight, she'd let them work it out among themselves.

Chapter 20

On Loco Road, Phoenix and Emmanuel watched teen-age boys converse animatedly. Some were shouting from open windows and doors, light glaring out, while others had left their parked cars and jogged to reach the center of the source of attention. It was time to arrange for the next drag race. Willing the rain the weather spokesman had predicted to hold off, they looked toward the sky on the cloudy starless night. The crescent moon barely peeped through. Headlights illuminated the stark darkness.

At least sixteen cars were in attendance, parked in various degrees of disorder: on the edge of freshly plowed peanut fields, on the side of the road, some actually on the pavement, others in a dirt path amid the budding trees, forgotten bramble pressed beneath the tires. The underbrush crackled as footsteps descended. Some of the youngsters had been fortunate enough to have parents purchase their vehicles for them. Others had to work for theirs. Those who used family cars sat on the sidelines to enjoy watching the races. Either way, most of the machines were souped up renditions, whether old or new, and all were spitting clean. Not a piece of paper found its way to the floor. The leather interiors shined and glossed, the outsides washed and waxed. And the white-walled tires, gleamed white.

The boys were equally well-dressed, at least what went for dressed for this generation. Some of them had the usual pants sliding past the crack in their behinds while others wore nice slacks or pressed jeans so as not to be turned around at their dates' doors. In this Baptist community, any self-respecting parent wouldn't dare let their daughter out with an inappropriately attired suitor.

Young men who had been fortunate enough to be allowed entrance, for the most part, had left their dates on the doorsteps promptly at midnight. Not a minute late to offset a possible greeting by an irate parent. Then, too, on Saturday nights, they had the races to look forward to.

Car doors slammed as they came to gather around the older men. The atmosphere reeked with tension while at the same time giving appearances of innocence. Since they hadn't been caught in the act, there wasn't a need to try to run away. They discounted the smell of burning rubber and exhaust fumes still perfuming the air amid the aroma of rich pine, honeysuckle, and freshly turned earth.

Some of them spoke, but none of them offered to start the conversations, simply swatted mosquitoes as they waited for the older men to react first.

Phoenix read varying degrees of responses when he looked around at the crowd. "How are you this evening?" he asked breaking the silence.

"Fine," they all replied, some shuffling their feet, others looking at their peers to observe their reactions, and wanting to follow suit, while others still gave hard stares, not afraid of anything. Some had boulder-sized chips on their shoulders.

Phoenix catalogued it all to gauge his approach to them. It was important that they see him as a friend, not as an enemy. He didn't have quite the reputation to live down that city cops had since many of these children hadn't yet received the negative treatment that caused them to be wary and untrusting of his authoritative role, not having experienced very much in life. Mothers had kept them busy in Sunday school and church on Sunday mornings as soon as they were old enough to talk, and daddies were ready to apply a good hickory switch that was always handy at the first inkling of anyone getting out of line. But others had been affected in some way. Whether small or large, negative treatment had a tendency to leave its impact for a lifetime.

"Fine night for a race, isn't it?" Phoenix asked.

They looked around as if the statement was a foreign one. "Race?" one brave soul said. "Not us." He scratched his bald scalp then pushed up his shirt sleeves. "We're just shooting the breeze." Phoenix caught a follow up of groans and nods of agreement.

But he knew better. However, if this visit was to be effective, his intent was not to get them on the defensive. It was time he dealt with the racing that occurred all to often in Nottoway. He almost felt like a hypocrite, knowing how juicy this stretch of the highway was to a teenager and the many Friday and Saturday nights he himself had enjoyed the burning rubber and the feel of the automobile hugging the curves as he charged ahead of his opponent. But he wanted these teenagers to live to be adults in good health, not hospitalized with splintered bones. Or worse.

"Now that you've had your hell-raising days, you're trying to deprive us," one brave sixteen-year-old spoke up, hands on his hips above the belted jeans.

"That's why I'm talking to you now," Phoenix responded. "I know better and I don't want you to make the same mistakes I made. Besides, it's against the law. And I'm here to make sure you obey it." Unflinchingly, he looked at every face to gauge reactions before he continued. He was the authority here and he wasn't going to let them ignore it. "It sounds glamorous and it's fun while you're doing it. Until someone gets killed or seriously injured. Innocent bystanders as well as you are at risk." He knew that brought Howie Martin to mind. Many of them were there the night of the accident. But he wanted to make sure it sank home. "Howie was lucky to be alive after his accident. His recovery will be a long, slow, painful process. Have any of you visited him?" When only two heads nodded, he said, "Maybe more of you should stop by. See what you could do to help him out. It might lift his spirits."

"We'll visit. But he just wasn't a good driver," one teenager said.

"You need to remember that, regardless of your driving capability, at high speeds, your vehicles are unsafe because they aren't designed to race. Passenger vehicles are different from race cars. Those men can drive at 180 miles per hour and walk away from an accident because their cars are designed to travel at high speeds." Some of the kids gave him their full attention. "They have roll bars, reinforced steel bars on both sides to protect the driver. Passenger cars aren't equipped with that." Whether they agreed with him or not, he wanted to make some things clear. "And, it's the law that no two vehicles should race on a state highway at the same time." No one spoke. "My department will prosecute to the full extent of the law if you are caught racing."

For a time no one said anything until one of the teenagers asked him a question about his work with the agency.

After that, slowly, they began to open up to him and ask other questions. Some of them remained silent, but many came around. He didn't want to be a sheriff they couldn't identify or connect with. They were the most important part of his job.

His undercover work seemed very exciting to them and he talked about some of the more interesting cases he and some of his coworkers had been assigned to. As one youngster laughed, Phoenix feared the boy's pants were going to slide off his hips any second, if he didn't trip from lack of movement first.

"What do we do if we want to be an agent?" Peter Granger asked.

"Finish school and get a college degree," Phoenix said. "With a degree, you can do anything you want to do."

After the boys left, Phoenix chatted to Emmanuel awhile. For some reason, he was restless and unwilling to go home to an empty house.

"You've won them over for life," Emmanuel said.

"I don't know about that," Phoenix shook his head. The sense of foreboding was taking over again.

Emmanuel leaned against the car and crossed his arms. "So you dropped the suit against Karina."

"It seemed the wisest move."

"You just might win her over yet," he offered optimistically. He seemed to sense Phoenix's mood.

Phoenix looked up as a drop of rain fell on his arm. Now that the cars had left, it was pitch black outside. But that didn't seem to deter the swarming mosquitoes. There wasn't much he could say.

"Is she speaking to you yet?" Emmanuel seemed oblivious to the annoying insects.

"Not quite. I'm working on it."

"You really stepped your foot in it this time, didn't you?"

"I did." Phoenix didn't like to be reminded of what a fool he'd been. "But at least the triplets know they're mine. They aren't ready to call me Daddy yet, but they'll come around eventually . . . I hope."

"They will. At least the case is all wrapped up."

"Except for the extra money in my account." His computer forensic friend was still plowing through the records to find the origin that seemed to spring from all over the globe. Someone must have taken months to set up his account.

"Well, we'll solve it nevertheless."

"Yeah," he said, but sometimes he was doubtful they'd

ever solve that issue. And at least nobody believed he was dumb enough to hide money in his regular bank account.

As the drop of rain turned into a drizzle, Phoenix and Emmanuel left. Phoenix wondered what he was going to do about Karina to thaw her toward him. He loved her desperately. What could be the perfect relationship had turned into something so elusive. He thought she would soften a little after he dropped the suit, but it didn't seem to help. He'd taken a dozen roses over to her, but she only thrust them back at him and slammed the door in his face. If he called her, she only wanted to talk about the children, not about the two of them. He sighed as he pulled into his drive at 1:30 A.M. wondering if this situation would ever straighten out.

The triplets were sitting on his front porch waiting for him silhouetted by the bright glow of the yard light.

"Hi, Phoenix," they greeted him quietly.

"Isn't it a little late for you to be out?" He stopped just before the first step. Damn, he was glad to see them.

"We wanted to talk about something," Karlton said.

Phoenix sat down on the porch step and faced them. "I can presume your mom doesn't know you're here."

"She wouldn't have let us come if we'd asked."

Phoenix knew he should admonish them more strongly, but his heart wasn't in it, he was so happy they were there. "You shouldn't have come without her permission," he said halfheartedly.

"But we needed to talk to you tonight."

To a child, everything was important. "What's so urgent that it couldn't wait until tomorrow?"

"Mom. We think you should be together like other parents."

Phoenix swiped a hand across his face, took in a deep breath. He thought so, too. "We're working on that," was the best response he could come up with.

"Maybe we should talk to Mom for you," Kara snapped impatiently.

"She might listen to us." Karlton propped his chin on his hands.

"I appreciate your offer of help, but I don't think that'll be a good idea. She might feel we're ganging up on her. She needs more time to adjust to the idea."

"Well, you've got to do something. We're supposed to be a family!" Frustrated, Karl kicked a rock off the porch and, leaned against the column.

"We are a family." Phoenix tried to reassure him.

"It's not the same. Families live together. In the same house," Kara came to sit by him.

Phoenix pulled on a pigtail. She didn't snatch it away. His little girl. "Tell you what. Give me a little time to work on it. If I can't pull it off on my own, I'll come to you for help. Is that agreeable to you?"

With tired yawns, they acquiesced reluctantly with a parting warning. "Don't take too long."

Phoenix smiled to himself. They were tuckered out, poor things, but wanted their family together so badly, they'd waited for him half the night. He could see them in his mind's eye, sitting on Kara's bed, planning the whole affair, whispering so Karina wouldn't overhear them. He wanted to reach over and hug them all, but wouldn't push the tenuous relationship at this point. Instead, when he got up, he ruffled each boy's hair. "It's late and you need your sleep." He went inside to call Karina and drove the children home. Home. He was looking forward to the day when home would be the five of them. Together.

Phoenix lifted the phone from his ear for the third time and winced. The indignant screeching reverberating over the wire grew louder and louder.

"Mom . . ." he sighed and listened again. "I've got too much on my plate now. I wasn't keeping secrets," he said tiredly. "I was going to tell you next time I talked to you."

She blasted him again.

"I know . . ." This must be the fourth time she'd shouted that she had a right to know about her only grandchildren and how he was depriving her the right of a grandparent. And why did she have to hear it from that gossipy Mrs. Jones anyway. Her son should have told her. How did he think she felt hearing it from someone else? She seemed to forget that these were the same children she'd lamented were the terrors of Nottoway a few short months ago. Now they were her darling grandchildren.

"Phoenix?"

He looked up to see Emmanuel at the door.

Saved, he wound the call to a close. "Mom? I've got to go. Duty calls." He hung up knowing he'd have another fight on his hands if he tried to take the children out of town without Karina. She'd probably accuse him of trying to skip town forever with her children. Phoenix sighed wanting to solve the dilemma with them, wanting some peace, some continuity in his life. Hell, when had anything ever been normal for him? Maybe they could make the trip together.

"Yeah, Emmanuel?" The younger man stood in the open door way.

"Victor fell down a flight of stairs at his house and he's unconscious. Flo found him this morning. Karina went to the hospital."

Phoenix swiped a hand over his face. So much for peace. "I'm going over there." It seemed almost every trip he made to Petersburg was somehow involved with Karina. She was terribly attached to Victor and would need some hand-holding. Consoling the woman he loved while she lamented over another man wasn't exactly his favorite role. It ate at him that she still harbored feelings for the man. Envy also ate at him, regardless of how petty he felt for his antipathy toward the man when he was so ill.

The children were in school, thank goodness. Hopefully he'd have good news for them by the time school let out for the weekend.

* * *

Upon arriving at the antiseptic-smelling hospital, Karina tried to soothe a distressed Flo Wallace. "I hope he isn't dead. Oh my Lord!" the older woman wailed slumped in a mint green chair placed under an abstract print. *Time* and *National Geographic* lay scattered over dozens of other magazines on a coffee table.

"The doctors are doing everything they can for him. He's getting the best of care," Karina said over and over in a calm voice, more than a bit anxious herself. Even though she was still angry at Phoenix, Karina was pleased to see him come through the door.

Their greeting was stiff. He cleared his throat as Karina handed another tissue to Flo. The low murmur of a doctor's page came over the intercom. Another family sat in the opposite corner of the enormous room. A man paced the dark green carpet. Phoenix nodded a greeting in their direction. Sad, lackluster eyes nodded back to him. "How's he doing?" he asked throwing a weary look toward Flo. He was still uncomfortable dealing with teary situations.

"We don't know. He didn't break anything in the fall, thank goodness. But other than that . . ." Karina shrugged her shoulders, helplessly, trying not to upset Flo more.

"He looked just about dead when I found him this morning at the bottom of the stairs. He'd had just a little bit to drink, but he never got intoxicated enough to lose his balance," came her high-pitched voice. She twisted the tissue to shreds in her hands.

Karina patted her arm, hoping to give her some small measure of solace. Even though Flo had made her disapproval of Karina well known, Karina was the first person she called from the hospital.

Phoenix sat in the chair on the other side of Flo. She seemed to need more consoling right now. Just as he was about to speak, a woman with a head of flying hair dyed dark red sailed into the room, clearly distressed.

"Oh, God," she cried. "where is he?" One white-garbed nurse marched in right after her.

"I'm sorry, Miss. But we can only give out patient information to immediate family."

"I'm his fiancée. That's close enough," the tear-stained woman barked, black streaks of mascara running down her cheeks.

"It's hospital rules."

"Oh, my Lord! Victor, Victor. I don't know what I'll do without him." She clutched the nurse's arms looking as though she'd pass out any minute, the black body-hugging dress that a moment before had hit midthigh now rose a few inches. "You've got to tell me something!"

Flo, Karina, and Phoenix stood at once.

"You're Victor's fiancée?" Flo asked, tears forgotten in the disruption.

"Yes, we're supposed to get married in a couple of months," the woman sniffed. "Who are you?" She let the nurse go. The woman was thankful her attention had been drawn elsewhere.

For a moment everyone was too shocked to speak. Phoenix focused on Karina to judge her reaction. She stepped toward the woman reaching out to her since Flo seemed struck speechless. "I'm Karina Wallace," she said. "And this is Flo Wallace, Victor's sister and Sheriff Dye of Nottoway." She led the woman to the chair she had just vacated, the precarious dress riding higher as she sat. "We haven't heard anything yet. The doctors are still with him. He fell down a flight of stairs at his house this morning." Karina thanked Phoenix for the chair he bought to her and continued with the drill. "Flo found him. He was breathing, and nothing seems to be broken, but he's still being examined by the doctors." Karina guessed Flo wouldn't approve of this woman either. No one was good enough for her brother.

"I'm Susan Parker. Well, maybe no news is good news."

"We're hoping for the best."

"Karina Wallace?" Susan eyed her from head to toe. "You're his ex-wife."

"Yes, I am."

She eyed Phoenix with distrusting eyes, forgetting the competition momentarily. "Well, what's the sheriff doing here?"

"He's a friend of the family," Karina answered.

"Oh," she sniffed, still piercing him with her gaze. "Victor never mentioned him before."

A harried doctor carrying a clipboard and wearing a green scrub suit covered by the white lab coat walked over to them, immediately drawing everyone's attention. "Mr. Wallace has regained consciousness. He has a concussion, a few bruises, a couple of cracked ribs."

"Oh, my Lord," Flo sobbed.

"It's not as bad as it sounds. He should be able to leave tomorrow." He patted Flo's hand. "He says that he was pushed down the stairs. He doesn't know who did it. We've notified the police."

Everyone was stunned.

"Who would want to push him down the stairs? He never hurt a soul in his life," Flo bellowed.

"You'll have to take that up with the police department. He's safe here. I'm concentrating on his physical well-being right now."

"Can we see him, Doctor?" Phoenix asked, wanting to know what was behind this action.

"Maybe in an hour or two. He's resting quietly now, and I don't want him disturbed."

Chapter 21

As usual, his gut instinct had been proven right. The problem was, what had Victor seen that would cause someone to try to kill him? Since he'd been hit from behind, Victor hadn't an inkling of by whom or what. And since he'd been in pain when Phoenix had questioned him, Phoenix didn't want to badger him any more than necessary. It never occurred to Phoenix that the man could be lying. There were still missing pieces from the Casey puzzle, and Phoenix still waited for something more to happen.

The other problem was trying to get Karina to stay in one place long enough to talk. Fresh lemon scent permeated the air as she sprayed and dusted the tables in the family room. She'd been scrubbing and cleaning and straightening the house since he arrived. From the neatness of the place, he couldn't see where she had any more cleaning to do before she'd be cleaning what she'd already finished. And before he left, Grady had said she'd cooked enough to feed an army, which was evident by the bowls of food she'd packed and sent home with Jonathan and the kids. They had carted enough with them to last two weekends, and the enormous amount tucked away in Karina's frige would keep them for a week.

He could be thankful that she easily gave in to his staying with her and accepted protection for the children without argument. She never quibbled about the children's protection. Only her own. This time she'd said very little, which worried Phoenix even more. This withdrawn attitude wasn't like her at all. What happened to his little tiger?

Upon his arrival, he'd dropped his duffle bag in her entry closet, not knowing where he'd be sleeping for the night. Preferably with her, but he didn't stand a snowball's chance in hell of that happening.

What was he going to do? He had a feeling the children wouldn't have botched the job nearly as bad as he had. They'd given him that look, each stopping a few seconds, afraid to say anything around their mom, but turned to Phoenix nevertheless, giving him the raised eyebrow just before they left with Jonathan. Phoenix took it as a warning that he was to make the most of the occasion. He'd hate like hell to disappoint them. Or himself. Because he'd be gravely disappointed if he didn't clear the air with Karina.

Phoenix looked out the huge bay window. Two squirrels scampered up trees, gathering acorns, storing them for the winter. He wondered if either of them was the triplets' pet. The animal seemed to come and go at its leisure. But instinctively knew when the triplets were around.

A female cricket sang her siren's song in the early evening. Phoenix longed for such a sign from Karina. Any indication to let him know she had some feelings left for him.

Their problems eleven years ago had all developed from misunderstandings. Phoenix was determined that wouldn't happen again.

"Karina," he called out.

When he didn't receive an immediate response, he turned, only to realize he was alone in the room. She yelled a reply from another part of the house.

He followed her voice.

She stood at the linen closet choosing sheets and towels.

"I want to talk," he said as she busily plucked a wash cloth off the shelf.

"I'm busy right now. I think I'll let you sleep in Kara's room," she said without looking up. "Her bed is larger than the boys'." She grabbed pillow cases. "You'll be more comfortable there."

Phoenix took the burden from her cold fingers and used his other hand to shut the closet door and steer her toward the family room, her posture stiffening, her feet dragging. "We can make the bed together later. Right now, we need to talk." He could see she was gearing up to protest.

"I don't want to fight anymore, Phoenix," she sighed.

He looked at her weary features. "Neither do I. But we need to clear the air." He gently pushed her onto the sofa cushion. "You're the one who said I was secretive, never talked enough about myself. Now, I'm talking."

Back erect, Karina clasped her hands together in her lap, still avoiding his eyes. This was it, she thought. It was over for the two of them. She'd regretted this moment. Her spine stiffened bearing up for the unpleasant news. She would endure it and hopefully come out of it whole. Someday. She did once before. She vowed, she would again. Except her heart didn't believe it for a moment. She would not break down in front of him.

"Victor's going to be fine."

"I know that. I was at the hospital, too, you know." Why was he dragging this out?

"Yeah, I know." He turned from her and clasped his hands behind his back and walked to the window. He'd been staring out that window a lot since he came over.

Karina didn't rush him, knowing, as her stomach did somersaults, what he had to say wouldn't be pleasant.

Abruptly he turned and Karina almost jumped.

"Why are you still angry with me? I know I made a stupid mistake when I tried to sue for equal custody, but I wanted you protected. If anything happened to me, I wanted you and the children cared for. There's health insurance"— he ticked off item by item—"retirement for you, college tuition. With legal parental rights, all that would be taken care of."

Karina didn't know what to say. "Why didn't you say that at the time? You didn't have to go to such extremes to accomplish that."

"Then, it seemed the best approach. Afterward . . ." he shrugged and sighed. "Karina, I love you, more than I did years ago. I consider you and the children my family. I don't want to lead a separate life from you all."

Speechless, Karina tried to gather her wits. "Phoenix, do you really love me?" was the only lame statement she could make.

"Yeah," he whispered. "Can you doubt it?"

"Yes, you dunce." She punched him in the shoulder. "You don't put someone you love though this emotional turmoil."

"Totally unintentional."

"You're always doing things to keep us apart."

"I may make mistakes sometimes. Hell, I'm not perfect. I just wanted to be close to you and the kids, Karina. I wanted it all. It seemed I couldn't have anything though." He took a deep breath. "Tell me anything. Just *don't* tell me I've lost you completely."

"Phoenix Dye." A light blazed in her eyes that hadn't been there for a while. "You haven't lost me at all. With your friends here, I thought you missed the agency and wanted to go back. I thought I'd lost you."

"Never," he groaned and delighted in her surprised yelp when he picked her up and whirled her around. "I can't tell you how much I've missed you." He sank onto the sofa cushions, plunking her up on his lap, a heavy burden leaving his chest. Lowering his head, he pressed a demanding kiss against her smiling lips. This wasn't a leisurely exploration as he moved his mouth insistently over hers, seeking and gaining entrance. But hot and demanding, urgent.

His hands traveled a quick but sensuous path down her body and lifted the T-shirt, pulling it above her breasts. Deft fingers quickly unhooked the front snaps on her bra and soft breasts spilled onto his waiting fingers.

Karina's hands slid under his shirt and tightened, delighting in the texture of his skin, seeking, caressing, exploring, and reveling in the sensations swamping her.

He moaned, need consuming him as her palm circled his chest, then dipped. Stomach muscles tightened in sensual anticipation.

His fingers unzipped her jeans, slid under silk panties, to find her hot, wet, ready. In one smooth motion, he got up and carried her to her bedroom placed her on the sheets. He broke contact and looked into her fevered eyes. They sparkled back at him revealing her need, giving the illusion of fragility, yet speaking of untold strength.

She closed her eyes, passion soaring through her.

He caught the top of her jeans and inched them down, bending to press hot kisses to her quivering thighs, her knee, calves, all the way to her toes. Then starting from the bottom, he traveled up the other side . . . inch by mind-numbing inch. Soft skin, insistent moans, and questing fingers drugged his senses. Rigid with need, he wanted to prolong this exquisite delight but wondered how he could stand the wait. It had been too long—far too long—since he'd had the pleasure of burying himself in her.

He stood, she came with him, tearing at his clothes. Through the need, he laughed, a strained affair as first his T-shirt hit the floor, followed by his jeans and navy blue briefs.

And then he was back, forearms beside her head, easing himself into her, centimeter by centimeter, until he touched her core. Her hips undulated, reached up. Her small hands pressed his tight bottom to suck him deeper still. A long low groan escaped him, a high-pitched whimper issued from her. And then they moved as one—her seeking, him fulfilling, faster and faster, deeper and deeper. Her fingers dug into his back, his buttocks; her thighs raised higher; his arms wrapped around her, tightened until pulsations and spasms spiraled bringing sweet blessed, explosive, release.

Before they fell into slumberous sleep, Phoenix remembered to say, "Marry me, Karina."

Groggily, she moaned, "Okay."

Phoenix was too sleepy to reflect on how unromantic this proposal turned out to be, but he smiled with contentment at the remembered okay. Karina was finally his.

Phoenix heard a noise, eased out the bed to investigate. Karina lay sleeping soundly beside him. He didn't know from which direction the clamor came. It might be that squirrel. Phoenix had barely made it to the door when he was backed back into the room, a gun pressing into his chest.

The light from the hallway caught the figure in the face. "Thornton? What's going on?"

"Just get over there next to . . ."

"Phoenix?" At the noise, Karina sat up, the sheet sliding low on her bare breasts. When she saw the bank president standing in the doorway, she hastily covered herself, confusion clouding her sleep-filled senses. "What in the world?"

"Mrs. Wallace," Thornton Sterns greeted her in his usual cultured manner.

Completely awake now, Karina merely looked from the gun to Phoenix. One wouldn't think a man of this ilk would even possess a weapon, much less break into someone's house to use it.

"I can assume you didn't come here to rob the place," Phoenix said as a macabre joke when, in fact, the situation wasn't funny at all.

"I've waited two years for this." He waved the gun, indicating Phoenix should back up.

"Let Karina go," Phoenix said. "It's me you want. No reason to hurt anyone else."

"Oh, no. You're less likely to take chances with her around." His ice blue eyes turned even colder. "Besides, I've got plans for your tramp and your three children," he clipped out through thin, cold lips. "Back up."

The blood chilled in Phoenix's veins as he backed toward the bed, putting Karina behind him. His gun was of no use in the dresser drawer.

Karina gasped, foiling his effort. "Stay away from my babies!" She rose tucking the sheet around her like a sarong.

Phoenix caught her and shoved her in back of him, applying pressure to keep her in place when she tried to move again. A warning that said to let him handle this.

Somehow Phoenix knew he was looking at Jimmy's infamous missing brother, who was going under the pseudonym Thornton.

"Your brother endangered innocent people. It was a decision he made."

"And I'm my brother's keeper. An eye for an eye ... and all that." The only emotion he displayed was a minor tic in his cheek.

"It's not your fault. It's not even my fault. I was faced with a life and death situation. It's unfortunate what he did. But I had no choice," Phoenix tried to reason. "He was ordered to drop the gun. We didn't want to kill him. But innocent people were around who could get killed. That's the chance he faced. I take that chance every day." By the looks of Thornton, Phoenix couldn't tell if his words were penetrating. Most likely not. But he was going to try anyway. "Don't do the same thing. You have your whole life ahead of you."

"Killing my brother was murder." His composure didn't slip a notch. "A murder I must avenge."

Phoenix had to find some way to save Karina and the kids, even if it meant his life. Reason wasn't gong to work with Thornton any more than it worked with an intoxicated person. The man's eyes glazed with a touch of madness. Phoenix eased closer to the drawer, hoping for an opportunity to retrieve his weapon. For now, he had to keep Thornton talking long enough to take action.

"Enough of this. Mrs. Wallace, get dressed. We're going for a little ride."

"Take me instead. You'll never get away with a multiple homicide. You're going to end up dead yourself."

"Do I look like a fool to you? I'm not in the States, remember?"

When Karina went to the drawer to pull out fresh underwear, he stopped her.

"No, no. The ones scattered on the floor will do."

Heat filled Karina's cheeks as she gathered the clothes in her hand. She was headed to the adjourning bathroom when he stopped her again.

"Right here, where I can see you. Don't be modest, Mrs. Wallace."

She wasn't about to stand nude in front of that horrid man. She scooted under the spread on her bed and wiggled into her clothing while underneath the covering.

During his speech, Thornton had eased closer in the room. Phoenix turned to see Karina bend on the opposite side of the bed to pull her shoes from underneath where she was out of the range of the gun. He wouldn't get a better chance than this. Suddenly, Phoenix barreled into Thornton, knocking him against the wall and wrenching the gun from his stunned fingers. Just as quickly, Thornton knocked it out Phoenix's hand.

Thornton cried out in outrage as Phoenix hit him twice in the face. But the health club Thornton visited four times a week had kept him in surprisingly good shape. He recovered and returned punches of his own. The men rolled on the floor, struggling, fighting and trying to get the gun.

When Karina heard the impact of bodies hitting the wall, the house seemed to shake. She bolted up to see Phoenix and Thornton in a tangle on the floor, Thornton's gun merely inches from them. She tried to get close enough to get it but with the men rolling back and forth, she couldn't. She didn't want to hinder Phoenix. Soon she gave that idea up and went to the drawer and pulled out Phoenix's gun. She'd never held a weapon in her life. She pointed it toward the wall and shouted, "Stop, or I'll shoot!"

No one seemed to have heard her. The men kept struggling. "I said stop!" she shouted again. Soon Thornton reached the gun and held it to Phoenix's head.

She pointed hers toward Thornton.

"Drop it or he dies." Thornton said, shifting behind Phoenix without taking his eyes off him. Blood seeped from his cracked lips. The red skin around one eye beginning to swell.

"Don't do it, Karina. Shoot him." Phoenix didn't look any better than Thornton.

Karina knew very well she couldn't take the chance of Phoenix getting shot.

"Now!" Thornton shouted pulling back the hammer.

Karina placed the gun on the floor by her feet.

"No!" Phoenix yelled.

Thornton scooted away from Phoenix and leveled the gun on Karina. "Now, get up," he said, inching up with the help of the wall. He didn't straighten completely, an indication that he may have cracked ribs. His previous calm was nowhere in evidence.

Phoenix got up, favoring his right side. Karina ran over to help him even though he indicated he was all right. However, she was skeptical and kept a watchful eye on him, wanting to lend assistance.

Thornton pulled a length of rope out of his pocket.

"Turn around." Once Phoenix's back was to the man, Thornton hit him on the head hard with the gun handle.

"Oh!" Karina screamed. She tried to catch him, but in the end fell with him, trying to bear his weight but losing the battle. She was sure every bone in her body was crushed as Phoenix lay prone across her, unconscious. "You didn't have to do that," she yelled at Thornton, fear lacing her voice.

He ignored her statement and bent, favoring his ribs and flipped first one of Phoenix's hands then the other behind his back and tied him securely.

Blood seeped from the cut on Phoenix's head. Karina knew he was alive because she felt his chest move with each breath he took. She used the edge of her T-shirt to press against the wound, but the blood still flowed freely.

"Now, we wait until he comes to. I wouldn't want him to miss anything."

"Why don't you let us go?" Karina asked.

"Because he killed my brother. He's going to watch you die. And then the children—one by one. He'll feel the pain I felt, suffer as I have, before I finally kill him."

Cold fear sailed through Karina. She'd never looked into the face of evil before. Panic attacked her. But if she gave in to it they were all doomed. *Think, Karina think,* she told herself. *She had to save them.* Her babies. God, he couldn't just murder them in cold blood. But she looked into his frigid eyes and knew he could. She trembled all over. And couldn't seem to stop. She had to do something. You can't let panic rule you, she thought frantically.

She tried to think rationally. Her children had three of the FBI's finest guarding them. Thornton couldn't get to them easily. Try to solve one problem at a time. *Think of what you can do right now to save you and Phoenix, then all will be fine.* She drew in a deep breath and leaned across Phoenix. She tried to look around without Thornton detecting her actions. Phoenix's gun was hidden under the bed. She could barely see the tip of it. If only she could scoot over to retrieve the weapon.

She sat up again, looked into his face. His piercing eyes drilled though her. But he didn't say a word. The smile, if you could call it that, jerked up one side of his mouth seemed to say that he knew what she was thinking but it would do no good. She shivered as a chill ran through her.

But she knew she'd have to do something, anything to save them. He was hurting as Phoenix was. While she was still unscathed—to a certain extent. The fall wasn't so bad.

"He's getting heavy. And I need some water to tend to his wound," Karina said.

"By all means, get up. But you can't leave the room. It won't do any good to patch him up anyway."

When she tried to move, Phoenix moaned.

"Ah, wonderful. He's coming around. And he'll be easier to handle this time without the use of his hands."

Phoenix shook his head and immediately regretted the movement when pain arrowed though it. He could barely understand the mumbling around him. Rough hands jerked his shoulder back.

"Come on, get up," Thornton barked.

Phoenix stifled a moan—just barely. When he tried to use his hands, he realized they were tied. He stifled another moan and a curse. Everything came back at once. This was the very last predicament he wanted to be in. Helpless, with his hands behind his back. Thornton jerked on him again. Phoenix stumbled to his feet with Karina assisting him. He looked up at Karina through eyes still seeing double, blinked to try to clear them. She seemed fine—so far.

Thornton directed him toward a chair.

If he was going to do something, Phoenix couldn't afford to be any more restricted than he already was. When Thornton turned him around and insisted that he sit, Phoenix made a motion to sit but didn't drop. Instead he put all his force into a forward motion and plowed right into Thornton's stomach.

"Oof." Thornton went back, the wall keeping him from falling on his backside, but he didn't let the gun go.

Karina went after the gun under the bed. As Thornton raised the gun to fire at Phoenix, she fired at him and caught him in the side. Startled, he raised the gun again to fire at her when suddenly something landed on his head and bit his ear. At the same instant, Phoenix kicked him in the stomach. Thornton doubled over, gun still in hand.

"Aag!" The gun wavered and fired into the floor as he fought the triplets' pet squirrel. Karina fired again, catching him in the arm. Blood seeped through the wound. He dropped the gun, still fighting at the squirrel, which had slipped behind him and nipped him on the shoulder.

Karina ran over and picked up his gun. Then untied Phoenix. The squirrel was getting macadamia nuts next time she went grocery shopping.

Phoenix got the handcuffs and cuffed Thornton while Karina dialed the police station.

By the time she'd hung up and retrieved wet towels and makeshift bandages for Thornton's wounds, he had come so unglued he was almost foaming at the mouth with hatred. Phoenix insisted she keep her distance and he attended to Thornton's injury.

"You won't get away with this. I must have justice!" he shouted. "You murdered my brother. You will die and your tramp and children with you. You must watch them all die!" Saliva drooled from the side of his mouth, his eyes rolled.

Karina covered her mouth with her hands, shaking with delayed shock and fright. In her safe little world, she'd never encountered such sickness before. This was not the poised bank president in three-piece suits she saw on a regular basis at the gas station, at ball games, at the bank. She was faced with a mad man.

"Karina . . ." She thought she heard her name called,

but she wasn't sure as she sat on her bed, the two guns beside her. Even though Thornton was cuffed, she wasn't leaving those weapons as long as he was in her home.

"Karina." Phoenix's voice finally penetrated her clouded mind.

"Yes?"

"Go in the other room. I'll be all right here."

"No." She could barely hear him through Thornton's deranged ravings. She couldn't leave. As long as Thornton was here, she had to see that he was contained.

"Karina, do as I said. Go in the other room," he said as he tried to stop Thornton's blood from flowing.

"I can't," she whispered. She remained in that one spot on the bed while he raved and raved for the fifteen minutes it took the officers to reach her house.

Epilogue

Karina marched down the aisle to Phoenix on Jonathan's arm. She hadn't expected a huge affair for the hastily planned wedding, but the people of Nottoway loved weddings and there were even more people in attendance than had been at Miss Drucilla and Luke's. A slew of agents had made an appearance, as well as a busload of Mrs. Dye's church friends from North Carolina. The fact that it was the hottest day in August didn't seem to bother them, and the church's overworked air conditioner just couldn't seem to keep the building properly cool. Makeup ran, sweat trickled, and many a wide-brimmed summer hat toppled, as friends who hadn't seen each other in ages greeted each other. Pleased smiles spread on faces as they fanned themselves with the fans donated long ago by the Harper's Funeral Parlor.

The triplets didn't complain about being in the wedding either. They'd considered it a treat most kids didn't get to experience. Kara didn't mutter a word about having to wear a white gown trimmed in blue, and the boys' chests poked out with pride in their blue tuxes. However, they complained long and hard that they didn't get to go on the honeymoon.

As a concession, Phoenix and Karina promised them a family trip shortly after they returned. That appeased them, somewhat. Besides, while their parents were away, they would be spending time with their new grandmother.

Karina watched the bus leave as she stood with Phoenix outside the Riverview in the sweltering August heat in her ivory wedding gown. All the men had peeled their jackets off and slung them over their shoulders, while she suffered in the hot sticky clothing. From the looks of things when she walked out, the band was getting its second wind and the guests were enjoying the free food and the company.

Suddenly a car came charging up the restaurant lane. She wondered who would come so late to the reception that should have been almost over. Since it was time for Phoenix and her to leave.

"I can't believe it," Grady said.

"What?" Phoenix turned toward the direction Grady was looking.

Tim Malloy, the computer genius, pushed his horn-rimmed glasses up on his nose as he exited the car. The other hand held a huge stack of green bar paper.

"I finally solved it. I knew I could do it," Tim said waving the papers as he approached them.

The men looked at the huge stack of paper and wondered if he'd worked too long without any sleep. He had a tendency to do that.

"This is where the first transaction took place." He pointed to a page as he came to a halt. "San Francisco. I've got every transaction nailed down," he continued. "It must have taken Thornton months to set this up. Most challenging setup I've ever encountered. Pure genius."

The genius was sitting in federal prison awaiting his trial. He hadn't quite been all there since his arrest.

"Can you imagine this? He had transactions from

Zurich, Hong Kong, Buenos Aires, Cayman Islands, and that's only the beginning."

Karina and Phoenix scanned the sheets and he shook his head. "Talk about extreme." He reached for Karina and tucked her under his arm. There wasn't a night that went by that he didn't say a prayer thanking God for her and his children. He looked in her eyes as she smiled up at him. For a moment, he forgot they weren't alone.

Grady cleared his throat. "Now you can go on your honeymoon with a clear mind. I still say Thornton went through a lot of trouble for a mere thirty thousand."

"He was always budget conscious," Phoenix said.

Tim looked up with a blank expression on his face. Grady filled him in. "We tracked Thornton's contacts in South Carolina through some of his bank transactions. The cars had been shipped from the port of Charleston to Argentina and other Latin American countries."

Miss Drucilla shook her head. "I tell you, I'm still smarting about Luke's car. They never got it back."

"At least they paid me for it," Luke said.

"Not what it was worth," Miss Drucilla sniffed. "At least this group won't be stealing anymore."

"And thank goodness for that," Mrs. Jones said as she straightened out Karina's train on her gown. Phoenix was again in her good graces.

Emmanuel merely looked up at the sky.

Patrick laughed. Mrs. Jones had always been a bone of contention with them. "Ready for me to drive you to the airport?"

Casey had confessed his and Thornton's involvement in the country club thefts after Thornton's arrest. Patrick had his old job back but wouldn't need it long at the rate his sculptures were selling.

"Yeah," Phoenix said eagerly. He was ready to get Karina all to himself.

"Take good care of my sister." Jonathan had to cough

a couple of times to keep his emotions in check. He had also caught the garter Phoenix had tossed.

Under the quiet music of the rushing tides, their bed rocked that night during their first lovemaking experience as man and wife. Phoenix and Karina had no idea it had been rigged to flashing lights outside their cozy townhouse on Jeckle Island. But what could you expect with FBI agents as friends? And the people of the quaint and peaceful island never understood the unusual patterns of their suddenly berserk traffic lights.

Acknowledgments to:

Detective Onzy Elam for his patience in answering many questions on police procedural.

Mrs. Karen Farrier for her insights on triplets.

My family
Gerard, Shevonne, and Rachel for understanding that mom has deadlines; my husband, John, for his assistance; my sister, Evangeline Jones, for her unswerving support; and my parents who are always there for me. Thank you.

Sandy Rangel, my critique partner. Where would I be without you?

About the Author

Bestselling author Candice Poarch's sister first introduced her to romances and it wasn't long before she craved to write romances of her own featuring African-American heroes and heroines. Candice is a member of several writers groups. She lives in Springfield, Virginia with her family.

SPICE UP YOUR LIFE
WITH ARABESQUE ROMANCES

AFTER HOURS, by Anna Larence   (0-7860-0277-8, $4.99/$6.50)
Vice president of a Fort Worth company, Nachelle Oliver was used to things
her own way. Until she got a new boss. Steven DuCloux was ruthless—and the
most exciting man she had ever known. He knew that she was the perfect VP,
and that she would be the perfect wife. She tried to keep things strictly professional, but the passion between them was too strong.

CHOICES, by Maria Corley   (0-7860-0245-X, $4.95/$6.50)
Chaney just ended with Taurique when she met Lawrence. The rising young
singer swept her off her feet. After nine years of marriage, with Lawrence away
for months on end, Chaney feels lonely and vulnerable. Purely by chance, she
meets Taurique again, and has to decide if she wants to risk it all for love.

DECEPTION, by Donna Hill   (0-7860-0287-5, $4.99/$6.50)
An unhappy marriage taught owner of a successful New York advertising
agency, Terri Powers, never to trust in love again. Then she meets businessman
Clinton Steele. She can't fight the attraction between them—or the sensual
hunger that fires her deepest passions.

DEVOTED, by Francine Craft   (0-7860-0094-5, $4.99/$6.50)
When Valerie Thomas and Delano Carter were young lovers each knew it
wouldn't last. Val, now a photojournalist, meets Del at a high-society wedding.
Del takes her to Alaska for the assignment of her career. In the icy wilderness
he warms her with a passion too long denied. This time not even Del's desperate
secret will keep them from reclaiming their lost love.

FOR THE LOVE OF YOU, by Felicia Mason   (0-7860-0071-6, $4.99/$6.50
Seven years ago, Kendra Edwards found herself pregnant and alone. Now she
has a secure life for her twins and a chance to finish her college education. A
long unhappy marriage had taught attorney Malcolm Hightower the danger of
passion. But Kendra taught him the sensual magic of love. Now they must each
give true love a chance.

ALL THE RIGHT REASONS, by Janice Sims   (0-7860-0405-3, $4.99/$6.50)
Public defender, Georgie Shaw, returns to New Orleans and meets reporter Clay
Knight. He's determined to uncover secrets between Georgie and her celebrity
twin, and protect Georgie from someone who wants both sisters dead. Dangerous secrets are found in a secluded mansion, leaving Georgie with no one to
trust but the man who stirs her desires.

*Available wherever paperbacks are sold, or order direct from the
Publisher. Send cover price plus 50¢ per copy for mailing and
handling to Kensington Publishing Corp., Consumer Orders,
or call (toll free) 888-345-BOOK, to place your order using
Mastercard or Visa. Residents of New York and Tennessee
must include sales tax. DO NOT SEND CASH.*

LOOK FOR THESE ARABESQUE ROMANCES